BATMAN™

NIGHTWALKER

— DC ICONS —

Wonder Woman: Warbringer
by Leigh Bardugo

Batman: Nightwalker
by Marie Lu

Catwoman: Soulstealer
by Sarah J. Maas

— COMING SOON —

Superman
by Matt de la Peña

BATMAN
NIGHTWALKER

– DC ICONS –

MARIE LU

Random House New York

Batman created by Bob Kane with Bill Finger

Copyright © 2018 DC Comics.
BATMAN and all related characters and elements
© & ™ DC Comics. WB SHIELD: ™ & © WBEI. (s18)
RHUS38064

Jacket art by Jacey

All rights reserved. Published in the United States by Random House Children's Books, a division of Penguin Random House LLC, New York.

Random House and the colophon are registered trademarks of Penguin Random House LLC.

Visit us on the Web! GetUnderlined.com

Educators and librarians, for a variety of teaching tools, visit us at RHTeachersLibrarians.com

Library of Congress Cataloging-in-Publication Data
Names: Lu, Marie, author.
Title: Batman : Nightwalker / Marie Lu.
Other titles: Nightwalker
Description: First edition. | New York : Random House, [2018] | Series: [DC Icons] | "DC Comics." | "Batman created by Bob Kane with Bill Finger"—Title page verso.
Identifiers: LCCN 2017021544 | ISBN 978-0-399-54978-6 (hardback) | ISBN 978-0-399-54977-9 (lib. bdg.) | ISBN 978-0-525-57856-7 (int'l) | ISBN 978-0-399-54979-3 (ebook)
Classification: LCC PZ7.L96768 Bat 2018 | DDC [Fic]—dc23

Printed in the United States of America
10 9 8 7 6 5 4 3 2 1
First Edition

FOR DIANNE:

Bruce Wayne would be lucky to have you as a friend.

PROLOGUE

The blood underneath her nails bothered her.

Cheap, stupid, useless gloves, the girl thought in annoyance. She had even worn two layers of them tonight, but a rare errant slash from the knife had sliced through both layers, and now the blood had gotten on her hands. *Stupid.* On any other night, she would have stopped and—carefully, methodically—scraped the scarlet flakes out from under her nails, one line after another. But she had no time right now.

No time, no time.

Moonlight cut across the floor of the mansion, illuminating part of the man's naked body. He bled strangely, the girl thought, compared with the others. The blood just pooled beneath him in a perfect circle, like a disk of smooth frosting on a cake.

She sighed again and stuffed her canister of red spray paint into her backpack, then grabbed a few of the rags strewn on the floor. On the wall beside her was the symbol she had just hurriedly finished drawing.

They had mistimed everything tonight, from the unexpected

complications of Sir Robert Grant's security system at the entrance of the mansion to the surprise of him seeing them first instead of being sound asleep. They were running late. She hated running late.

She hurried around the bedroom chamber, gathering their tools and stuffing them all into her backpack. The moonlight illuminated her features in regular intervals as she moved past the row of windows. Her mother used to tell her that she had doll-like features, had been doll-like since birth—large, liquid-dark eyes; long, long lashes; a slender nose and a rosebud of a mouth; porcelain skin. Her eyebrows cut straight and soft across her brow, giving her an expression that looked permanently vulnerable.

That was the thing about her. No one ever saw what mattered until it was too late. Until their blood stained her fingernails.

Her hair had come undone in all the rush, tumbling in a river of black over her shoulders, and she paused to whip it back up into a knot. No doubt a strand or two had come loose and were now lying somewhere on the floor, leaving a clue for the police to follow. But no matter—if she could just escape from here in time. What a messy getaway, so uncharacteristic of her.

I'm going to kill them, she thought bitterly. *Leaving me to clean this up—*

Somewhere in the night came the wail of sirens.

She froze, listening intently. Her hand flew instinctively to rest on one of the knives strapped around her thigh. Then she started to run. Her boots made no sound—she moved like a shadow, the only noise being the faint bump of her bag against her back. As she went, she pulled her black scarf up across the bottom half of her face, hiding her nose and mouth from view, and fitted her pair of dark visors over her eyes. Through the visors, the mansion transformed into a grid of heat signals and green lines.

The sirens were closing in rapidly.

She paused again for a breath, listening. They came from different directions—they were going to surround her. *No time, no time.*

She darted down the mansion's staircase, her figure lost entirely in the shadows, then made a sharp turn at the bottom to head not for the front door but for the cellar. The security system had been rewired to seal the front door's lock from the inside, but the cellar was their getaway route, all alarms cleared and window locks ready for her command.

As she reached the cellar, the sirens outside turned deafening. The police had arrived.

"Window A open," she muttered into her mouthpiece. At the other end of the room, the rewired window unlocked with a soft, obedient click. The police would gather at the front and back doors, but they wouldn't think to look on the side of such a huge house yet, not without knowing there was a tiny window at ground level. She ran faster.

She reached the window and started pulling herself up and through it, snaking her way out in the span of a second. On the front lawn, she could hear a police officer shouting into a megaphone, could see the heat signals of at least a dozen guards in heavy body armor crouched around the mansion's perimeter, their faces hidden behind helmets and their assault rifles all pointed toward the door.

She leaped to her feet in the darkness, pulled her visor up, and prepared to dart away.

A blinding light flooded over her.

"*Hands in the air!*" Several voices were shouting at her at the same time. She heard the clicks of loaded weapons, then the furious barking of police dogs barely restrained by their partners. "*On your knees! Now!*"

They had found her. She wanted to spit out a curse. *No time, no time.* And now it was too late. At least the others on the mission had already fled. For a fraction of a second, she thought about pulling out her knives and throwing herself at the closest officer, using him as a hostage.

But there were far too many here, and the light had blinded her enough to make her vision inaccurate. She didn't have the time to make such a move without the police unleashing the dogs, and she had no desire to be mauled to death.

So instead, she put her hands up.

Officers shoved her hard to the ground; her face scraped against dirt and grass. She saw a glimpse of herself reflected in the police's opaque helmets, and the barrels of guns pointed directly in her face.

"We got her!" one shouted into his radio, his voice hoarse with excitement and fear. "She's in custody! Stand by—"

You got me, she echoed to herself as she felt cold cuffs snap onto her wrists. But with her cheek pressed against the ground, she still allowed herself a small, mocking smile behind her scarf.

You got me . . . for now.

CHAPTER 1

If Bruce Wayne belonged in any car, it was this one: a brand-new, custom Aston Martin, mean and sleek and charcoal black, embellished with a stripe of metallic shine along its roof and hood.

Now he pushed the car to its limits, indulging in the roar of its engines, the way it responded to his slightest touch as it hugged the sunset streets right outside Gotham City. The vehicle was a gift from WayneTech, fitted with the latest WayneTech security features—a historic collaboration between the legendary carmaker and the Wayne empire.

Now the tires screeched in protest as Bruce hit another sharp turn.

"I heard that," said Alfred Pennyworth from the car's live video touch screen. He gave Bruce a withering look. "A bit slower on the turns, Master Wayne."

"Aston Martins weren't made for slow turns, Alfred."

"They weren't made to be wrecked, either."

Bruce smiled sidelong at his guardian. The setting sun glinted off his aviator sunglasses as he turned the car back in the direction of Gotham City's skyscrapers. "No faith in me at all, Alfred," he said lightly. "You're the one who taught me how to drive in the first place."

"And did I teach you to drive like a demon possessed?"

"A demon possessed with *skills*," Bruce clarified. He spun the steering wheel in a smooth motion. "Besides, it's a gift from Aston Martin, and it's armed to the teeth with WayneTech security. The only reason I'm driving it at all is to show off its safety capabilities at the benefit tonight."

Alfred sighed. "Yes. I remember."

"And how can I do that properly without testing what this masterpiece can do?"

"Displaying WayneTech security at a benefit isn't the same thing as using it to tempt death," Alfred replied, his tone drier than ever. "Lucius Fox asked you to take the car to the party so that the press can do a proper write-up about it."

Bruce made another hairpin turn. The car calculated the road ahead instantly, and on the windshield, he saw a series of transparent numbers appear and fade. Responding with uncanny precision, the car was in perfect sync with the road as it mapped out the surrounding terrain down to the last detail.

"That's exactly what I'm doing," Bruce insisted. "Trying to get it there on time."

Alfred shook his head tragically as he dusted a windowsill at Wayne Manor, the sunlight casting his pale skin in shades of gold. "I'm going to kill Lucius for thinking this was a good idea."

An affectionate smile lingered on Bruce's lips. Sometimes he thought his guardian bore a remarkable resemblance to a timber wolf, with his attentive, world-weary, winter-blue gaze. A few strands of white had started to streak Alfred's hair over the past few years, and the crow's-feet lining the corners of his eyes had deepened. Bruce wondered if he was the reason for it. At the thought, he slowed down just a little.

It was that time of evening when people could catch a glimpse of bats heading out into the night to hunt. As Bruce reached the inner city, he spotted a cloud of them silhouetted against the dimming sky, circling out of the city's dark corners to join the rest of their colony.

Bruce felt the familiar tug of nostalgia. His father had once designated land near the Wayne mansion as one of the largest bat havens in the city. Bruce still had childhood memories of crouching there in awe on the front lawn, his toy gadgets forgotten as Dad pointed out the creatures streaming into the dusk by the thousands, sweeping across the sky in an undulating stripe. They were individuals, Dad had said, and yet they still knew, somehow, to move as one.

At the memory, Bruce's hand tightened against the steering wheel. His father should be here, sitting in the passenger seat and observing the bats with him. But that, of course, was impossible.

The streets turned grungier as Bruce got closer to downtown, until the skyscrapers blocked out the lowering sun and shrouded alleyways in shadows. He streaked past Wayne Tower and the Seco Financial Building, where a few tents were pitched in its alleys—a stark contrast, poverty right next to a rich financial beacon. Nearby was the Gotham City Bridge, its repainting half finished. A collection of dilapidated, low-income homes sat haphazardly underneath it.

Bruce didn't remember the city looking this way when he was younger—he had a memory of Gotham City as an impressive jungle of concrete and steel, filled with a rotation of expensive cars and doormen in black coats, the scent of new leather and men's cologne and women's perfume, the gleaming lobbies of fancy hotels, the deck of a yacht facing the city lights illuminating the harbor.

With his parents at his side, he'd only seen the good—not the graffiti, or the trash in the gutters, or the abandoned carts and people huddled in shadowed corners, jingling coins in paper cups. As a sheltered child, he'd seen only what Gotham City could give you for the right price, and none of what it did to you for the wrong one.

That had all changed on one fateful night.

Bruce had known he would be lingering on thoughts of his parents today, the day his trust funds opened. But as much as he braced himself for it, the memories still cut at his heart.

He pulled onto the road curving toward Bellingham Hall. A red carpet spanned the front sidewalk and went up the steps, and a bevy of paparazzi had gathered beside the road, their cameras already flashing at his car.

"*Master Wayne.*"

Bruce realized that Alfred was still talking to him about safety. "I'm listening," he said.

"I doubt that. Did you hear me tell you to schedule a meeting with Lucius Fox tomorrow? You're going to be working with him all summer—you should at least start putting together a detailed plan."

"Yes, sir."

Alfred paused to fix him with a stern look. "And behave yourself tonight. Understood?"

"My plan is to stand still in a corner and not make a sound."

"Very funny, Master Wayne. I'll hold you to your word."

"No birthday wishes for me, Alfred?"

At that, a smile finally slipped onto Alfred's face, softening his stern features. "And happy eighteenth, Master Wayne." He nodded once. "You *are* Martha's boy, hosting this event. She would be proud of you."

Bruce closed his eyes for a moment at the mention of his mother. Instead of celebrating her birthday every year, she would throw a benefit, and the money raised went straight into the Gotham City Legal Protection Fund, a group that defended those who couldn't afford to defend themselves in court. Bruce would carry on her tradition tonight, now that the responsibility for his family's fortune had officially fallen on his shoulders.

You are Martha's boy. But Bruce just shrugged off the praise, unsure how to accept it. "Thanks, Alfred," he replied. "Don't wait up for me."

The two ended the call. Bruce pulled to a stop in front of the hall, and for a heartbeat he let himself sit there, stilling his emotions while the paparazzi shouted at him from outside the car.

He had grown up under the spotlight, had endured years of headlines about him and his parents. EIGHT-YEAR-OLD BRUCE WAYNE SOLE WITNESS TO PARENTS' MURDERS! BRUCE WAYNE SET TO INHERIT FORTUNE! EIGHTEEN-YEAR-OLD BRUCE WAYNE NOW THE WORLD'S WEALTHIEST TEEN! On and on and on.

Alfred had filed restraining orders against photographers for pointing their long lenses at Wayne Manor's windows, and Bruce had once run home from elementary school in tears, terrified of the eager paparazzi who had nearly hit him with their cars. He'd spent the first few years trying to hide from them—as if holing away in his room at the manor somehow meant that the tabloids wouldn't make up new rumors.

But either you hid from reality or you dealt with it. And over time, Bruce had built up a shield, had negotiated an unspoken truce with the press.

He would show up with his carefully cultivated public demeanor, let them take the photos they wanted. In return, they'd shine the spotlight on the issue of his choice. And right now that issue was WayneTech's work to make Gotham City safer—everything from new security technology for the city's bank accounts to drones that aided the Gotham City Police Department to auto safety features that WayneTech would release for free, open-source technology to all carmakers.

Over the years, Bruce had spent countless nights hunched

at his bedroom desk, listening obsessively to police scanners and following cold cases on his own. He had burned out dozens of lightbulbs while deconstructing WayneTech prototypes under his desk lamp in the darkness before dawn, holding up glittering microchips and artificial joints, studying the technology his corporation was making to improve the city's safety.

If forwarding that agenda meant being in the news, well then, so be it.

As a valet rushed over to open his car door, Bruce veiled his discomfort, stepped out with a single, graceful move, and gave the reporters a flawless smile. The cameras went into overdrive. A pair of bodyguards in black suits and dark shades shoved people back, clearing a path for him, but the reporters still crowded in, their microphones extended, shouting questions.

"Are you looking forward to your graduation?" "Are you enjoying your new wealth?" "How do you feel about being the world's youngest billionaire?" "Who are you dating, Bruce?" "Hey, Bruce, look this way! Give us a smile!"

Bruce obliged, offering them an easy grin. He knew he photographed well—long and lean, his blue eyes dark as sapphire against his white complexion, his black hair perfectly smoothed back, his suit tailored and oxfords polished. "Good evening," he said as he stood for a moment in front of the car.

"Bruce!" one paparazzo shouted. "Is that car your first purchase?" He winked. "Enjoying your trust fund already?"

Bruce just looked at him steadily, refusing to take the bait. "This is the newest Aston Martin on the market, fully equipped with WayneTech safety technology. You are welcome to explore its interior tonight for an exclusive first look." He held his hand out toward the car, where one of his suited guards had opened the door for the press to peek in. "Thank you all for covering my mother's benefit tonight. It means a lot to me."

He continued talking for a bit about the charity that the event would support, but everyone shouted right over him, ignoring his words. Bruce faced them wearily, and for an instant, he felt alone and outnumbered. His gaze scanned past the tabloid paparazzi, searching for the journalists from official papers. He could already see the headlines tomorrow: BRUCE WAYNE BLOWS NEW MONEY ON MILLION-DOLLAR CAR! TRUST FUND BABY WASTES NO TIME! But interspersed with those would hopefully be a few true headlines, detailing the work being done at WayneTech. That was what mattered. So he lingered, enduring the photos.

After letting the cameras flash wildly for a few moments, Bruce made his way up toward the hall's entrance. Other guests mingled at the top of the stairs—members of Gotham City's upper class, the occasional council member, clusters of admirers. Bruce found himself categorizing everyone in the crowd. It was a survival skill he'd learned since his parents' deaths. There were the people who'd invite him to dinner only in an attempt to get gossip out of him. The people willing to betray friends in order to become his. The occasional wealthy classmate who'd spread lies about him out of bitter envy. The ones who'd do anything to get a date with him and then share the details with the rags the next morning.

But on the surface, he kept his cool, greeting everyone politely. Only a few more steps until he'd reach the entrance. All he had to do was make it inside, and then he could find—

"Bruce!"

A familiar voice cut above the chaos. Bruce looked up to where a girl was standing on tiptoe and waving at him from the top of the stairs. Dark hair skimmed her shoulders, and the hall's floor lights highlighted her brown skin and the round curve of her hips. There was glitter woven into the fabric of her dress, shimmering silver as she moved. "Hey!" she called. "Over here!"

Bruce's careful demeanor dissolved in relief. *Dianne Garcia.* Category: genuine.

As he reached her, she instinctively turned her back on the

crowd stuck behind the velvet rope at the bottom of the stairs in an attempt to shield him from the flashing cameras.

"Fashionably late on your birthday?" she said with a grin.

He gave her a grateful wink and leaned down closer to her ear. "Always."

"This benefit is epic," she went on. "I think you might set a new record for how much money it'll raise."

"Thank god," he replied, throwing an arm around her neck. "Otherwise I'd have put up with all the cameras down there for nothing."

She laughed. This was the girl who had once punched a tooth out of a kid for harassing her friends, who had memorized the entire first chapter of *A Tale of Two Cities* in senior-year English to win a bet, and who could spend an hour staring at a menu only to order the same burger she always got. Now Dianne shoved him off in affectionate protest, grabbed his arm, and led him through the open doors of the hall, leaving the paparazzi behind.

Inside, the lighting was dim, an atmospheric blue, and chandeliers hung from the high ceilings, glinting bright silver and white. Ice sculptures and spreads of food covered long banquet tables, while another table was lined with rows of auction items, all trembling slightly from the beat of the music.

"I thought you had a college interview today," he said over the noise as Dianne swiped a lemon tart from one of the dessert stands. "Not that I'm complaining about you being here, of course."

"It was earlier," Dianne replied through a mouthful of pastry. "It's okay. My *lola* needed me home in the afternoon to pick up my brother, and besides, I couldn't bear the thought of robbing you of my company tonight." She leaned in, her voice dropping to an ominous whisper. "That was my way of saying I didn't get you anything."

"Nothing at all?" Bruce put a hand over his heart in mock pain. "You wound me."

"If you'd like, I could always bake you a cake."

"Please don't." The last time Dianne had attempted to make cookies, she'd set Bruce's kitchen on fire, and they'd spent the next hour hiding the scorched kitchen drapes so that Alfred wouldn't know.

Dianne squeezed his arm once. "You'll just have to settle for diner food tonight, then."

Years ago, Bruce, Harvey, and Dianne had all agreed to forgo birthday presents in exchange for an annual date at their favorite local diner. It would be where they'd meet up tonight, too, after the benefit ended, and Bruce could shed the billionaire and just be a boy on the cusp of graduating from high school, getting teased by two of his best friends over fat burgers and thick milk shakes. He smiled in anticipation at the thought.

"Well?" he asked Dianne. "How'd the interview go?"

"The interviewer didn't faint in horror at my answers, so I'm going out on a limb to say it went well." She shrugged.

And *that* was Dianne's way of saying she'd aced it, just like she aced everything else in life. Bruce had come to recognize her shrug whenever she tried to downplay an achievement—getting a perfect score on her entrance exams, being admitted to every university she applied to, and speaking as their class valedictorian at graduation next month.

"Congratulations," he said. "Although you've probably already heard that from Harvey."

She smiled. "All Harvey's done tonight is beg me not to leave him alone on the dance floor. You know how much his two left feet love to dance."

Bruce laughed. "Isn't he alone on the floor right now?"

Dianne grinned mischievously. "Oh, he can survive for two minutes."

The music grew louder and louder as they neared the dance floor, until finally they stepped through a set of double doors and onto a balcony that overlooked a packed space. Here, the music shook the floors. A haze of mist hugged the ground level. On the stage below was an elaborate stand, behind which stood a DJ, bobbing his head in time to the beat. Behind him, an enormous screen stretched from floor to ceiling and played a series of moving, flashing patterns.

Dianne cupped her hands around her mouth and shouted down at the crowd. *"He's here!"*

An enormous cheer exploded from the dance floor, drowning out even the music. Bruce looked on as the crowd's roar of "Happy birthday!" filled the room. He smiled and waved, and as he did, the DJ sped up the track. Then the DJ dropped the beat hard, and the crowd became a sea of pumping limbs.

Bruce let the pounding music fill his senses, and whatever unease he'd felt now faded away. Dianne led him down the stairs and into the mass of guests. As he greeted one person after another, pausing to take selfies with some, he lost Dianne in the tangle of bodies, until all he could see was a blur of familiar and strange faces, every outline lit up in slices of neon and darkness.

There she is. Dianne had reached Harvey Dent, who looked chalky under the club lights as he tried his best to move with the beat. Bruce smiled at the sight, then started making his way across the dance floor toward them. They waved him over.

"Bruce!"

He turned at the voice, but before he could even reply, somebody was clapping him hard on the shoulder. A face came into focus, grinning harshly, his white teeth even whiter against his pale face. "Hey—happy birthday, man!"

Richard Price, the son of Gotham City's current mayor. Bruce blinked in surprise. It had been months since they last talked, but Richard had already grown a few inches taller, so that Bruce had to look up slightly to meet the other boy's gaze. "Hey," he replied, returning Richard's embrace. "I didn't think you'd come."

"And miss your shindig? Never," Richard replied. "My dad's here—out in the auction hall, anyway. He never missed any of your mom's benefits, and he won't do it now."

Bruce nodded warily. They had once been best friends—they lived at opposite ends of the same neighborhood of exclusive estates, had attended the same middle school and the same parties, had even taken kickboxing classes at the same gym. They'd played video games in Bruce's theater room, laughing themselves silly until their stomachs hurt. Even now Bruce felt a pang at the memory.

But things had changed as they grew older, and Richard had gradually fallen into a specific category of his own: the kind of friend who called you only when he needed something from you.

Bruce wondered what it would be tonight.

"Hey," Richard said now, his eyes darting to one side. He kept his hand on Bruce's shoulder as he gestured up to the exit. "Can I talk to you somewhere? Just for a sec?"

"Sure."

Bruce's ears rang as they headed off the dance floor and into a quieter hall. There, Richard turned around and looked at Bruce with an eager grin. In spite of himself, Bruce could feel his spirits lift at the expression—it was the same grin Richard used to give him when they were kids and Richard had found something exciting that he had to share. Maybe he really was here just to celebrate Bruce's birthday.

Richard stepped closer and lowered his voice. "Look," he said. "Dad's on my case. He keeps asking me if I've got an internship lined up for the summer. Can you help me out?"

Bruce's moment of hope flickered out, replaced by a familiar sinking feeling of disappointment. Richard needed something again. "I can recommend you to Lucius Fox," he started to say. "WayneTech is looking for interns—"

Richard shook his head. "No, I mean, I don't actually want to *be* at the internship. Just, you know, put in a word for me with my dad, tell him I'm doing stuff at WayneTech this summer, and let me into the building a couple of times."

Bruce frowned at him. "You mean, help you fake that you're at an internship, just so your dad won't bother you anymore?"

Richard gave him a halfhearted nudge. "It's the last summer before college starts. I don't want to spend it working—yeah, you know how it is, Wayne, right? Just tell my dad I'm working with Lucius. It won't be a big deal."

"And how are you going to keep it up?"

"I told you—just let me into WayneTech every now and then. Take a photo of me in the lobby or something. It's all my dad needs to see."

"I don't know, man. Lucius will just tell your dad the truth if he gets wind of it."

"Oh, come *on*, Bruce! For old times' sake." Richard's grin was still on as he reached to shake Bruce's shoulder once. "It's your company, isn't it? You're gonna let that nerd tell you what to do?"

Bruce bristled. Richard had fawned all over Lucius when he'd first met him. "I'm not covering for you," he said. "If you want to tell your dad you're interning at WayneTech, you'll have to actually *do* the internship."

Richard made an annoyed sound in his throat. "What's it to you?"

"Why are you insisting?"

"All you have to do is mention it once or twice to my dad. It's not like it'll cost you anything."

Bruce shook his head. When they were younger, Richard would show up unannounced at his front gate, talking breathlessly over the intercom, holding the latest game or the newest set of action figures. At some point, their hangouts shifted from debates about what their favorite movies were to requests from Richard to copy Bruce's homework or for Bruce to finish their group projects on his own or put in a good word for him for jobs.

When had he changed? Even now Bruce couldn't understand when or why it'd all gone wrong.

"I can't," Bruce said, shaking his head again. "I'm sorry."

At that, Richard's eyes seemed to shutter. He searched Bruce's gaze as if expecting a different answer, but when it didn't come, he grimaced and shoved his hands into his pockets. "Yeah, whatever," he muttered, stepping around Bruce to head back down the hall. "I see how it is. You turn eighteen and get the keys to your empire, and suddenly you're too good to help out your friends."

"Richard," Bruce called out. The other boy paused to look over his shoulder. Bruce stared at him for a moment. "If you hadn't wanted my help, would you have come to the party tonight?"

There was a pause, and Bruce knew that the answer was no. Richard just shrugged at him, then turned around and continued down the hall without answering.

Bruce stood there for a moment, alone, listening to the pounding music coming from inside. He felt a sudden rush of not belonging here, not even at his own event. He pictured the crowd of his classmates and friends on the dance floor and wondered if, aside from Dianne and Harvey, any of them would be here if it weren't for his family name. The paparazzi outside wouldn't, that was for sure.

If he were just Bruce Wayne, the boy next door, would anyone care?

Instead of heading back to the dance floor, Bruce made his way down the hall and through a nondescript door that led outside. He walked around the building until he reached the front entrance, where the cameras had already gotten what they wanted from the Aston Martin and were now clustered at the top of the stairs, waiting for special guests to enter or leave. Unnoticed, Bruce reached the car and got in. One of the bodyguards watching the paparazzi at the entrance spotted him right as he shut the car door and revved the engine.

"Mr. Wayne, sir!" the man said, but Bruce just gave him a terse nod. Through the window, he could see some of the paparazzi turn in his direction and realize that he was leaving. Their eyes widened, and their chatter morphed into shouts.

But Bruce slammed his foot down on the gas pedal before anyone could reach him. In the rearview mirror, the hall shrank quickly away. Maybe it was rude of him to leave his benefit so soon, to get some time alone when everyone wanted his time for themselves. But he didn't slow down, and he didn't look back.

CHAPTER 2

Neon lights smeared across the evening streets of Gotham City. Few cars were on the road at this hour, and all Bruce could hear was the rush of pavement and wind, the sound of his car tearing down the freeway. That was what drew him to machines. They followed algorithms, not emotion; when Bruce pushed his foot down on the pedal, the car only responded in one way.

Somewhere behind him, he could see the headlights of paparazzi attempting to follow him. Bruce allowed himself a cynical smile and edged the speedometer higher and higher. The world blurred around him.

A harsh beep rang out in the car, followed by an electronic voice. *"Speed not recommended for this road,"* it said, and at the same time, one corner of the windshield lit up with a recommended speed and a blinking marker telling Bruce to slow down.

"Override," Bruce replied. The alerts faded. He could feel the car lock itself tighter in position on the road, so that if he seemed to be even slightly shaky, the car would compensate by steadying itself.

At least WayneTech's features were working as they should, he thought darkly. Lucius would be happy to hear it.

The car's phone rang, echoing in Bruce's ears. When he glanced down at the caller ID, he saw that it was Dianne. Bruce let it ring a few times before he finally answered. Dianne's voice filled the car, along with the din of the party behind her.

"Bruce?" she shouted over the noise. "Where'd you go? I saw you step away with Richard, but then I heard you left, and—"

"I did leave," Bruce replied.

"What? Are you okay?" That was Harvey's voice, anxious.

"I'm fine," Bruce reassured them. "Don't worry. I just needed to get some air and clear my head."

There was a pause on the other end before Dianne spoke up again. "Do what you need to do," she replied.

"And if you need us," Harvey added, "we'll head to you."

Bruce relaxed a little at their words. The three of them had all gotten to the point where they could sense each other's moods, so that none of them needed to explain a thing. They just knew.

"Thanks." Then he hung up.

He had no idea where he was driving to, but after a while he realized he was taking a long route back in the direction of the manor. Bruce exited the freeway onto a local street, passing rows of dilapidated apartment buildings, their walls permanently stained from decades of water and filth. Clothes hung limply on lines strung from one window to another. Steam billowed up from vents. He swerved neatly through traffic, then made a sharp turn at an intersection, where he paused at a stoplight.

Outside his car window, an old man was crawling into his makeshift tent, while at the end of the block another man was stuffing old newspaper into his shoes. A pair of kids played in an alley piled high with trash.

Bruce looked away. He shouldn't be here. And yet here he was, driving through the slums in a car that probably cost more than what a person living here could earn in a lifetime. Did he have a right to ever feel sad, with everything he had in his life?

These were the streets that his parents had fought all their lives to improve, and they were the same streets where their blood had been shed. Bruce took a deep breath as the light turned green and he revved his engine. Gotham City was broken in many ways, but it wasn't beyond repair. He would find a way to fix it. It was the mantle he'd been handed.

Soon the streets changed back to unbroken streetlights and unbarred windows. The paparazzi were slowly but surely gaining on him; if he didn't throw them off now, they would end up parked outside his mansion gates, fabricating tabloid headlines for why he left his party early. Bruce's eyes darkened at the thought, and he sped up until the car's warning beep went off again.

It wasn't until he reached another series of stoplights that he heard the echo of police sirens.

Bruce wondered for an instant if the sirens were for him, the police busting him for speeding. Then he realized that the sound was coming from somewhere up ahead—and not just from a single vehicle, but from what must be dozens.

Curiosity cut through his dark mood. Bruce frowned as he listened to the wails. He had spent enough time following criminal cases on his own that the sound of sirens always made him sit up straighter. For this area of the city, an upscale shopping neighborhood, the sheer intensity of them seemed out of place. Bruce took a detour from the route that would have taken him back toward Wayne Manor, and instead headed in the direction of the sirens.

As he rounded another bend, the wails suddenly turned deafening, and a mass of flashing red and blue lights blinked against the buildings near the end of the street. White barricades and yellow police tape completely blocked the intersection. Even from here,

Bruce could see fire engines and black SWAT trucks clustered to-gether, the silhouettes of police running back and forth in front of the headlights.

Inside his car, the electronic voice came on again, followed by a transparent map overlaid against his windshield. *"Heavy police activity ahead. Alternate route suggested."*

A sense of dread filled his chest.

Bruce flicked away the map and pulled to an abrupt halt in front of the barricade—right as the unmistakable *pop-pop-pop* of gunfire rang out in the night air.

He remembered the sound all too well. The memory of his par-ents' deaths sent a wave of dizziness through him. *Another robbery. A murder. That's what all this is.*

Then he shook his head. *No, that can't be right.* There were far too many cops here for a simple robbery.

"Step *out* of your vehicle, and put your hands in the air!" a police officer shouted through a megaphone, her voice echoing along the block. Bruce's head jerked toward her. For an instant, he thought her command was directed at him, but then he saw that her back was turned, her attention fixed on the corner of the build-ing bearing the name BELLINGHAM INDUSTRIES & CO. "We have you surrounded, Nightwalker! This is your final warning!"

Another officer came running over to Bruce's car. He whirled an arm exaggeratedly for Bruce to turn his car around. His voice harsh with panic, he warned, "Turn back *now*. It's not safe!"

Before Bruce could reply, a blinding fireball exploded behind the officer. The street rocked.

Even from inside his car, Bruce felt the heat of the blast. Every window in the building burst simultaneously, a million shards of glass raining down on the pavement below. The police ducked in unison, their arms shielding their heads. Fragments of glass dinged like hail against Bruce's windshield.

From inside the blockade, a white car veered around the corner at top speed. Bruce saw immediately what the car was aiming for—a slim gap between the police barricades where a SWAT team truck had just pulled through.

The car raced right toward the gap.

"I said, *get out of here!*" the officer shouted at Bruce. A thin ribbon of blood trickled down the man's face. "That is an *order!*"

Bruce heard the scream of the getaway car's tires against the asphalt. He'd been in his father's garage a thousand times, helping him tinker with an endless number of engines from the best cars in the world. At WayneTech, Bruce had watched in fascination as tests were conducted on custom engines, conceptual jets, stealth tech, new vehicles of every kind.

And so he knew: whatever was installed under that hood was faster than anything the GCPD could hope to have.

They'll never catch him.

But I can.

His Aston Martin was probably the only vehicle here that could overtake the criminal's, the only one powerful enough to chase it down. Bruce's eyes followed the path the car would likely take, his gaze settling on a sign at the end of the street that pointed toward the freeway.

I can get him.

The white getaway vehicle shot straight through the gap in the barricade, clipping two police cars as it went.

No, not this time. Bruce slammed his gas pedal.

The Aston Martin's engine let out a deafening roar, and the car sped forward. The officer who'd shouted at him stumbled back. In the rearview mirror, Bruce saw him scramble to his feet and wave the other officers' cars forward, both his arms held high.

"Hold your fire!" Bruce could hear him yelling. "Civilian in proximity—*hold your fire!*"

The getaway car made a sharp turn at the first intersection, and Bruce sped behind it a few seconds later. The street zigzagged, then turned in a wide arc as it led toward the freeway—and the Night-walker took the on-ramp, leaving a trail of exhaust and two black skid marks on the road.

Bruce raced forward in close pursuit; his car mapped the ground instantly, swerving in a perfect curve to follow the ramp onto the freeway. He tapped twice on the windshield right over where the Nightwalker's white vehicle was.

"Follow him," Bruce commanded.

It was a feature meant to make it easier for two cars to caravan with each other. Now a green target highlighted over the white car, and the Aston Martin's voice spoke up: *"Car locked on."* A small map appeared on the corner of the windshield, showing exactly where the getaway car was in proximity to Bruce. No matter how much the white car tried to escape now, it wouldn't be able to shake him.

Bruce narrowed his eyes and urged the car faster. His entire body tingled from the rush of adrenaline. "Override," he said the instant the car tried to get him to slow down. He snaked between cars from one lane to another. The Aston Martin responded with blinding accuracy, knowing exactly when he could cut into a narrow space and how fast he needed to be.

Already Bruce was catching up to the Nightwalker's car, and the Nightwalker knew it. The other car started to cut wildly back and forth. The few vehicles still on the freeway swerved out of their way as they wove between lanes.

A spotlight flooded Bruce and the freeway in front of him. He glanced up to see a black chopper flying low and parallel to their chase. Far behind him were the flashing lights of the GCPD cars, but they were a distant sight, getting rapidly smaller.

What the hell am I doing? Bruce thought in a feverish daze. But he didn't let up on the gas. Instead, he leaned back and floored the pedal. His eyes were fixed on the swerving white car before him.

Just a little more. Bruce was so close now that he could see the driver look back to glare at him. The white car swerved around a truck carrying a load of enormous pipes, forcing the driver into Bruce's lane. The Aston Martin beeped a warning as it automatically veered to the side. Bruce yanked the steering wheel sharply. For an instant, he thought he would hit the side of the truck—but his car slid into the lane by the barest of margins, a perfect fit.

In this moment, in spite of everything, Bruce felt invincible, even *natural*, his focus narrowing in on nothing but the sight of his target and the thud of his heart.

Overhead, the voice from the chopper's megaphone called out to him. "Pull over," it shouted. "Civilian, *stand down*. You *will* be arrested. *Stop your vehicle!*"

But Bruce had caught up to his target. *Almost there.* He tightened his grip on his steering wheel, hoping his calculations were correct. If he clipped him in the rear correctly, the Nightwalker car's speed and friction would probably flip him. *It ends here.*

Alfred's going to kill me.

Bruce patted the steering wheel once. His heart twisted for an instant at what he was about to do. "Sorry, sweetheart," he murmured to the Aston Martin.

Then he sped up. The car tried to stop him this time, and he felt the resistance in the steering wheel against his move. *"ALERT! Collision ahead!"*

"Override," Bruce shouted, then rammed his vehicle into the back of the Nightwalker's car.

The crunch of metal slamming into metal.

Bruce felt a shock wave ripple through his body as his neck whipped sideways and he was hurled in an arc, his seat belt cutting into his chest from the force. The other car's tires screamed against the pavement—or maybe that was Bruce, he wasn't sure—and he saw the vehicle flip, momentarily airborne. The world streaked around him. For an instant, he caught a glimpse of the driver's face—a man, eyes wide, his pale skin dotted with blood.

The white car crashed upside down. Glass exploded out in all directions as the metal frame crushed into a gnarled mass. Even though Bruce knew, as he shook his head groggily, that everything must have taken less than a second, he felt like he could see the metal twisting section by section, the million individual splinters of the windows cutting through the air.

Police swarmed the white car, their rifles pointed directly at the driver inside. He looked conscious, if barely.

"Don't move, Nightwalker!" an officer yelled. *"You're under arrest!"*

Bruce felt another wave of dizziness hit. As one of the officers approached him, shouting angrily now, Bruce heard his car issue a voice call alerting Alfred as well as sending his coordinates to him and the police.

Bruce's guardian answered on the first ring, voice tense and frantic. "Master Wayne! Master Wayne?"

"Alfred," Bruce heard himself say. "Could use a pickup." He couldn't understand what Alfred said in reply—he wasn't even sure if he could *hear* Alfred's words. All he remembered was slumping in his seat, and the world going dark.

CHAPTER 3

Interfering with a crime scene. Disobeying a police officer's orders. Obstruction of justice.

If Bruce had been hoping to avoid news coverage after the flurry on his eighteenth birthday, slamming his brand-new car into a criminal's vehicle was probably not the best way to do it. Especially not so soon before graduation.

At least the headlines had veered away from talk of his parents and his money, focusing instead on questions about Bruce's well-being and splashing photos of his ruined car on their front pages. Rumors of his possible death had swirled online almost instantly after the wreck, along with speculation about whether he was driving while intoxicated or escaping the police.

"An eventful couple of weeks?" said Lucius Fox from across the table.

They sat together in a waiting room at the courthouse, watching as the TV news repeated the footage of his Aston Martin crashing into the getaway car. Two weeks had passed since the crash, and Bruce still had a mild headache from the concussion he had suffered. He'd missed a full week of school because of it, and spent the second enduring questions from classmates and swarms of reporters hanging out at the manor's gates. Still, he couldn't help feeling a hint of satisfaction at the TV's news coverage. It was clear to everyone who watched it—even Lucius—that the car would have escaped from the police had Bruce not intervened.

Not that it mattered to the court.

"Well, our car did everything it should have, right?" Bruce ventured. "How was *that* for a test of its safety features?"

Lucius raised an eyebrow at him, unable to hide a slight smile at his comment, then sighed and shook his head. At least he didn't have the panicked look on his face today that he did when he first visited Bruce at the hospital and saw him strapped to an IV. "It's my fault," he replied. "I shouldn't have asked you to take that car to the benefit in the first place."

"Well, I ended up in the right place at the right time."

"Or the wrong place at the wrong time, Bruce. Why did you do it? You suddenly felt a need to dole out justice?"

It was the question the police had asked him first, too, but Bruce still wasn't sure how to answer. "Because I knew I could stop him, I guess," he replied. "And the police couldn't. Was I just supposed to stand by and watch?"

"You're not in law enforcement, Bruce," Lucius said. "You can't just intervene like that." The man's eyes turned stern for a moment. "If you didn't look the way you did, the police might have shot you dead for pulling a stunt like that."

Guilt hit him, and Bruce couldn't answer. If he could have intervened in that alley where his parents died so many years ago, his life might have turned out very differently. Lucius was right, of course, and it sent a thread of shame through him. His pale skin may have saved his life. "I won't do it again," he said instead, softly.

The video panned to police shouting at the other driver to come out, and the man being pulled out of the wreckage. "A low-ranking member of the Nightwalkers," the reporter said. "Little is known about the group, although authorities have released their symbol, one that appears at the locations of each target."

Nightwalkers. Bruce recalled the word being shouted by the police that night. He'd heard this group's name mentioned on the news more frequently over the past year; in fact, the primary suspect in the murder of that businessman—Sir Robert Grant—was considered a Nightwalker, too. On the TV, an image appeared of a coin engulfed in flames, then of that symbol sprayed on the side of buildings at various crime scenes. There was something ominously personal about the symbol, the burning of wealth, like the Nightwalkers would gladly do it to Bruce himself if given the chance.

"Well, Bruce," Lucius said as the footage began to repeat. He leaned back in his chair, running a hand absently over his closely cropped dark curls. The lights in the room cast a faint blue highlight against his brown skin. "I suppose our summer plans will have to change."

Bruce turned to face his mentor. For being the new head of research and development at WayneTech, Lucius Fox was remarkably young. His smile was quick, his eyes bright and alert, and his step energetic in a way that made it seem like he was perpetually eager to change the world.

"I can still come into the lab in my spare time," Bruce suggested, giving Lucius a hopeful look. "Just make sure I'm not the one driving."

Lucius let out a soft laugh at that. "We'll figure things out around your new schedule." He nodded toward a tablet lying between them on the table. "The world's more dangerous than you give it credit for, Bruce. We're just trying to watch your back, okay?"

Bruce studied the tablet. It was currently logged in to his bank accounts, accessible only with his fingerprints and a code, showing off the new security technology Lucius and WayneTech had developed. *If your accounts are opened suspiciously, say, with the wrong code,* Lucius had told him, *it'll send our security network an alert and remotely disable the offending computer in an instant.*

Bruce gave Lucius a nod. "Thanks for this," he said. "I'm looking forward to seeing all your team's been up to."

Lucius's brown eyes lit up. "Our security drones aren't ready to patrol Gotham City just yet—although we've already successfully pitched our Advanced Defense Armament to Metropolis. They're going in on a huge buy for us."

The Advanced Defense Armament project. It was a mission that Lucius and Bruce shared a common passion for—encryption tech to secure Gotham City's banks just as it secured Bruce's accounts, drone machines to secure the city's streets. Technology, on all fronts, to save them. "That's good. This city needs to be safer," he said quietly. "We'll make it happen with this—I'm sure of it."

Out of the corner of his eye, Bruce could see the news once again showing footage of the Nightwalker. He had killed himself in jail by slashing both his wrists with a smuggled razor the day before detectives were going to interrogate him. The police still had no idea what the Nightwalkers had been up to inside that building—and now, with their only suspect dead, they had lost their biggest lead.

Bruce studied the mug shot on the screen, trying to come to terms with the fact that this man he'd seen alive just two weeks ago was now dead. The thought made his stomach turn. This guy must have been either intensely loyal to or terrified of his boss, whoever that was.

Lucius nodded at the TV. "With Nightwalkers in the streets, it needs to happen sooner rather than later." A silence lingered between them, the memory of his late parents suddenly heavy in the air, before Lucius finally got to his feet. He walked over to Bruce's side and put a hand on his shoulder. "Steady, Bruce," he said kindly.

Bruce remembered this look from when he would visit Wayne-

Tech with his father and listen as Lucius—then a promising intern—gave his father a rundown of new projects he was working on. Now Bruce smiled back at his mentor. "Sorry for the trouble, Lucius."

Lucius gave him another pat on the shoulder. "Someday I'll let you in on all the trouble I got into when I was your age." Then he bid him goodbye and stepped out of the room.

Bruce's phone dinged. He looked down to see a group text from Harvey and Dianne.

Harvey: *hey, so, what's the official verdict?*

Bruce: *What else? Guilty.*

Harvey: *sorry, man. What's your sentence?*

Bruce: *Probation for five weeks, and community service.*

Harvey: *nooooo.*

Dianne: *that's like half the summer! and finals and graduation are coming up! Did they say where you have to do it?*

Bruce: *Not yet.*

Harvey didn't respond to that, but Dianne texted back a string of sad-face emojis. *Let's hang out soon,* she said. *To celebrate that you survived without breaking your neck. We're overdue for our birthday diner trip.* A pause. *You're going to be ok, ok?*

Bruce cracked a smile at that. *Thanks,* he texted back.

Just when he was starting to wonder how much longer he'd have to stay in the room, two police officers stepped inside. One of them nodded for Bruce to follow them out. "You're free to go," he said. "We'll take you home. Your guardian will meet you there, along with Detective Draccon."

"Detective Draccon?" Bruce asked as they went.

"She's discussing your sentence with Mr. Pennyworth." The officer looked uninterested in saying more on the subject, leaving Bruce to speculate on who the detective might be.

Half an hour later, they pulled up at the elaborate, gilded gates of the Wayne estate. The four pillars bordering the manor's front entrance came into view, along with the set of stone stairs leading up to the massive double doors. Twin towers rising three stories high peaked at either end of the manor. Iron light poles, their lamps not yet lit in the early afternoon, adorned the sides of the cobblestone path leading from the gate up to the stairs.

Bruce saw a blue car waiting outside the gate, the words GOTHAM CITY POLICE DEPARTMENT emblazoned prominently in bold white across the doors. Standing in front of the driver's side was Alfred, and beside him waited a woman in a light silk shirt that contrasted with her black skin, her long tan coat draped neatly across her shoulders. She straightened as their car approached. While Alfred gave the car a quick wave, the woman's eyes fixed on Bruce.

"You've kept me waiting," she said to the officer in the driver's seat.

"Sorry, Detective," he replied. "Hit some traffic on the way over."

"Bruce," Alfred said, leaning down to peer into the car, "this is Detective Draccon."

The detective rested a hand against the open window on the passenger side. Bruce noticed the simple silver rings on her dark fingers, and her impeccably polished nails, painted a clean brown nude. "Nice to meet you, Bruce Wayne," she greeted him. "Glad you're not the one driving." Then she turned away.

The windows in Wayne Manor's parlor had been thrown open to the air, letting in dappled sunlight and a breeze. Bruce walked through the front entrance into a grand foyer that opened up to a high ceiling. A staircase adorned with wrought iron railings curved up to a balcony that overlooked the living and dining rooms. At the moment, everything seemed in a state of disarray; white canvas was draped over all the living and dining room furniture, protecting it while workers refinished the walls, and part of the stairs remained blocked off because a few loose banisters needed replacement. Alfred was busy directing two people from the garage to the kitchen as they delivered groceries in preparation for the week's meals.

It all seemed like a normal afternoon scene, except that Bruce found himself sitting across from a stern detective, who now observed him from behind red-rimmed glasses, her stare discerning. Everything about her was perfectly put together—not a single wrinkle in her clothes. Her black hair was pulled back into rows of orderly braids that formed a thick ball on top of her head. No curl seemed out of place.

Bruce tried to figure out what category to put her in. He'd met few people in life who weren't either cozying up to him in an attempt to get something or bullying him out of envy. But the detective—she didn't want anything from him, she wasn't jealous of him, and she certainly didn't seem to have any ulterior motives. Right now she wasn't trying to hide how much she disliked him. He wondered about her work, what cases she must have investigated over the years.

Draccon tightened her lips at the light of interest in his eyes. "An officer at the precinct told me he still remembers you as a small boy. Definitely didn't see your publicity stunt coming."

"It wasn't a publicity stunt," he replied. "I get enough attention already."

"Oh?" she said in a cool, calm voice. "Is that so? Well, you're not very good at avoiding it, are you? Lucky for you, you have an army of lawyers to help you get off easy."

"I'm not getting out of anything," he protested.

Alfred cast Bruce a warning glance as he placed the cheese platter and a tray of tea on the coffee table between them.

Detective Draccon leaned forward to pick up her teacup, crossed her legs, and gestured once at Bruce. "Have you ever done menial work in your life?"

"I used to help my parents in the garden, and my dad in the garage," he answered. "I volunteered with them at soup kitchens."

"So, in other words, you haven't."

Bruce opened his mouth to protest, then closed it. No. He hadn't. Alfred managed a staff of a dozen employees to keep the mansion perfectly maintained; they were paid well to do a professional job and to keep out of sight as much as possible. Dirty dishes vanished from the kitchen, and fresh towels appeared folded and ready in the bathrooms. Bruce could recall the occasional sound of a broom in the halls, a pair of shears snipping at the hedges outside. But, with a twinge of shame, he realized he didn't know a single staff member at Wayne Manor.

"Well, you're about to do some real menial work," the detective went on. "You're going to be under my supervision for your community service, Bruce. Do you know what that means?"

Bruce tried to keep his face calm as he met her eyes. "What?"

"It means I will make sure you never want to run afoul of the law again." Draccon took a delicate sip of her tea.

"And where are you assigning me?" he asked.

She put her cup down on its saucer. "Arkham Asylum," she replied.

CHAPTER 4

"Arkham Asylum," Harvey mused as he and Dianne lounged around Bruce's kitchen island that evening. "Doesn't that prison house the criminally insane? I didn't know a place like that could even be a community service option."

Bruce picked at his food. He had ordered burgers and milk shakes for them so that they wouldn't have to go to the diner, but none of them seemed able to work up much of an appetite.

"I heard the inside of Arkham is a nightmare," Dianne added with a frown. "Does Draccon really think it's okay to send you there? How are you going to concentrate on studying for finals?"

"You're studying for finals?" Bruce gave her a wry grin. "Most dedicated senior I know."

"I'm serious, Bruce! Arkham is *dangerous*. Isn't it? My mom said those prisoners are guilty of some of the most horrific crimes in Gotham City's history. And there are always jailbreaks and fights. . . ."

Harvey grunted as he glided a quarter back and forth along his knuckles, his movements slick as water. He flicked his wrist once, sending the quarter into a perfect spin on the island counter. "No different from the world outside," he muttered, slapping the coin down on the surface when it refused to topple over fast enough. It came up heads.

Bruce tried not to cast a sympathetic look at Harvey. His friend was here for moral support, of course, but Harvey was also holing up at Bruce's mansion because he was avoiding his father, who had stumbled home again tonight as a drunken mess. When Harvey had tried to hang up his father's coat, which he'd tossed onto the floor, the man had turned on him, yelling something about how his son didn't think his father could take care of himself. There was always some tiny thing that set him off. The bruise on Harvey's jaw had already turned purple.

"You're staying the night, right?" Bruce asked as Harvey started flipping his coin along his knuckles again.

Harvey messed nervously with his blond hair, his eyes downcast. "If Alfred doesn't mind," he said. "Sorry I keep—"

"You don't need to apologize. Stay as long as you want." Bruce jutted his chin in the direction of the living room's staircase. "Guest room in the east wing's all ready for you. Just watch the shaky banisters on the stair railings. There's a closetful of clothes for you here, all ready to go."

"I can afford my own clothes," Harvey replied sharply as he pushed up the sleeves of his worn hoodie.

Bruce cleared his throat. "What I *meant* was, you don't have to grab anything from home. It's all here. If you need anything else, just ask Alfred."

"Thanks. I'll only stay the night. Dad'll expect me back tomorrow. He'll be sober by then."

Dianne exchanged a glance with Bruce, then reached out to touch Harvey's arm. "There's no rule saying you have to be there in the morning," she said gently.

"He's my dad. Besides, if I'm not there, I'll just make it worse for myself."

Bruce tightened a fist against the table. He'd lost count of the number of times he'd reported Harvey's father to the police, but every single time social services went to visit their home, the elder Dent seemed put together and calm. "Harvey," Bruce tried again, "if you report him, you won't have to go back home. You can just—"

"I'm not turning on him, Bruce," Harvey interrupted, spinning his coin hard enough to send it skipping off the counter. It clinked on the floor tiles.

Bruce sighed inwardly. "Well . . . you can stay longer, okay? If you want."

"I'll think about it." But Harvey was already shrinking away from the questions, and Bruce knew that lingering any longer on the topic would be going too far. On his other side, Dianne was giving him a pointed look. *Leave him be*, she was trying to say. Suddenly, the punishment of doing community service inside Arkham seemed light, even trivial, compared with what Harvey had to face every time he went home.

Harvey bent to retrieve his coin and started spinning it again. "So," he muttered, changing the subject, "did the detective say why she was sending you there?"

"She didn't need to say anything," Bruce replied. "I think she picked a place where I'd be most likely to learn my lesson."

"What's your lesson?"

"To not help the police?" he guessed.

Harvey sighed. "To not *interfere* with the police. It's not up to you to save the world, Bruce."

"I know, I know." Bruce grimaced, picked up Harvey's coin, and inspected it. "I'm just being difficult about it. I was really looking forward to spending most of our last summer together."

Dianne nudged Bruce once with her elbow. "Well, you were

going to work on security projects with Lucius at WayneTech this summer, weren't you? Maybe seeing the inside of Arkham will give you some ideas."

Some ideas. Bruce lingered on her words for a moment. She had a point. He'd obsessed over criminal cases since he was young— but reading mystery novels and listening to a police scanner in the middle of the night would be nothing like seeing the inside of a prison with his own eyes. Maybe his time at Arkham could be his own personal study on how justice worked, a close look at how the asylum's prisoners behaved and at the prison's security system. It was a better way of thinking about his sentence.

"I'll try to get on Draccon's good side," he said. "Maybe the whole thing won't be too bad."

"Well, at least you can say you've crossed paths with the most dangerous criminals in the city," Dianne added as she bit into her burger. "I mean, when will you get to do *that* again?"

Bruce had once watched a documentary about the Elizabeth Arkham Asylum when he was still a freshman in high school. It was a sixty-minute exposé about the prison system in the entire country, and Arkham, on the outskirts of Gotham City and fully overseen by the city government, had been singled out as a particularly controversial penitentiary. If it were truly a prison, critics said, it should be called one, and if it were truly a hospital, it should be restructured as a ward, a mental health facility, or a rehabilitation center. *Asylums* were relics of a darker time and should be left in the past. Bruce knew of several petitions that had circulated recently in an attempt to change Arkham's name and upgrade the facility to the modern era.

But as Alfred drove Bruce along the bleak road curving out of the city and into a stretch of forest, then up a hill of yellowing grass and sheer rock, Bruce didn't think Arkham's grounds looked like a place that *could* change. Or that had *ever* changed. The long road approaching the asylum's gates was lined with skeletal trees that were bare even now, in early summer. Aging signs warned against picking up any hitchhikers. In the distance was an old tower, also a part of the penitentiary, that had in the past shone its lights upon escaping inmates who had been lucky—or unlucky—enough to get past the prison's walls.

What a way to spend a Saturday, Bruce thought glumly. He wondered what this area must have looked like when the asylum was still new. He couldn't picture the place with flowering trees or green lawns. Maybe it had always been dying.

Arkham loomed at the top of the hill. The prison's outer gates looked like an antique from a bygone era, tall and menacing and gothic, with the name ARKHAM ASYLUM spelled out in rusted iron across its spiked bars. On either side of the gates, twin statues leered down at them, their bodies bony underneath their carved hoods, their brows serious and their cheeks sunken. One of them held a balance scale in its frozen grasp. Bruce couldn't tell if the figures were supposed to represent justice or death. Perhaps here, there was no differentiating between the two.

Arkham Asylum was shaped like a giant U, a monstrosity of stone and spires, with some floors lacking windows altogether. Four tall watchtowers overlooked the complex, along with a main building rising high in the center of the grounds, its roof coming to a sharp point. More towers lined the perimeter of both the outer and inner gates, and even from inside the car, Bruce could see the guards in the posts with their rifles drawn, the narrow gun barrels stark against a gray sky.

As they drove through the concrete field, Bruce spotted Draccon—looking as polished as ever, her black braids tied up into the familiar neat bun—already waiting for them near the enormous front doors, with two guards and a short, round woman in a plain black shirt.

Bruce took a deep breath. He shouldn't be this nervous, but when he looked down at his hands folded in his lap, he noticed they were shaking. He squeezed them together. Passing through the gates of Arkham reminded him of how impenetrable this place must be and gave him the unpleasant feeling that *he* was now a prisoner who had been sentenced here. How inmates had ever escaped in the past, he had no idea.

You won't be here long. Five weeks will fly by, he tried to tell himself.

"Good luck today, Master Wayne," Alfred said as they stopped at the steps leading up to the front doors.

Bruce looked away from the windows to the rearview mirror, where he could see Alfred's familiar eyes. With a sigh, he nodded at his guardian, then pushed open the car door and stepped out to meet the people waiting for him.

As he approached, the woman in the black shirt uncrossed her arms and stretched one hand out toward him. She was shorter than Bruce, but Bruce still winced at the strength of her handshake. Her skin was light brown, her hazel eyes as hard as marbles. Bruce noticed that the guards on either side of her wore bulletproof vests with bold white SECURITY inscriptions.

"You're early," the woman grunted. She peered over his shoulder at Alfred's car, which had turned around to leave. "Glad you hired a babysitter who knows how to tell time."

"His name is Alfred," Bruce said. "He's my guardian."

The woman just grinned at him. "Yeah, and I'm sure he doesn't ever think of you as a baby he has to sit for."

"Bruce, this is Dr. Zoe James," Draccon said with a sigh as she adjusted her glasses. "The head warden of Arkham. You'll report directly to her."

"The detective thinks I'm difficult." Dr. James winked once at Bruce. "But we'll make this visit of yours fun, won't we, Wayne?"

"You *are* difficult," Draccon replied, rolling her eyes. "Don't make me regret this, James."

"I've never been anything but the sweetest." And before Draccon could reply, James whistled a cheery jingle and waved for them to follow her. She glanced over her shoulder at Bruce. "You'll need to sign in at the front desk every time you're here, and then get my signature, or your hours will count as invalid. So play nice, or we can make this game real hard for you."

They stood before the front doors. Only now did Bruce see that the doors were solid metal, a modern design that stood out from the gothic architecture. James placed her hand against a palm pad on one side of the doors, then punched in a long code. The doors gave a loud clank, gradually pulling to either side to reveal a dimly lit lobby.

Bruce followed Dr. James and Draccon to a small counter protected by a wall of thick glass. Behind them, the front doors slid shut with a bang, sealing them in.

A surly attendant looked up at them and smacked gum loudly between his teeth. His chewing paused for a moment at the sight of Bruce. One edge of his lips tilted up. "It's the kid," he said, narrowing his eyes as he passed Bruce a note card through the small gap at the bottom of the window. He nodded once at James. "Don't look as rich as the TV makes him."

Bruce kept his head turned down, hoping the man didn't notice the slight coloring on his cheeks, and filled out the note card as quickly as he could. He passed it back. Draccon and James led him farther into the building, where they passed through a pair of barred sliding doors flanked on either side by guards armed with live weapons.

They were inside the halls of Arkham.

The first thing that struck Bruce was how coldly lit the halls were. Fluorescent lights beamed icily across the tiled floors and speckled walls, casting everything in a sickly green. The walls gave Bruce the distinct feeling that they were closing in from all sides, that eventually they would crowd around him and crush him like a bug. From somewhere in another hall came the echo of angry shouts and a wild peal of what could be either laughter or sobs.

"Mayor Price's administration oversees this place," James said as they went. "The fact that they keep such close watch over every-thing here—our guards, tech, facilities, workers—should tell you everything you need to know about how dangerous the city consid-ers these criminals."

A couple of prison guards marched down the hall, not making eye contact with them as they half dragged an inmate with a jag-ged scar running down his face. The prisoner turned alert as they passed. "Well, well," he said, craning his neck. He scowled at Bruce. "What's this delicate little piece of flesh doing in a place like this?" And before anyone could stop him, he lunged for Bruce.

Bruce instinctively fell into his fighter stance. But James was al-ready there, grabbing the prisoner's right arm, twisting him around, and pinning him against the wall hard enough to make his cheeks turn bright pink.

"Nice reflexes," Draccon commented in mild surprise at Bruce.

Bruce's heart pounded furiously in his chest. "Guess the gym's good for something," he managed to reply.

"Another display like that," James warned the prisoner, "and I'll add years to your sentence. I know how much you enjoy our time together." She gave him a bitter smile, and the prisoner snarled back at her. His eyes settled on Bruce again, and when they did, he allowed himself a grim little grin.

"Skin's too soft and clean for this place, pretty boy," he spat out. "If you need some scars, you come find me."

Bruce looked away, his heart still hammering, as the guards continued dragging the man down the hall. He tried to imagine the man as a child, as *himself,* a boy sitting on the front lawn with his father and watching the bats stream out into the evening. Maybe some people were never young.

At his side, James watched him with her arms crossed. "What are you thinking, Wayne?"

"I'm wondering at what point someone makes the flip from a child into a killer."

"Ah. Interested in criminal psychology, are you?" James replied. "Well, you're in the right place. Our inmates would make you tremble in your boots. That man you just saw? He killed four people in a café."

A chill swept through Bruce. "Yeah, he seemed pleasant," he muttered.

"Dr. James has been the head warden here for a decade," Draccon added. "As you can see, it takes a certain level of steel to manage a place like this."

They left the small corridor, and suddenly the space opened into a huge, vaulted ceiling where they could see floors and floors of jail cells. Bruce froze in place at the sight of Arkham's entire expanse. This was a gateway to hell.

"What's the matter?" Draccon said dryly. "Finally regretting your joy ride?"

"This is the female east wing," James called out as they walked to the right. "Men are kept in the west wing. Medical facilities are in the center halls connecting the two." *That explains the U shape*, Bruce thought. "There is an additional level below our feet that houses our intensive-treatment inmates. You are going to sweep and then mop the halls in the female wing, as well as scrub the toilets the guards use. Tomorrow you'll clean the basement level. We'll work around the remainder of your school year, but once your summer starts, I expect to see you in here every morning. Our janitors have no trouble keeping this place spotless, so I think a billionaire should easily be able to do the same. I suggest you learn quickly."

Bruce looked inside one of the cells. A female inmate in an orange uniform leaned against its bars, and when she caught his gaze, she sneered at him.

"Hey, ladies!" she shouted as they passed. "Looks like they upgraded our guards!"

The others took up the cry, yelling vulgar suggestions at him. Bruce gritted his teeth and kept his gaze firmly on the hall. He'd seen guys catcall Dianne, had even gotten into fistfights with a few of them over it. But this was the first time he'd ever experienced it directly. *Why don't you smile, Bruce?* It reminded him of the way the paparazzi swarmed around him like flies, peppering him relentlessly, punishing him when he didn't respond accordingly. He caught a glimpse of Draccon's face; despite the detective's desire to punish him, even she seemed to sympathize a little.

They finally, mercifully, reached the end of the wing. James led them through the medical halls and past workers fixing the doors, through more of the fluorescent, cold green corridors.

They used an elevator to reach the basement level. It was dark, dank, and moist, an air of permanent staleness permeating the space. A sign hung over the entrance: ARKHAM ASYLUM INTENSIVE TREATMENT.

"The worst of the worst stay down here, Wayne," James said over her shoulder. "I'd try to do my work quickly in this hall, if I were you."

Two workers were reprogramming the door's security lock. Bruce noted the security cameras regularly dotting the ceiling. The cell doors were solid metal down here, smaller versions of the heavy sliding doors at the asylum's main entrance and noticeably more fortified than those along the upper corridors of Arkham. Each cell door had a window of what must be bulletproof glass, through which Bruce could occasionally see a prisoner sitting inside a stark room. The uniforms they wore down here differed from the orange ones of the other inmates. They were white, as if to mark them as a special breed of dangerous.

"More than usual down here, James," Draccon said as they went.

James shrugged. "More crimes than usual," she replied. "We had three Nightwalkers moved here just yesterday from Gotham City Penitentiary."

At that, Draccon shook her head in frustration.

"Still no luck figuring out what the hell they were up to that night, huh?" James asked.

"I'm afraid not."

"The Nightwalkers?" Bruce asked, grateful for something to think about other than his sentence. "Just how many of them are out there?"

"Don't worry about it, Wayne," came Draccon's stern reply. "Be grateful that this isn't your business."

Several voices came from one of the cells near the end of the hall. As they approached it, James nodded toward the cell door. "That's one of the new transfers I was talking about," she said. "Trickiest Nightwalker we've ever gotten."

Through the window, Bruce caught a glimpse of the scene. Three men—one dressed like a detective, the other two in police uniforms—were crowded around someone, interrogating the inmate. The frustrated voices were coming from the police.

"You think this is funny, don't you?" Bruce heard one officer snap. "Cutting an old man's throat, watching him bleed out? How did you get into his accounts? What's your team doing with all those millions? No answer, huh? You better wipe that smirk off your little face."

"Before we do it for you," the other officer added.

"Who else was *with you?*" the first growled. He said it as if he'd asked the question repeatedly.

Bruce tried to see who the inmate was, but then they passed

the window, and his chance was gone. The shouts turned muffled and faded away.

James shook her head. "She still hasn't talked."

"I ordered that one transferred myself," Draccon said, glancing coolly at Bruce. "Don't worry. They always crack."

As they left the hall, the angry questions continued to drift after them. Bruce found himself dwelling on what the police were trying to get out of the inmate. He would be down here often—he'd probably see this same scene play over and over again. Maybe by the time he came through once more, the police would have gotten the inmate to talk.

And maybe Bruce would catch a glimpse of who the inmate was. Who *she* was.

CHAPTER 5

"What's the matter, handsome? Never dirtied those clean hands before?"

Arkham, day one. Inmates leered at Bruce through the bars as he cleaned, their grins fixated on him and their taunts echoing down the halls. Boots and toothbrushes clanked against cell bars.

His appearance today was a stark contrast from the way he'd shown up at the benefit on his birthday, clad in his tailored suit and standing beside his custom Aston Martin. Now he wore a blue worker's uniform from head to toe, his hands hidden underneath a pair of yellow cleaning gloves.

Ignore them. Just concentrate, Bruce reminded himself as he made his way steadily along the corridor. They wanted to see his expression change, get a rise out of him.

"Girls, we got a billionaire mopping up our mess." Another catcall.

"Damn! Guess money don't buy what it used to."

"He's cute, though, isn't he?"

"I'd go to jail just for a piece of that. Come on, Bruce Wayne. Give us a smile."

"Tell you what—we'll stop giving you such a hard time if you take your shirt off and use it to scrub the floor."

Snickers rippled down the hall.

They continued throughout the day, one hall after another, until they all melded together into a single train of sound. Bruce kept his head down. James checked on him three times—and even though she never gave Bruce so much as a sidelong glance and a sniff, he still found himself looking forward to her presence. The inmates quieted whenever she appeared, and stayed taunt-free for a good few minutes after she left, giving him moments of reprieve.

Finally, at the end of the day, James came up to him. "Get out of here, Wayne." She nodded for him to follow her down the hall. "You're so tired that you're just smearing dirt around on the floors."

It wasn't exactly pity, but Bruce decided it was close enough. He barely remembered signing out. He couldn't even recall climbing into Alfred's car. All he could register was being grateful to sink onto the cool leather seats, and waking up the following morning in his own bed.

"How is it so far?" Dianne asked him the next day as they headed to their English class together.

Bruce tried to tune out the whispers and glances from classmates passing them in the hall. He could hear his name on their breath, along with snatches of rumors about why he'd crashed his car. *Drunk. Cocky. Temper problems.* The light coming in from the academy's windows stretched everyone's shadows out into long stripes down the hall, encasing the school behind bars. Bruce sighed, forcing himself to stare straight ahead. Yesterday had seemed to go on forever—and he would have to go back to that real prison over and over again for weeks.

"Could've been worse," he replied, then launched into the details as they reached their English room and settled into their seats.

Dianne gave him a pitying shake of her head. "Ugh. Sounds awful. Five more weeks of that?"

"It wouldn't be so bad if it weren't for all the catcalls." Bruce texted a few of the more memorable taunts he'd gotten to her, so he wouldn't have to say them out loud.

She grimaced. "Yeah, well, I know what *that's* like. And it's not right."

Bruce shook his head. "I'm sorry, Di. I hate that you've had to deal with that."

Dianne put a reassuring hand on his arm. "You'll make it. We're all getting out of here in a few weeks, and—" She cut off as the bell rang, then went on in a lower voice. "And your time at Arkham will be over before you know it."

Her words brought some small measure of comfort. Bruce took a deep breath and tried to take them to heart. "Before I know it," he echoed.

After all the jeers yesterday, the intensive-treatment basement of Arkham Asylum seemed eerily quiet by contrast when Bruce arrived after school.

The silence raised the hairs on the back of his neck. If he didn't know better, he could swear that this was a hall straight out of a horror film—the pale green cast of light, the bare walls, the faint echo of his boots. If ghosts were real, they would live here, whispering in the air.

As he started down the hall, he listened for the voices of detectives coming from the last cell. Maybe they were interrogating the prisoner again today.

Bruce had just made his way toward the first cell window when a loud slam echoed from it. Instantly, he jumped back a step—

and saw an inmate staring at him through the window. "Well, well, well," the man said. "It's the new boy. You look good enough to carve."

He practically spat out the words, and as he did, he stirred the rest of the hall to life, until other shouts echoed along the corridor. Bruce looked away and concentrated on the floor before him instead.

"What's the matter, boy?" the inmate said. "What got you into this slum in the first place, eh, cleaning up our sh—hey, *hey!* Where the hell you think you're going?" He rapped madly on the glass when Bruce took a step away. "You know what *I* did to get into this place? I carve. I carve *real good.*" He made a cutting gesture along his neck and down his arms.

Bruce sped up, trying to purge the haunting sound of the man's voice from his mind.

The next cell was no better—it held an enormous man, who looked even bigger in his jumpsuit, with every inch of his exposed olive skin tattooed, including his face. He let out a laugh as Bruce went by, and didn't break his stare until he was completely out of sight. Then he rammed his giant shoulder against the glass, making the entire pane shiver.

A third inmate was tall and eerily handsome, his veins visibly blue against his skin. Bruce recognized him from the news, a serial killer convicted of at least two dozen murders carried out in gruesome fashion. The fourth inmate was bald and thick-necked, with eyes as pale and clear as water, pacing from one end of his cell to the other, until his shoes bumped against the walls.

These were murderers who had terrorized Gotham City when they roamed free, who had dominated the news cycles. Now the only thing separating Bruce from each of them was a layer of metal and glass.

Finally, he reached the end of the hall. He slowed, then stepped closer to the last cell, where the officers had been interrogating the prisoner several days before, their voices raised and frustrated. His thoughts lingered on the inmates he had just passed, their twisted smiles and stares, their unspeakable crimes. If they were the sort who stayed down here, then what did it take to command the police's undivided attention? Who sat in that last cell?

The window on the cell's door stretched about half his body length, enough for him to see most of the inner room. It was plain, like the others, with nothing but a mattress and a toilet and sink. His eyes went to the lone figure sitting inside, pressed against one corner, legs stretched out, dressed in a long-sleeved white uniform.

It was the woman. No, that wasn't right—the *girl.*

She didn't look a day older than Bruce himself, sitting languidly with her head leaning back against the wall, her expression empty like a doll's, her eyes staring out at nothing in particular. They were very, very dark eyes. Her hair was long and straight and so black that its highlights appeared blue, and her skin was so pale under the light that it looked dusted with flour. Her mouth was small and rosy, her face heart-shaped, her neck arched and slender.

Bruce blinked. *This* was the inmate the Gotham City police were interrogating? He didn't know what he'd expected to see, but she didn't look anything like what he'd imagined. She looked like she belonged in his class at the academy, a girl far too young to be in a place like Arkham. In this fortress of the violent and broken, she seemed calm as death and starkly out of place.

And yet. There *was* something off about her gaze . . . something that sent a shiver down his spine.

The girl's slender eyes shifted. She looked at him without moving her head.

Bruce startled, taking a step back from the window. *Those eyes.* They didn't just appear dark—there was something more in those depths, something lurking and guarded, calculating. They were windows into an intelligent mind, and right now they were analyzing

Bruce. He had the strange sensation that she was memorizing every-thing about him, that she could read his thoughts.

When he glanced down at her hands, he noticed that she had folded a napkin into the intricate shape of a flower . . . but when-ever she twisted her wrists, the flower unfurled into the shape of a scorpion. Back and forth it transformed. Impossible, he wanted to think, to fold something that intricate with just a napkin. It re-minded him of the precise way his mother used to fold letters be-fore sending them, carefully sharpening the creases of the paper with her nail so that each segment of the paper lined up perfectly.

They stared at each other for a moment longer. Then Bruce stepped out of her line of sight and let out his breath. His mind spun.

Maybe the staff had moved the original inmate somewhere else and put this girl here instead. That would make more sense. Bruce frowned as he returned to work. What had she done to end up at the intensive-treatment section of Gotham City's most notorious prison?

He thought of his system of categorizing people. Where did she fit?

When he couldn't linger anymore, he packed up his supplies and turned to the exit. As he went, he got one more glimpse into the cell. He half expected the girl to still have her eyes turned to him, dark and depthless, searing straight through his bones.

But she had returned to staring off into space. She didn't stir. The origami in her hands was back in the shape of a flower. Bruce thought about it for a moment, then shook his head as he stepped through the exit door. Perhaps she hadn't noticed him at all, and he had imagined the whole thing.

CHAPTER 6

Bruce was still thinking about the girl as the evening drew to a close and he headed out of Arkham's doors to get into Alfred's waiting car.

"How was it today?" Alfred asked.

Bruce cast his guardian a dry look through the rearview mirror. "Had the best time," he replied. "I highly recommend it."

Alfred frowned at him. "Where do you inherit all this sarcasm from, Master Wayne?"

"I don't know." Bruce leaned forward and hung an arm over the side of Alfred's seat. "Maybe it's from you."

"Me? Sarcastic?" Alfred sniffed, the barest hint of a smile appearing on his lips. "It's as if you think I'm British."

Despite the long day, Bruce couldn't help but grin at the retort. He watched the dead limbs of trees blur past the window. The girl's face lingered in his thoughts, and when he let himself dwell too long, he could see her eyes flashing by in rhythmic intervals between the trunks, darker than night.

A few minutes later, they pulled up to the training gym where

Bruce spent many of his evenings. Bruce took a deep breath as he got out of the car, pulled open the gym door, and stepped inside. He needed a good, clean workout to clear his head, to shake the girl from his thoughts.

The gym was an exclusive club where the coach—Edward Chang, an Olympic gold medalist in boxing and wrestling—only accepted students to train on a case-by-case basis. Bruce's gaze swept across the massive unbroken space, ending at the ceiling, which yawned a good two stories over his head. Blue mats were set up in various configurations all around the floor, and an octagon ring lay in the center, where official spars happened between Bruce's coach and his students. There were dozens of stations with weights and jump ropes, punching bags and padded gear, multiple rock-climbing walls. At one far corner, there was even a swimming pool with eight lanes.

He went to the locker room and changed quickly, wrapping each of his hands in white gauze and dusting them with powder, and then took a pair of slim aviator goggles from his locker and pulled them on.

The facilities were impressive, but what made the gym so expensive was the technology behind these goggles. With them over his eyes, Bruce could now see labels—MATS and RING and POOL—hovering over each area of the room. A central panel showed him a carousel of rotating landscapes he could set himself in while he trained.

Bruce scrolled through them until he found his preferred setting. He reached out in midair to tap the option, and the world around him darkened into blackness.

In a flash, it reset—and he found himself standing on the edge of a tower that disappeared into a bank of sunset clouds, staring out at a sea of glittering skyscrapers all connected to each other with cables in such a way that he could do a run between them. Stairwells curved around the outside of each building in spirals. Overhead hung a virtual night sky. When he looked down, the height seemed so realistic that he felt his head spin.

The skyscrapers and obstacles all matched up with the layout of the gym itself, the mat formations and the octagon fighting ring and so on, the virtual stairwells syncing up with real, physical step-like mats laid out in circles. Bruce could select a mode on this landscape, too; if he wanted to run between the skyscrapers and up and down the stairwells, then the cables and stairwells would be highlighted, turning bright white to make it easy for him to see. If he wanted to scale the sides of the buildings, then footholds along the sides of the buildings would be highlighted instead, all matching up with the rock-climbing walls.

Bruce chose the option to highlight the cables and stairwells. They lit up in white, startling against the sunset scene. He stretched in relief, ready to shed the image of Arkham's dark halls from his mind and let himself stare down the dizzying side of the skyscraper. Then he jumped.

He landed on a cable that ran between him and the nearest skyscraper. Instantly, he began to run it, his balance unwavering, footing accurate from years of practice. When he reached the end, he took a flying leap to grab onto the bars of the building's outer stairwell. In real life, he hooked onto the metal monkey bars hanging over a series of blue mats, and his wrapped hands sent up a cloud of white dust. Bruce pulled himself up in a single motion, his arm and back muscles wound tight, then rolled onto the stairwell and continued running. Up a stairwell, then a flying leap, then another cable line. Sweat beaded his brow. With each passing minute, the warm-up exercise calmed him, and he could concentrate on nothing other than the steady pounding of his heart.

"Bruce!"

Bruce paused the simulation, then pulled his goggles up to see Coach Chang emerge from his office down the back hall to wave at him.

Bruce smiled. "Coach."

The man nodded at the greeting. His hair was shaved short on the sides, tapering into a fauxhawk on top, and when he folded his arms, his muscles bulged. His ears were scarred, hinting at his wrestling past. "Nice work on those runs."

Bruce was about to respond, when a second figure followed Coach out onto the gym floor. Richard.

Richard forced a smile. "Hey, Bruce," he said, flexing his wrists once.

"Richard told me he'll be out of town the night he usually trains," Coach said. "I hope you don't mind that I have him here tonight. The pair of you can partner up like you used to."

Like you used to. It'd been years since he and Richard had wrestled together as friends. *So much for a relaxing workout session,* Bruce thought.

Richard nodded. "Like old times." Bruce heard the note of exaggeration in his voice, the sarcasm.

Their coach seemed oblivious to the tension between them as he dropped a bunch of equipment on the floor. Then he glanced down at his phone. "Warm up a little, loosen yourselves up. We'll get started on a routine in a bit." He held his phone up to his ear and stepped away, leaving them alone in the room.

They moved to a sparring mat, where Richard started circling Bruce.

"Heard you left the benefit early," Richard said. "Did I really bother you that much?"

"I just needed to clear my head." Bruce searched for an opening, his eyes fixed on the other boy.

Richard let out a humorless chuckle. "Please. You think I don't know you well enough to tell when you're lying?"

Bruce flexed his hands open and closed. He remembered circling Richard around this same space when they were young, the way they'd laugh and throw challenges at each other. How different it'd felt back then. "If you'd said that years ago, I'd have believed you," he replied.

"Not my fault we stopped hanging out."

"Then why?" Bruce scowled. "Was it something I did?"

At that, Richard's expression darkened. "Maybe someone's head got too big for his brain."

Bruce could feel his temper rising. "Why—because I stopped letting you cheat off me all the time? Because you couldn't use me anymore?"

"Don't flatter yourself."

So that was it, Bruce thought, resigned. Richard wanted a fight, was *itching* for one. He narrowed his eyes as he saw Richard shift into an offensive stance, then pulled his goggles back on. Both of them connected on the same channel, and the ring around them transformed into a helicopter pad on a skyscraper's rooftop.

Richard lunged, one bandaged fist aimed at his head. Bruce brought his shoulders up instinctively; the blow struck his upper arm, and he immediately countered. Bruce circled his opponent, holding back, waiting for him to attack again. *Defense first.*

Another lunge—another exchange of blows. Bruce had always been lighter on his feet, and he dodged Richard's attack, but he could tell that Richard had been practicing. Well, he wasn't the only one who had changed. One, two hits—Richard barely managed to block Bruce's second strike.

Richard's face showed his surprise. He skipped forward and shoved Bruce hard enough to send him stumbling back. *An illegal move.* Before Bruce could recover his balance, Richard aimed a vicious kick at his knee. Pain exploded through Bruce—he clenched his teeth in an attempt not to cry out, but his leg still gave way, and he nearly fell. He caught himself at the last second, stumbling.

Bruce's dark hair fell across his forehead as he glared at his opponent. That wasn't a move learned here from their coach.

Their strikes turned faster and more frequent. Richard had a weight and height advantage over Bruce, but he was also slower, and Bruce could see him starting to tire. Bruce seized the moment to strike Richard twice in rapid succession against his side. The boy doubled over with a grunt.

As Bruce swung at him again, Richard grabbed Bruce's wrist and twisted his arm around in one gesture, flinging Bruce toward the edge of the ring. Bruce stumbled, but this time he was ready. He used his momentum to swing back around, striking Richard hard in the stomach.

Richard doubled over and held a hand up, a silent signal to pause. Bruce hesitated, breathing heavily, pain lancing up and down his body. He lowered his fists.

The instant he did, Richard struck. His fist connected with Bruce's chin. Stars burst in his vision.

The next thing he knew, he was lying on the floor of the ring with his goggles removed, staring up at his coach's concerned face as the man helped him up into a sitting position. When had Coach returned to the room?

Coach frowned, nodding for them to step out of the ring. "Break it up, break it up, both of you." He gave them pointed looks. "You two used to spar so well. Now I can't leave you boys alone for a few minutes before you try to kill each other."

Bruce winced, touching his swelling jaw gingerly as Coach left to get an ice pack. He glared at Richard. "Only way you win these days is by cheating, isn't it?"

"Poor Bruce Wayne. Nobody treats him fair." Richard returned his cold look before turning away. Somehow, it was worse than the physical pain Bruce felt. "In the real world, there's no such thing as cheating, is there? That's just life."

CHAPTER 7

"What happened to you?" Draccon asked Bruce when she saw him in the Arkham cafeteria that weekend. Her eyes went straight to the deep purple bruise staining Bruce's jaw.

Bruce didn't reply right away as he took a seat across from her with his lunch tray. The rest of the week had blurred mercifully by, full of finals and yearbooks and graduation preparations. Bruce was glad for it all, a welcome distraction from his spar with Richard. He was even relieved to be here at Arkham on a Saturday.

"It always looks the worst when it's healing," he finally said to the detective. "I'll be fine."

She didn't pry further, to Bruce's relief. Instead, she went back to her food. "Hope you're still having a miserable time here, Wayne," she said.

"Almost as miserable as you," he replied.

"That so?" She chuckled once. "Then you've got it pretty bad."

Bruce watched the detective for a moment. Her nails were perfectly unchipped, still the same nude brown polish to match the tone of her hands. She was as careful about the way she ate, he noticed, as she was about her appearance—the way she speared her food, the way she arranged her napkin in a perfect square beside her plate so that the edges ran exactly parallel to the table. No wonder she'd become a detective, absorbed in the details of things. In spite of himself, he liked her presence here. At least she lacked any interest in nonsense, and had no desire to taunt him. In fact, if Bruce hadn't come over to talk to her, she would probably avoid him for the entire duration of his summer probation.

Bruce's thoughts wandered back to the girl in Arkham's basement level. He had passed through the hall several times since they'd first locked eyes, although her cell was always filled with a team of detectives and police—including Draccon, who spent the sessions rubbing her neck in frustration as the girl remained silent.

Bruce had to marvel at the girl's stubbornness. She didn't even bother looking at her interrogators; she just stared straight ahead, as if not even aware that they were there. There was a different folded napkin in her hands each time—a swan, a boat, a star. He always found himself lingering there, waiting for her to twist her wrists and transform the paper into something else. Something more dangerous.

Draccon caught him studying her. "What do you want, Wayne?" she asked. "You look like a question's about to pop right out of your mouth."

"I saw you and your team down in the basement level twice last week," Bruce replied. "What's the story behind that girl in the last cell?"

Draccon raised a perfectly sculpted eyebrow at him. "This place boring you enough to make you nosy?"

"Just wondering," Bruce added, stirring his mashed potatoes in an attempt to make them creamier. "It's hard to miss the spectacle."

Draccon put her fork down and massaged her forehead. Whatever the reason, Bruce thought, this interrogation was clearly a sore point for her. "That girl. She's in there for a good reason, believe me, but what we discuss with her is none of your business."

Bruce looked at his own food, picking his next words carefully. "It didn't seem like much of a discussion," he replied. "Detective."

"Excuse me?"

He casually cut himself another piece of meat. "With all due respect, I've only seen you and the other officers asking *her* questions. She doesn't ever seem to respond."

Just by the expression that crossed Draccon's face, Bruce knew the answer—the girl had *never* responded to anyone's questions. She probably stared off into space the entire time they questioned her, pretending that they weren't even there, folding her bits of origami. He was surprised they didn't ball up her creations in frustration.

Draccon muttered a curse. "The Nightwalkers give us an endless string of cases."

Nightwalkers. Bruce leaned forward. "What do they want?"

Draccon shrugged. "You've seen their symbol, right? A coin in flames, usually spray-painted on a wall? They're a massive network of thieves and killers. They go after the rich—we're talking hundreds of millions of dollars. And they use it to fund their operations."

"Operations?"

"So far, things like targeted assassinations, bombing factories. Terrorizing the city. They see themselves in a Robin Hood light, however twisted, and like to frame their tactics as taking from the rich and giving to the poor—although all they've really given the poor in this city is a more dangerous place to live."

"Taking from the rich and giving to the poor." Bruce couldn't help uttering a chuckle at that.

Draccon eyed him. "What?"

"It's just that—people always seem to conveniently forget to follow through on the second half."

Draccon pulled down her red-rimmed glasses to look at Bruce over the top. "Philosophical," she said, sounding slightly amused. Then she waved her hand once. "It's nice of you to ask, Wayne," she said as she stood up and pulled her tan coat off the back of her chair. "But you're here on probation, not detective duty. Let's work on getting you out of this place, not more entangled in its web."

When Bruce headed down to the basement level after lunch, one of the lights in the corridor was flickering in an unsettling rhythm. It cast a trembling glow against the walls, making the hall seem surreal, as if it might blink out of existence if he shut his eyes. A couple of the cells were empty, while several of the remaining inmates were napping. Already, he didn't recognize some of them. Inmates didn't stay down here for long. Maybe the girl had been moved by now, too, even though Bruce felt strangely disappointed at the thought.

He reached the end of the hall, where the girl's cell sat beside the flickering light. He slowed his steps. She was still here, this time alone.

She's in there for a good reason.

But she was so *young*. Decades younger than everyone else in here. Bruce frowned as he watched her, waiting for something, anything—a violent tantrum, an insult—to reveal a clue about why everyone found her so threatening that they locked her up down here. His gaze returned to the new shape she was folding with her napkin. It looked like an unfinished lion. He wondered what it would transform into when she was done with it.

As he looked on, she glanced up at the door. At *him*.

Again, her look caught him off guard. This time Bruce forced himself not to jerk away. He walked toward her door's window and stopped right in front of it.

She stared at him for a long moment. Of course she wouldn't

speak, Bruce reminded himself. She had been in here for weeks, at least, maybe even months, and hadn't uttered a single word. How much longer would Draccon try to get something out of her? What exactly did they want to hear from her, anyway? If—

"You're Bruce Wayne."

Bruce stilled.

Did he just hear her *speak*? And not just that. She recognized him. The sound of her voice surprised him so much that, for an instant, he couldn't move. She was soft-spoken, but her words rang clear as a bell. Lovely. Soothing, even.

"Guilty," he finally replied. He wondered if she could hear him.

There was another pause, but the girl never turned her stare away. Instead, she continued to look at him in her calm, quiet manner, barely blinking, her eyes dark pools set against white marble. Finally, one edge of her lips tilted up by a hair. "*You're* different from the regular crowd."

Keep her talking. "Could say the same about you," he managed.

She put her lion-shaped napkin aside. "Who has the nerve to hit a billionaire?"

Bruce blinked, his hand rubbing instinctively at his jaw. She was talking about his bruise now. "It's nothing," he mumbled.

She pressed her lips together. "Hmm. Someone close to you, I bet, someone who knows you well." She tilted her head to one side, and her hair spilled over her shoulders in a river of midnight. There was something about her movements that made him think of a dancer, all grace and cunning, like she was aware of him watching her every gesture. "Everyone has their enemies. But look at your eyes—so tight and frustrated. Whoever did it is still on your mind."

Bruce didn't answer. There was something unnerving about the way she was studying him, splitting the puzzle of him into smaller pieces as she went.

At his silence, a glint appeared in her eyes. "It really bothers you, doesn't it? You like to understand why things happen, to solve the mystery and put it into neat little boxes—but you haven't figured this one out yet."

His mind spun, trying to find the right category for *her.*

She sighed. "I can see your problem."

"And what's that?" Bruce said, finally finding his voice.

"You hold back. Poor bleeding heart, always wanting to give a second chance." She was analyzing him with a look that burned him to his core. "Don't."

"Don't what?"

"Don't hold back, of course."

Bruce frowned, mesmerized by her strange words. *Don't hold back.* In the span of thirty seconds, this girl had him down cold. How did she know? How could she speak as if she could hear all the thoughts churning in his mind?

"Who are you?" he asked.

"I'm Madeleine."

Madeleine.

Bruce was pretty sure he had just heard more from her in the past minute than anyone else here ever had. He waited, thinking that she might say something more. But the girl just put her hands behind her head and arched her back, stretching herself out languidly until he could see the sharp divide between her ribs and her stomach under her suit. She settled, crossing her legs.

"Why are you in here?" he called out, hoping she would respond. But she stayed quiet. Whatever had possessed her to speak to him, however little, had clearly disappeared, there and gone so quickly that he thought perhaps he'd imagined it.

He lingered for a bit, just in case, but when she stayed silent, he turned away and left her alone, the ghost of her voice still lingering in his thoughts, bringing with it more questions than answers.

CHAPTER 8

Graduation day.

Hats went flying in the air, and cheers rang out from the crowd of students seated on the expansive green lawns of the academy grounds.

Bruce stood with Alfred and Lucius, smiling along as they congratulated him, making the right gestures—handshakes, hugs, attempts to shake off the mound of leis and medals Alfred kept looping around his neck. He'd been looking forward to the end of high school, had been counting down the days with Dianne and Harvey.

It was supposed to be the most momentous day of his life.

But his mind was distracted as he glanced around the quad. Madeleine's words still echoed in his memory.

You're different from the regular crowd.

Even now, he could hear her voice speaking clearly in his thoughts, as if she stood before him, secured behind glass. She knew who he was, had clearly been paying attention to him for as long as he'd been paying attention to her. Why did she bother?

"Bruce."

Bruce forced his thoughts to return to Lucius, who was talking to him. "Let's plan to do this sooner rather than later, shall we?" The man patted him on his shoulder. "A proper demonstration of the drones we're working on. The Wayne Foundation is hosting a huge charity gala to show them in action." He tugged once at his sports jacket. "Some important folks on that RSVP list—the council, Metropolis officials, the Luthors. . . . Everyone's interested in what we're building, Bruce." Lucius nodded off in the distance at a man with several police officers around him. "Including the mayor."

Bruce tensed. If the mayor was nearby, then it probably meant Richard was, too.

Dianne and Harvey came over, each of them completely laden with their own shares of leis and medals. Dianne caught sight of Bruce's stare, then took off one of her medals and draped it around his neck. "You're supposed to *wear* these, Bruce," she said to him with a smile. "See? Harvey's setting a good example."

"Hi, sir," Harvey said to Alfred, shaking his hand and then Lucius's in a formal gesture that sent his medals clinking. He seemed uncomfortable here, where everyone's family had shown up except for his father. It made Bruce step protectively to his friend's side. "You both must be proud of Bruce."

"As I am of you," Alfred said, smiling, and offered Harvey a kind wink. "Well done, Mr. Dent."

Dianne touched Harvey's arm and started pulling him away. Behind her stood a huge crowd of family members, all cheering uproariously about something. They waved her over. "Come on, Harvey, Bruce. . . . My fam's dying to see you guys."

Harvey opened his mouth to protest, but Dianne had already started dragging him off with her. Her family let out an enthusiastic round of greetings as Harvey reached them, then engulfed him in welcoming hugs. He blushed, but through his reddening face, his mood seemed to brighten.

"Go catch up with them," Lucius said, nudging Bruce forward. "I can keep Alfred company here."

Bruce thanked him, then started to head toward the others. He hadn't gone far when Mayor Price stepped into his path, with Richard right behind him. "Bruce Wayne!" the man exclaimed, putting a hand on his shoulder and giving him a warm smile that stretched the freckles on his pale face. "Been years since I've seen you. Look how you've grown! Congratulations, son—not that any of us ever doubted how well you'd turn out. Isn't that right, Richard?" He shot his own son's medal an uninterested, sidelong look, and Richard seemed to tighten like a corkscrew.

Bruce nodded stiffly. The mayor had always been kind to him. "Thank you, sir," he replied, shaking the mayor's hand. "Congratulations to you, too, and to Richard."

At that, the mayor didn't even smile. "You're a kind boy, but I'll accept congratulations for this one when they're actually due." The look on the mayor's face was so dismissive that Bruce could hardly believe it was being leveled at his own son. Richard stood there awkwardly, unspeaking, as his father talked around him. "It's a shame we don't see you around our house that often anymore, Bruce."

"I've been a bit too busy lately to come by, what with my summer work and my . . . time at Arkham. . . ."

"Ah, that." The mayor waved a hand in the air. "Showed initiative, what you did in stopping that Nightwalker. You've got all the makings of a leader. I remember when you were still small. Smartest kid I'd ever seen. Still are." He slapped Richard once, hard, on the back. Richard lurched, his eyes downcast. "Could teach this one a thing or two."

Bruce's attention went back to Richard, who was actively

avoiding the conversation now. A few memories clicked into place of when Bruce would do his homework at Richard's home. The man would always praise Bruce, always within earshot of Richard. At the time, and even now, it'd seemed like nothing big enough to dwell on—Alfred was hard on Bruce sometimes, too, and often in front of his friends. But something about the mayor's words, about Richard's distant stance, made Bruce dwell on those memories. Maybe their rift was bigger than he'd thought.

"Heard you're working with Lucius Fox this summer."

"I am, sir."

"Well!" The mayor's smile broadened. "It's to be expected from a tech whiz like yourself. You come by my office anytime, and I'll walk you through the city's work with your foundation. You're going to do big things for this city, son. I know it."

Son. Beside the mayor, Richard looked more miserable than ever, and Bruce felt discomfort knot in his own stomach. For the first time, he wondered if the way the mayor ignored Richard to heap esteem on Bruce was part of the reason behind their frayed friendship. "Thank you, sir," he responded, unsure what else to say.

The mayor nodded at him, then paused to wave once at someone across the park. Without saying a word to Richard, he left his son's side and walked away.

"Dad's always had pretty low standards for you," Richard said as he put his hands in his pockets. "You could steal his wallet and he'd praise you for it."

Bruce thought of Richard's desperate attempts to get ahead, his comfort with cheating all the time. "Is *this* why we don't hang out anymore? Because of your dad?"

Richard shrugged, although his eyes revealed this had hit him harder than he'd let on. "Last night I showed him where my name was in the award lineup. Do you know what he said without even looking at me? He asked where *you* ranked."

Bruce winced. "Sorry. I didn't know."

"Yeah, you never did." Richard's scowl deepened. "But then again, you don't have to listen to stuff like that day in and day out, do you? You've got Alfred."

"You make it sound like Alfred never gets on my case."

"He's just your butler, not your—"

At that, Bruce's momentary sympathy wavered. "Alfred's my guardian. You know that. And if you were about to make a comment about my parents, I'm telling you to stop right here."

The warning in Bruce's voice only seemed to irritate Richard further. "What? I'm not saying it's your fault."

Bruce shook his head. "What's really bothering you?"

Richard paused for a moment. Then he looked off to where his father now stood with a cluster of other parents. "I found out Dad locked me out of his trust fund."

Suddenly, it clicked. Bruce's trust funds had opened recently—his parents had handed over the keys to their empire to their son without a second thought, even as Bruce felt the weight of the responsibility more than the benefits. If Richard had recently learned, on the other hand, that *his* father had decided to lock his son out of his will, then Bruce's recent fortune must have seemed like a personal insult.

"I'm sorry about your dad. Look, I don't know what you want me to say."

Richard's expression shifted to something cruel. "I don't want your sympathy. At least you don't have to be a backup son. Your dad isn't even around anymore—"

A cut of anger rushed through Bruce. "Careful."

"I'm just *saying*. You can do whatever the hell you want, and nobody's going to stop you."

"Are you saying my life's *easier* because my parents are gone?" The anger was crowding in, blurring the edges of Bruce's vision. "And you don't think I wish, every day, that they were still here?"

"Stop being so precious, Bruce." Richard's scowl turned into a sneer, his own voice developing a harsh edge. "You know you like not having to work for your parents' approval. Everyone loves poor Bruce Wayne, because his mom and dad are six feet und—"

Bruce didn't know what happened next. One second, he was standing in front of Richard, posture tense, hands clenching and unclenching, trying to reason with his former friend; the next, they were both on the ground, and one of his knees was pressed against Richard's chest. Blood gushed from the boy's nose—Bruce must have hit him hard, because when he looked down at his fist, blood was smeared on his knuckles. Vaguely, he heard a couple of startled screams go up around them, but they sounded like an underwater hum. The space, the other onlookers—they blurred away, and for an instant, he was staring at the girl in the cell—at Madeleine— while she stared back at him with her dark eyes.

Don't hold back, she had said to him.

Then it was over, as quickly as it had begun. Richard was holding his nose as blood oozed out of it. Hands were pulling Bruce up, dragging him away as his boots kicked up dirt. It took him another second to realize that the people holding him back were Dianne and Harvey, their faces stunned and wary.

Harvey's hand was clenched hard around Bruce's arm, and his jaw was set. With a jolt of guilt, Bruce realized that Harvey must be familiar with scenes like this. But when he looked at his friend, Harvey shook his head once. "I know," he just said. "Deep breaths. I know."

"Hey, it's okay," Dianne was murmuring in his ear as she held his other arm.

Bruce stopped struggling and stared back at where Richard was still holding his injured nose and looking at Bruce with eyes full of loathing. Bruce's heart hammered wildly in his chest, Richard's final sentences whirling in his head. The world felt like a muffled vacuum, and he was on the other side of the glass, looking in at a friendship that had now completely fallen apart.

On the ground, Richard slowly pushed himself to his feet. His sleeve was ruined with blood from his nose, but to Bruce's surprise, there was a slight smile on the boy's lips, some darkly satisfied expression. "You're going to regret that," Richard said. Before Bruce could respond, Richard turned his back and walked away.

CHAPTER 9

Both Draccon and Dr. James noticed Bruce's unusual silence at Arkham the next day, saw the healing bruise on his knuckles. To his relief, though, they'd chosen not to bring it up.

News of the fight had spread swiftly through the grapevine. And instead of the incident fading away like it would for a normal person, Bruce had no doubt some tabloid somewhere was printing a blurry photo submitted by a student standing nearby where it had happened, pairing it with a headline that made Bruce look bad. He was steering clear of glancing at any papers today.

As Bruce walked toward the detective and warden in the cafeteria, he overheard a few words of what Draccon was saying to James. "... that there's something wrong with that girl ... no, still not even so much as a peep ... she knows, I *know* she knows, she's worked directly with the Nightwalkers' boss before, probably even as a close hand ... they're targeting all of Bellingham Industries' holdings, banks, factories ... they'll go for the rest soon ... I tell you, I've cracked a lot of people in my time, but she ..."

They're talking about Madeleine. Maybe Draccon had been

down there just this morning to interrogate her again, clearly with no success.

Draccon's gaze flickered to him as he approached the table; James turned in her chair to glance up at him, her hazel eyes flashing, and their conversation cut off.

"Detective," Bruce said, sitting down to join them. "Dr. James."

"Afternoon, Bruce," Draccon said, returning to nurse her coffee.

Bruce's encounter with Madeleine lingered in his mind. He knew it was only a matter of time before they saw the footage of it from the security cams and asked him about it. He cleared his throat. "I—" he started, trying to figure out the best way to tell them about what had happened. "I couldn't help but overhear what you were saying, Detective. It's about that girl again, isn't it?"

Draccon frowned as if Bruce were accusing her of doing a poor job. But then she sighed and lifted her coffee to her lips again. "The girl still won't talk," she grumbled. "Today makes exactly four months she's been in detention, and she hasn't said a single word to anybody."

"Yes, she has," Bruce said.

Draccon raised her eyebrow at him over her cup while James picked at her teeth. "You mean in your dreams, Wayne?" the warden said. "I think she's out of your league, little boy."

Bruce shot a withering look at James but went on as Draccon sipped her coffee. "She knew who I was. She told me her name was Madeleine."

Draccon choked on her coffee. Brown liquid splashed out of her cup as she slammed it down on the table and sputtered. Bruce waited for her to recover. When she finally did, gasping and wheezing, she dabbed her mouth with her napkin and then shot him a venomous glare. "You've been digging around in files," she snapped, her voice still hoarse. "Where have you been sneaking around?"

"I haven't," Bruce replied.

"Don't lie to me."

"You don't think I could make up a better lie than that? I would've told you she said something way more interesting than just a name."

"How'd you know her name is Madeleine? From one of the inmates?" She leaned back in her chair and crossed her arms. "Because *I* certainly didn't tell you."

"*She* told me. She said it to me last week, when I was cleaning down there."

James was looking at him with suspicious eyes. "I don't believe you."

"Check the security tapes," Bruce replied.

"You giving me attitude?"

"Calm down, both of you," Draccon said, holding out her palms at him. "Bruce, walk me through your entire conversation. She didn't just blurt out her name for no reason."

"I see you and other officers in her cell often," he replied. "Interrogating her. But last week she was alone, and she noticed me glancing at her cell. She said, 'You're Bruce Wayne.'" He paused for a second, sure that Draccon would interrupt him, but the detective stayed silent, willing him on. "So I said yes. She told me that I was definitely not the usual crowd around here and then told me her name."

A strange light had entered Draccon's eyes, like she had realized something that Bruce didn't quite understand.

"Maybe she likes you because you're her age," James mused.

"Maybe she likes you because she knows you're a brand-new billionaire," Draccon added. She considered Bruce for a moment longer before rising from her seat. Whatever schedule she'd originally had for the day seemed forgotten now as she focused her attention on him. "Fine," she said. "You want to know more about this girl?"

"Anything I'm allowed to know."

Draccon gestured toward the cafeteria door. "Come with me to the precinct."

Steady rain was pouring outside by the time they arrived, painting everything in a gray haze. Through the fogged windows of Draccon's office at the police department's downtown precinct, Bruce could barely make out the lights of Gotham City's independent theater shining through the wetness. He looked away only when Draccon stepped back into the office, bearing two steaming mugs of coffee and a thick manila folder tucked under one arm.

She placed a mug in front of Bruce, then dropped the folder onto the table between them with a thud. "Her name's Madeleine Wallace," Draccon began. "She's eighteen."

Eighteen. She could have been at his graduation, laden in medals and leis. "That's it?" Bruce replied.

Draccon nodded for him to take a look inside the folder. "Just got her file back from our clerks. It contains her whole background. Youngest inmate in the history of Arkham, not that it makes her any less dangerous. She's got crime in her family—her mother, to be specific. Madeleine's accused of committing three murders, all in the same way, and was on our wanted list for months before we finally arrested her back in February at the Grant estate." She fixed Bruce with a grave stare. "There are some graphic photos in there. Don't look if you think you can't stomach it."

Bruce opened the folder. Staring back at him was the mug shot of Madeleine Wallace, alabaster white and unsmiling, her dark hair straight as a sheet on both sides of her face. If it weren't for her prison jumpsuit and the number she was holding up, she would look like an average high school student. He scanned the rest of her profile, but there was precious little there, aside from the fact that she had a particular talent with technology. How someone like this could have committed three murders gruesome enough to put her away in Arkham Asylum made Bruce shiver, made him wonder what kinds of thoughts went through her head. He turned the page.

He flinched. It was a full-page crime scene photo from one of the murders.

Draccon nodded grimly at Bruce. "Think it's fun to interfere with police business? Welcome to my world."

There were pages and pages of photos. All Bruce could let himself linger on were a few obvious facts—an older man, a pool of blood, a ghastly look on his frozen face, the last expression he made before he died. Bruce felt his stomach twist as the photos went on, unable to tear his eyes away and yet afraid to see more. The edges of his vision blurred, and his breathing turned shallow.

The theater. Blood on the pavement. Someone was screaming, always screaming.

"Bruce?"

Through the fog, he felt Draccon's hands on his shoulders, giving him a rough shake. His eyes snapped up to the detective, who stared down at him with a worried look. "Are you okay?" She shook her head. "Shouldn't have brought you into this. We can head back—"

Bruce scowled and shrugged off the detective's grip. "I'm fine." He took a deep breath, then willed himself to stare back down at the photographic evidence. *Focus.* "I recognize this man," he said.

Draccon sat down and leaned one arm across the back of her chair, still eyeing Bruce warily. "You've probably seen him before at a Wayne function. Sir Robert Bartholomew Grant, hedge fund manager turned city council member. He was well known in philanthropy circles and must've thrown a charity ball every month." At that, her lip curled ever so slightly, as if the thought of such a wealthy man left a bad taste in her mouth. Draccon shook her head, and the expression disappeared, replaced with something resembling guilt at thinking ill of the dead. "He was found like this in his own home. Madeleine's last victim." She hesitated as they both stared at the photo. "Throat slashed, multiple knife wounds. His bank accounts were completely drained of their millions. In the weeks following his death, the Nightwalkers bombed a building that bore his name on Gotham City University's campus, then the charities he sponsored."

Bruce nodded slowly. It took nearly all of his effort to keep the memory at bay. He had a vague recollection of the man, knew that his parents must have been acquaintances with him.

He flipped the page and found himself staring at photos of the next victim.

"Annabelle White," Draccon went on. "Former president of Airo Technologies, also a heavy philanthropist who nevertheless shied away from public appearances. She was found in her home, in a similar state to Grant. Her accounts were also drained of cash, and her lab headquarters were bombed shortly thereafter."

"I heard about this murder," Bruce murmured as he went quickly through the photos so that he didn't have to focus on each one. "She lived nearby. I remember seeing the flashing lights of police cars on her hill all the way from my home." He'd heard the panic from the officers, in fact, on his police scanner, had followed some of the chaos live.

Draccon nodded. As Bruce flipped to the last page, she continued. "Edward Bellingham III, heir to the Bellingham oil fortune. Same type of murder, also committed in his own home. This was the one where we finally found a print that led us to Madeleine, although there were clearly multiple assailants involved in each crime—two different sets of tire tracks on the path leading to both the front and back entrances, locks on doors picked at opposite ends of the estate."

Bellingham. *Bellingham Industries & Co.*, the name on the side of the building where Bruce had chased the Nightwalker's getaway car. "He owned the place the Nightwalkers bombed, didn't he?" Bruce asked.

Draccon nodded. "Same story. Fortunes drained, still untraceable. His legacies and landmarks destroyed. The Nightwalkers are waging a war against the upper rungs, Bruce—they want to punish the elite who they think have corrupted the system, and they do it by stealing those individuals' money and using it to fund the destruction of all those people ever cared about."

These victims could have been his parents. Who did they leave behind? Did each of these people have young sons, daughters, siblings, people who now had to figure out how to live life without a loved one? The thought lodged in Bruce's throat, bringing with it a sense of rage. Was there ever a reason to kill? Did Madeleine sleep well at night, with the blood that stained her hands?

Blood on the pavement. Blood on the ground.

He closed the folder and felt an immediate sense of relief. He looked across the table at Draccon, who was using her coffee mug to warm her hands. "All wealthy philanthropists," he said.

"And all murdered in their homes," Draccon added. "In each case, the home's security system had not only been compromised, but had been completely reprogrammed to work against the owner, trapping them inside their own home instead of protecting them. Grant's system should have dialed the police, for instance, but instead, it unlocked the door in his garage, letting the assailants inside. The security cameras throughout his home were rewired to aid the intruders in figuring out exactly where Grant was in the house. And so on."

Turning his security against himself, and then turning his money against him, too. Bruce shivered, imagining his own mansion sealing him in like a tomb. "And Madeleine's connected to the Nightwalkers?"

"At the time of her arrest, she was found escaping the estate grounds with a canister of spray paint in her backpack that matched the paint used to draw the Nightwalkers' symbol inside the house. It gives us reason to believe that she and at least one of her accomplices are Nightwalkers. She might even be a highly ranked member herself. We've been trying to get information out of her for months—with plea deals, then with threats—but she hasn't so much as uttered a peep. That is, until you came waltzing along."

"I don't waltz."

Draccon's eyebrows lifted at his retort, and a hint of amusement flashed across her face. "Skipping, then," she said dryly. "You seem like a skipper."

Bruce didn't say it out loud, and he appreciated Draccon not saying it, either—but it couldn't have been a coincidence that Bruce himself was also a wealthy heir and following in his parents' philanthropic footsteps. A member of Gotham City's elite. A perfect victim for her—*their*—taste.

"We've managed to get a little bit about Madeleine from other Nightwalker inmates," Draccon continued. "Not much, not enough, but it's better than nothing. She's a skilled manipulator. Apparently, she can read a person better than they can read themselves, can figure out the people who matter to you and then use your relationship with them to burrow into your mind."

Bruce thought of her penetrating stare, the way she had guessed his issues with Richard and then planted a seed in his thoughts. *Don't hold back.* And he hadn't even said a word to her about his issues. A chill ran through him. "I can believe that," he replied, his voice hoarse.

"Bruce," Draccon said, eyeing him carefully. "Your mentor, Lucius Fox. We approached him about creating a better security system for your new bank accounts. This is why."

Bruce blinked. *The security Lucius recently installed on his accounts.* "That was a request from GCPD?"

Draccon nodded again.

So this was why Lucius had been keen to develop securities

specifically for Bruce's accounts. They were going to use it to further secure the city's banks, sure—but they had developed it first to protect Bruce from the Nightwalkers.

"Well." Draccon gauged his reactions. "You are on this case now," she finally said, "whether you like it or not."

Bruce nodded. Now that he knew more about Madeleine as a killer, the thought of seeing her in Arkham again brought up a different feeling in his chest. His heart turned cold, hard. *I might have been too young to save my parents, but I can seek justice now. I can stop the deaths of others before the Nightwalkers strike again. I won't let them add me to their tally.*

"I want to help," he said. "You *need* my help."

Draccon grimaced. "If you weren't eighteen and legally an adult, I wouldn't even consider it. I'm hesitating even now, given who you are and who the Nightwalkers target. But she hasn't said a word to anyone but you." She studied Bruce. "So. Let's see if you can get her talking."

CHAPTER 10

That night, Bruce tossed restlessly in bed as one nightmare after another visited him. He was back on the midnight streets outside the theater, his hands shoved firmly in his pockets, shivering from the cold and the drizzle, his mother's arm secure around his shoulders. He tried to shout at his father to turn back and take a different route, but his father couldn't seem to hear him. Instead, they walked farther and farther away from the streetlights, wandering through pitch-black alleys hazy with steam and fog. They walked faster and faster, until they were sprinting through the street. His legs felt as if they were dragging through mud, but he willed them on.

And then the alleys weren't alleys at all, but passages, the familiar halls of Wayne Manor, the corridors lit by moonlight. He was shouting for Alfred now, but Alfred was nowhere to be seen. He couldn't remember why he was running—only that he had to run, that he was in terrible danger. Every time he reached the door that should have led out to the street, he would swing it open only to stare back down at the corridor leading into the mansion again. *Why couldn't he leave?*

He stumbled over something on the floor, then caught himself. When he looked down, he saw that he had tripped over Richard's bloody, mutilated corpse. He had a faint memory of hitting him, not stopping even when hands were trying to pull him away.

"Hello, Bruce."

He whirled around at the voice. It was one he had only heard once, and yet he recognized it immediately. Madeleine looked up at him from under her canopy of lashes, her lips full, face stunning. "How easy you make it," she said, glancing down at Richard's body with a smile.

Then she raised her arm and plunged a knife into Bruce's stomach.

Bruce bolted upright in bed with a startled gasp. Outside, a strong wind whipped branches against his window. He sat there for a moment, trembling, sucking in deep lungfuls of air, until his heartbeat finally slowed down. He forced himself to collect his thoughts.

He couldn't go in to see Madeleine if she was already getting to him before any interrogation even started. Bruce tried to blink away the images of the three murders Draccon had shown him. But if he truly wanted to aid in the investigation, if he *truly* wanted to learn about justice, then he needed to be able to face the darkness.

"This goes inside your shirt. This goes in your pocket."

Bruce leaned forward on his chair in Draccon's office. The detective held up a tiny, flat square that looked like a slice of aluminum. She handed it to Bruce, and he carefully slipped it inside the front pocket of his uniform. When he pressed it against the fabric, it stuck on firmly.

Draccon handed him a rectangular card, which Bruce tucked

into a pocket of his work pants. "The square in your shirt pocket is a wireless microphone," she said. "It'll pick up your conversations, crystal clear. The other piece will record everything."

Bruce nodded. "Anything else I should know about Madeleine?"

"Even without uttering a word, she'll find a way to make you doubt yourself. She's impossible to intimidate, and I've never seen her lose her composure. Be careful what you say to her. We'll be watching you at all times, of course, and will make sure you're never in danger. Still . . . protect yourself."

It was such a strange warning. Madeleine was contained behind solid steel. She had absolutely nothing to use as a weapon. "I will," he replied, although the detective's words lingered with him, making him dwell on how the entire police department had so far been unable to crack this girl.

"And remember," Draccon said as they both rose from their chairs, "no one except for you, me, and Dr. James knows about this. It's your decision whether or not to inform your guardian, but as far as anyone else is concerned, you're still just doing your community service."

"Know about what?" Bruce replied, and a ghost of a smile appeared on Draccon's face.

"You're hilarious, Wayne," the detective replied.

The wind from the night before had changed into a dark morning of low black clouds. By the time Draccon and Bruce arrived at the asylum, fat drops of rain had started to fall, and a rumble echoed constantly across the sky.

Nothing changed about their morning routine. Bruce quietly signed in, gathered his cleaning supplies, and headed down to the basement level, while Draccon disappeared to speak with James. But as they left, Bruce knew that they were setting up equipment in the warden's office, listening in on the conversation they hoped he would have.

The intensive-treatment level felt particularly sinister today, the pressure of the air seeming to push in on Bruce from all sides. As he neared Madeleine's cell, he chanced a peek in through her glass window. She was, as expected, alone again, this time standing in the middle of her cell and studying something on the ceiling that he couldn't see.

He let his gaze stay on her for a moment longer, hoping she would notice him. When she still didn't stir, he pretended to drop his mop with a loud clatter, then picked it up again. He straightened, glancing in her window to see if she was paying any attention.

She wasn't.

Maybe the first time had been the last time. Bruce felt a strange disappointment at that.

"You're clumsier than I remember."

The voice was sudden and startling, an echo of his nightmare—but when Bruce whirled and looked through the glass, Madeleine still had her face turned up to the ceiling, as if ignoring him. She continued to speak, though. "You're not scheduled for this level today. Why are you here?"

She kept track of his days? A train of thoughts rushed through Bruce. He could say, of course, that the asylum had changed his schedule—but it seemed like something she would see straight through, something that would alert her right away to the fact that he was here to secretly interrogate her. So he decided on a different tactic. "I'm not supposed to be," he replied, keeping his voice low. He edged closer to her window. "My supervisor is out for the day."

At that, Madeleine arched her neck and rolled her head back. Her eyes were closed, her lashes curving gently against her cheeks. She had pulled her black curtain of hair over one shoulder and woven it into a thick, shining fishtail of a braid, and the end of it was gradually coming undone without a tie. She turned to look at him. "Well, aren't *you* feeling rebellious? Did you come to thank me for my advice?"

Her advice? As if that had triggered him to attack Richard?

How could she even tell that something had happened? When he looked through her window again, she was now looking back at him. Her eyes chilled him as they did the very first time.

He had to be careful with his expressions around her. She read far more in them than he could ever expect a person to.

Bruce checked to see that no one else was watching before stepping a bit closer to Madeleine's cell. "I came here because you spoke to me last time," he replied. "And you almost always have a crowd of police in there, trying to persuade you to talk."

Her eyes returned to searching the ceiling. "And you're curious?"

"Yes."

She tilted her head in a slow, methodical manner that lifted the hairs on the back of his neck. "What are you so curious about?"

How could someone who had brutally killed three victims make such calm, collected gestures? Did she never dwell on the deaths? Or toss restlessly from nightmares? "I heard about the murders you committed," he said.

"Did you, now?" She blinked once at him. "And how does that make you feel about me?"

"I'm not sure yet. I've never spoken to a killer before."

"Oh yes, we Arkham inmates are the scary ones," Madeleine murmured, distracted, turning her attention to the ceiling again. "How many lives have you billionaires ruined?"

Bruce felt a cut of anger, even as her sarcastic words sent ripples through him. *False comparison.* She was messing with his mind. "Why did you kill those people?"

She shrugged again, falling silent, and her nonchalance annoyed him further. "What are you staring at?" he asked, nodding at the ceiling for emphasis.

Madeleine pursed her lips, considering. "The security cams wired into the ceiling," she said aloud, as if purposely meaning for someone to hear.

"Why are you looking at them?"

"To break them, of course."

Bruce eyed her warily. She was playing a trick, although he couldn't quite see her hand. "Maybe not the best idea to say that out loud."

"Why not? It wouldn't be hard. This is old technology, you see?" She pointed to the wires running along the ceilings, secured within metal piping, ending in the small, round cameras embedded outside each cell door. "All you'd need to do to disable the system is to use the right scrambler, set at the right frequency. Any device within its signal range could knock them out." She tapped a slender finger once against her temple. "Never trust tech. Anything made to your advantage can also be used against you."

Bruce listened in confusion and fascination. She was telling this directly to whoever sat on the other end of that security camera, monitoring her—it was almost as if she was toying with that operator like a cat toyed with its mouse, daring them to be on the defensive, maybe even distracting them from what she actually wanted to do. Or maybe she was just having fun. Bruce's eyes darted to the bed in her cell, the only piece of furniture she had. If she jumped on it at the right angle, she could probably reach the security cam—but she hadn't done it yet.

"Are you *trying* to get them to take away your bed?" he said incredulously.

There was something unreadable about her face as her expressions shifted from one to another, like the shapes of clouds before a thunderstorm. "Are these really the questions you came here to ask me today?" she asked.

Bruce's gaze went to her slender white fingers as she began to weave the loose ends of her braid tight again. "Why are you talking to me?" he asked. "You haven't said a word to anyone in months."

"Ah." Madeleine's smile widened. "That's more like it." She

tossed her braid casually over her shoulder, the weave loosening once more into a sea of waves, and yawned. "They gave you a new uniform today, didn't they? Your first one was too big on you, and a slightly different shade of blue. Did your supervisors have a change of heart? It took them weeks to finally hand you a better-fitting one."

Bruce glanced down at his clothes. *He* hadn't even noticed the difference. How long had she been watching him? "Good eye," he said, looking back up at her.

She beamed at him, seeming genuinely pleased. Then she said, "I hope the police heard that through the wire you're wearing. They have a bad habit of talking to me like I'm a fool."

She knows about the wire. How?

Bruce cursed inwardly. He should've known better, actually; in fact, *Draccon* should have. As he fought to keep his expression calm, Madeleine just kept her steady stare on him, waiting for his reaction. There was no point in denying it. *You're clumsier than I remember,* she'd said to him just moments earlier. He'd thought she was referring to his dropped mop handle, but now he thought that perhaps she'd been talking about the wire all along.

At least now Draccon had heard proof of her speaking to him.

"How did you know?" he asked.

"You're here on the wrong day. You're speaking slightly louder to me than before, because you're trying to make sure the mike you're wearing is picking up your voice. Your posture is off from our last talk—you're leaning forward to the left and craning your neck just a little toward the mike. You're left-handed, aren't you? And your mike is in your left shirt pocket, isn't it? I figured as much, from the way you've been cleaning."

His voice. His posture. His dominant hand. Bruce stood there for a moment, rendered speechless. She was right, of course, on every count.

Madeleine's brow furrowed in disappointment at his expression. "Well. If I was unsure before, I'm definitely sure now. Everything about your face screams that I'm right. You're like a goddamn open book."

Bruce cast her a sidelong glare. "Maybe you're too confident."

She stretched lazily, looked away, and took a step toward her bed. "You're boring me," she said with a sigh.

Protect yourself. Draccon's warning came back to him again, and this time it took on a new importance. He wondered what Draccon was thinking right now as she listened to the interrogation. *I need to do something, and quick.* If he didn't, he might lose Madeleine's trust entirely and put an end to his questioning.

On a whim, Bruce reached into his shirt pocket and pulled out the square wire. If Draccon could speak into his ear, she'd probably be yelling right now. Bruce held the square up to the window so that Madeleine could see, and then threw it far down the hall. He reached into his pants pocket, yanked out the recorder, and tossed that away, too.

"There," he said, holding both of his hands up. "You caught me."

Madeleine's expression didn't change—much. But her eyebrow lifted just enough to let Bruce know that she hadn't expected him to blow his cover so readily. He'd surprised her. *There's no point in doing any of this if she doesn't trust me.*

"I think we're done for today," she said, but a smile still lingered at the corners of her lips. Then she sat on her bed and lay down sideways.

"Hey—" Bruce held up a hand. His irritation came spilling out with his words. "Wait a sec. You spoke to me *first*, long before I ever caught the attention of the police. I never initiated any of this. You always knew that if you spoke to me, the police would approach me and wire me up to come back and talk to you. And now you're telling me that we're done here. What was the point of all that?"

"I wanted to see if you were worth talking to," Madeleine called out.

"And?"

But she didn't reply again.

Bruce took a step closer to her window, so that he now stood barely a foot away. He'd withstood countless paparazzi cameras trained on him. He'd managed to persuade Draccon to involve him in an actual case. But somehow, here, he found himself having trouble thinking of what to say next to this girl, no longer sure of what she knew or how she knew it, whether she was figuring out new things about him even at this very moment, whether she was playing a game with him. Whether she was thinking of ways she could kill him, were she free. The photos of the three murders flashed through his mind.

What category did she belong to? He didn't even know where to begin.

Maybe he really was done here. Draccon would have no use for him if Madeleine wouldn't talk to him. Bruce stared at her for a moment longer, as if she might turn around to look at him again— but she just stayed where she was, her eyes now closed in some illusion of sleep, her hair spilling behind her like a dark ocean.

Right as he was about to leave, Madeleine shifted, tucking her hands behind her head on her pillow. "You're not like the others," she said.

He froze. Turned back around. "What do you mean?"

"I *mean*," she continued, "they interrogate me because it's their job. Why do *you* do it? It's not like you need the paycheck."

Bruce thought of his late nights, listening to police scanners and obsessing over WayneTech's security work. "I don't like standing by, feeling helpless," he replied. "I want to understand *why*."

"Mmm," Madeleine murmured, as if deep in thought. She turned so that he could partially see her face resting against her pillow, her eyes still closed. "You have a heavy heart, for someone with everything."

Bruce could only look on. How did she know that? Had she heard it in his tone, his words? "What do you mean by that?" he asked her, but she was no longer paying attention to him. Her chest rose and fell evenly, as if she had decided to go to sleep.

A few minutes passed before he finally tore his eyes away from her and started heading back down the hall. In his mind, he could still see her slender form curled on her bed. Her last words had been said without amusement or sarcasm. They were serious.

They were the words of someone who, somehow, understood him.

CHAPTER 11

"You're a fool."

"I wanted her to trust me."

Draccon grimaced over her office desk as she dumped a sad-looking sandwich in front of Bruce. Several papers flew up from a stack at the edge of the desk. "So you tossed the entire setup? You couldn't have even tried lying? We don't have any of what she said next to you on record."

"She already knew the truth," Bruce replied. "I could see it in her eyes. You wanted me to earn her trust, didn't you?"

"Don't assume what I wanted you to do," Draccon snapped at him.

"Don't get mad at me for telling the truth."

Draccon threw up her hands and then rubbed her face. "This is what I get for trusting a kid to find something useful for us."

Bruce leaned forward and gave the detective a steady look. "Give me another chance to talk to her. She wouldn't have ended with that comment if she had no interest in speaking to me again. She was curious. I could hear it in her voice."

"Don't trust a word she says."

"You've never even talked with her before."

"I've made a lot of prisoners talk in my time," Draccon said. "Madeleine is feeding you strategic sentences, turning questions back around on you, wanting to know why you're interested in her, luring you along with that last bit about you. She could have been trying to bait you into talking about your parents."

"Don't."

Even Draccon hesitated for an instant, knowing that she had crossed a line. She sighed, a flash of guilt on her face. "I'm sorry, Bruce," she said, softer this time. "What I mean to say is—don't take her conversations at face value. If you keep letting her lead the conversation the way she wants it to go, then you'll be playing into her hands, and not the other way around."

Bruce opened his mouth to argue, but then thought better of it. Draccon was right. And if he wasn't careful, she would kick him off the case altogether, probably take him off duty in the basement, and that meant returning to the normal terms of his probation, the endless days of work. He pictured Madeleine's slender hands braiding her hair, the tilt of her head as she turned to him and smiled that unsettling smile. There was an ocean of mystery in her eyes, an unspoken grief behind her final, intimate words. He felt a need to uncover more, to hear her tell him the secrets she refused to hand to the police.

"I'll be careful," Bruce decided to say instead. "I promise. And I'll follow your lead on what to say to her."

The basement of Arkham felt narrower and more suffocating each time Bruce visited it.

When he next stood before her window, Madeleine was sitting up, staring off into space with her arms wrapped around her knees. He left his supplies in the corner of the corridor and walked up to her cell's door, his hands in his pockets. As he reached the glass window, he pulled his hands out and held them both up for her to see.

"I thought maybe they'd stopped sending you," Madeleine said before he could speak. She turned her head slowly to meet his gaze. There were those deep, dark eyes again—and when he met them, she gave him a searching look, as if she were pickpocketing his thoughts. "No wires on you today," she said.

"How can you be sure?"

She shrugged. "The detective was angrier than usual with me. She wouldn't sound so frustrated if she knew she could still get information through you, which means she didn't try wiring you up again." Madeleine rested her chin against her knees in a gesture that made her seem eerily innocent. "She wanted to take you off the case, didn't she?"

Bruce grimaced. It seemed like Madeleine could predict every single thought in his head. "Yes," he acknowledged.

"Why are you back here?"

Don't trust a word she says, Draccon had warned him repeatedly. But the final words Madeleine had said to him continued to echo in his mind. "I was thinking about what you said, the last time we talked," he began. "How you said it."

Madeleine gave him a mock innocent look. "What do you mean?"

"You told me that I had a heavy heart." His voice lowered. "I could hear the change in your voice, like there was something . . . something about me that you related to."

She leaned her head against one hand. "No," she said. "I just know what happened to your parents. Everyone knows about that, don't they? I was giving you my condolences, in my own way. Does that count, from someone like me?"

She was smiling at him again, in a lazy, knowing way, like she'd found something interesting and wanted to play with it—but this time she was talking about his parents. Draccon had warned him not to let her lead the conversation. And just as the detective had predicted, here Madeleine was, toying with the details of his past.

"I don't need your condolences," he said. "I'm just trying to understand you."

"How sweet of you," she murmured, her dark eyes hooded beneath thick lashes. "Bring flowers next time. Don't you know anything about seduction?"

"You're screwing around with me."

Madeleine flashed a glimpse of white teeth as her smile broadened. "Oh, I wish."

To his annoyance, Bruce felt his cheeks warm. What was he doing, trying to get more out of her? Madeleine Wallace was an inmate at Arkham Asylum—she was, in every sense, not normal, and now here she was, playing some twisted, flirtatious game with him. She had murdered three people in cold blood, slit their throats with the precision of a psychopathic surgeon. Bruce suddenly felt like a fool for coming down here and expecting a logical answer from her. Nothing she'd said before and nothing she said now would be useful. He needed a new tactic.

Bruce shook his head and turned away. "You know what? Forget it," he called over his shoulder. "Obviously we're not getting anywhere."

"Wait."

He paused. When he glanced back, he saw Madeleine had turned to face him now, her legs hanging down across the side of the bed, her arms perched against the bed frame. Her long, straight hair framed her face, and she was staring at him with a serious expression.

"I lost my mother, too," she said.

Bruce found himself turning back toward her. "You're lying," he replied, wanting to see her defend herself.

"I lost my mother, too," she repeated, "and so I know what it feels like, to have your heart weighed down like that. That's why I said it."

"What happened?" Bruce asked.

"Well, aren't you nosy?"

He didn't flinch. "You already know what happened to my parents."

"So?"

"So it seems like a fair question. The police said your mother had committed crimes."

The amusement in her eyes vanished in an instant, replaced by anger. "You don't know anything about my mother," she said quietly. "Or me." Then she sighed and looked away, lost in thought. "My mother was a robotics professor at Gotham City University. She was the best in her department, one of the best in her field. She used to spend long weekends with me, showing me how to take apart clocks and put them back together again. Even during her busiest days, she would sit with me at night and show me how a piece of software worked, how a line of code could make an artificial arm move." Madeleine gave him a nod. "You should understand that, right, Bruce Wayne? I mean, you're in charge of WayneTech now, aren't you?"

Her words sent a shiver down Bruce's spine, even as Madeleine's mention of robotics lit up his eyes. Wasn't he the exact same way?

Madeleine had noticed the shift in his demeanor. "A kindred spirit," she murmured, scooting to the edge of the bed. "What did you take apart when you were a kid? Clocks? Robots?"

"Phones," he answered, the memories flashing back to him now, how he'd sit at his desk and stare at the pile of circuit boards and batteries that were once inside whole gadgets. "Laptops."

"Me too," said Madeleine. "I used to build my own."

"You built your own computers, too?"

"Yes. For myself, and for others."

Bruce nodded at her hands. "Is that how you got the calluses on your fingers?"

"You noticed my calluses." She pursed her rosy lips. "Ah. Bruce Wayne is not as boring as he seems."

It was Bruce's turn to smile now. "You think you're the only one with a sharp eye?"

Madeleine laughed, a beautiful, bell-like sound. "It is my business to know what other people don't know," she answered, giving him a wink.

"Sherlock Holmes," Bruce replied, pinpointing her quote's origin and enjoying the impressed look on her face.

"Very good." She rubbed her fingertips together. "My calluses are from playing the violin, though. I suppose I have more in common with Holmes than I thought."

Violin. He was starting to wonder if there was anything this girl couldn't do.

Careful, Bruce. He could feel himself drawn to this girl, could feel himself aching to talk more to her, to find out everything about her.

But he wasn't talking to just anyone—no, this was Madeleine, a murderer imprisoned at Arkham Asylum, a criminal who was challenging him at some unspoken game. Her past victims had seen their buildings and labs blown up by the criminals she was involved with. She probably wouldn't hesitate to do the same to him and WayneTech. Bruce repeated this to himself several times until he felt firmly cemented on the ground again. *She's got crime in her family,* Detective Draccon had told him.

Enough small talk. "And did you learn all this from your mother?" he asked, trying to steer the conversation back to her past.

Madeleine looked away. Bruce felt a strange note of disappointment at ending their private little moment. "Why does it matter to you?" she said, folding her legs underneath her and leaning back against the wall. "She's dead now. Died in jail."

Died in jail. "What did she do to end up in jail?"

Madeleine's eyes shuttered behind long lashes, seemed to darken. Whatever the reason, she didn't want to discuss it. "Always curious, aren't you?" she said. "That's why you're back here, talking to me and getting nothing out of it other than satisfying your own interest. That's why you crashed your car in that chase and ended up mopping floors here in Arkham. You think you're going to solve the mysteries of the Nightwalkers, don't you?"

"And what about you?" Bruce replied. "What do *you* want? Who are you protecting? Why won't you tell Detective Draccon anything about the Nightwalkers' plans? The Bellingham Industries building?"

"Ah, that. Can't let it go, can you, Bruce?"

"Let it go? The guy I stopped is dead, so . . . I'm finding it hard to let go, yeah." It was a shot in the dark, but he couldn't help seeing if a blow would land. He cast her a sidelong glance. "I'm not like the Nightwalkers. Willing to toss people aside when they no longer serve their purpose. I'd like to know what was so important about that building."

She studied his face a moment longer. "Let's say, Bruce Wayne, that you are a person living in a black-and-white world. You know that, somewhere, color must exist. So you read every book about color that you can find. You research it day and night until you can recite the wavelengths of blue and red and yellow light, that a blade of grass must logically be green, that when you look at the sky, it is logically blue. You can tell me everything there is to know about color, even though you've never seen it yourself." She leaned on her knees. "And then, one day, you see color. Would you know it? Would you even recognize it? Can you ever truly comprehend anything about something, or some*one* . . . unless you experience it for yourself?"

Bruce narrowed his eyes. She spoke as if she had already grown old. "You're telling me Frank Jackson's thought experiment now?" he said.

"And *you* know of Jackson's philosophical work, too? Well. You *are* an interesting one, Bruce Wayne."

"What are you trying to say?"

Madeleine pushed herself off the bed and walked toward him. Her expression had settled into a calm sea that hid monsters far within its depths, and Bruce took an instinctive step back as she drew near. She stopped right in front of the window separating the two of them, then leaned forward until he could clearly see the details of her—a small, slight dot of a birthmark on her slender neck, the thickness of her lashes and each glossy strand of her hair, the puff of her lips as they folded up into a smile. *God.* She was frighteningly pretty.

"The first rule of fooling someone," she said, "is to mix a few lies in with many truths." She turned her chin down and gazed up at him from under a canopy of lashes. "It's hard, isn't it? To believe anything I say?"

Madeleine had been messing with him after all, even with her hurt words, her angry expressions.

"Then maybe I'm just wasting my time," he replied.

"You should be grateful. I'm teaching you." Madeleine's enigmatic smile widened. "Trust nothing, suspect everything. If you want to figure out the truth, you shouldn't just be standing here, trying to get me to talk. Go out and see color for yourself."

The Nightwalker's escape from the intersection of Eastham and Wicker now appeared clearly in Bruce's mind. What had been going on behind the faded brick facade of the Bellingham building? Bruce couldn't bring himself to look away from Madeleine's gaze. A prickling sensation crawled down his spine.

"You're afraid of me," she said.

Instead of his finding a category to put her in, she was breaking *him* down, every step of the way. "You're locked away in Arkham's basement," he replied. "I'm not afraid of you."

"Maybe you're afraid that you like me." She smiled sweetly.

"Why would I like you?"

"Well, you sure talk a lot when you're here."

"I could say the same about you."

A teasing light appeared in her eyes, and she pulled her hair over one shoulder in a shiny rope. "Maybe I just like trying to read your mind," she replied.

Bruce leaned his shoulder against the glass window separating them, then sighed. "Do you even know why they were there?"

Madeleine rested a hand on her hip and chewed her lip, considering him. He wondered what she was looking for. Finally, she said, "Go back to the building. If you want to find something, you're going to have to get inside."

Inside. "And is that a hunch, or do you know this because you used to work with the Nightwalkers?"

She just shrugged. "I might know some things."

"Do you know who the Nightwalkers' boss is?"

"So many questions. I can't answer everything for you—go figure out something on your own."

"How do I know you're telling the truth? You just told me to suspect everyone."

She looked pleased. "You *should* suspect me, more than anyone," she replied. "But it sounds to me like you want to get to the bottom of the Nightwalkers, and that the police don't want you involved anymore. I may have exactly the information you need, but you're the one who needs to use it."

This was what he had come back for—information that Draccon had been trying to work out of her for months. *Keep a level head. She might crawl in.* Bruce wondered if he *wanted* her to, just to see what she could do. "You know I'll probably pass this information along to the police. Why would you tell me this, when you've stayed silent in front of them for months?"

A playful light had entered Madeleine's eyes. "Because, Mr. Wayne," she said, "I suppose I've grown rather fond of your visits."

Even though everything in him warned him to stay away, that this was a girl who had blood on her hands, who might work with an entire organization of killers—he still wanted to stay here, wanted to keep talking to her. *I have to*, he told himself, justifying the feeling. *I'm getting further with her than any of the police have. I'm their only shot.*

"And what will I find, once I'm inside?" Bruce asked her.

She touched a finger to her lips teasingly, then waved farewell to him as she headed back toward her bed. "Check the north wall's lower bricks in the building. I'll let you decide whether or not that turns out to be useful information."

Bruce turned away, too. She could have just lied about everything, but it still didn't stop his heart from beating loudly in his chest. *Useful information.* Her words had taken hold in his mind, and he felt compelled to follow them.

CHAPTER 12

"You hate this band," Dianne said as she looped her arm through Bruce's. He had to lean down to hear her properly.

Together with Harvey, they were heading to a summer concert held on the greens of the new park in central Gotham City. The air was surprisingly chilly tonight, the result of a week of irregular storms, and in the sky, a few lingering clouds were lit up by the sunset in hues of pink and gold.

"I don't *hate* this band," Bruce lied. "I just think the Midnight Poets are overrated." But in the back of his mind, he was thinking about the surrounding neighborhood. The park was only a few blocks away from the corner of Eastham and Wicker, where the Bellingham Industries & Co. building had been bombed. If he could find a good moment to get away from the crowd, he could take a closer look at the intersection, perhaps get inside and follow Madeleine's clue.

Bruce hoisted his backpack higher, feeling self-conscious about the things he'd brought in case he'd need them. A bolt cutter, to get past any locks that might be on the building's doors. A knife.

A ski mask. Gloves. Items a criminal might pack, if anyone were to look through them. His thoughts flickered back to Madeleine for a moment, and the memory of her small, secret smile. What else did she know that she refused to tell the police?

"Bruce?" Dianne nudged him hard enough to jolt him back to the present. "I *said*, what's not to like? They're billed as the next great indie."

"Hey, obviously someone likes them," Bruce replied, recovering quickly. He gave Dianne a wry grin. "Far be it from me to stop you guys from listening to an awful show."

Dianne grimaced at him and rolled her eyes. Bruce knew she could tell that his mind had wandered somewhere else. "Well, if we see them playing at a Super Bowl halftime in the future, I'm totally going to rub it in your face."

"You've been acting weird ever since graduation day, Bruce," Harvey chimed in as he munched on a churro, spraying sugar crumbs everywhere. "It usually takes a lot to set you off like that. What's happening at Arkham? Is it getting to your head?"

Bruce hesitated. The most he'd mentioned to either of them was that Draccon had finally begun . . . not warming up to him, exactly, but letting him in on a few aspects of her detective work. The rest of it, though—the conversation with Madeleine about the Nightwalkers—he hadn't brought up to either Dianne or Harvey.

So Bruce shrugged. "Maybe some. Arkham's been a noisy place, with the inmates heckling me all the time."

"Maybe Detective Draccon will find a way to shorten your sentence," Harvey said, "so you don't have to deal with that every day. That doesn't sound healthy at all."

You have no idea. "I'll ask her," he replied.

Harvey looked ready to ask more questions, but Dianne just sighed and quickened her pace, forcing them to do the same. "Can we skip the asylum talk today?" she said, saving Bruce from elaborating more. He felt a twinge of relief when she cast him a subtle wink and then nodded toward the park, where people were filling up the grass with picnic blankets and lawn chairs. A few silhouettes lingered behind tree trunks, waiting for security to look away before climbing up to sit on the branches. "I mean—do you guys realize that this will be one of the last times the three of us all hang out together in Gotham City?"

"We have the whole summer," Harvey replied. "You're not leaving until the end of August, right?"

Dianne held up all her fingers. "Ten weeks," she replied. "Yeah. My *lola* reminded me of that this morning—she nearly sobbed into her rice and eggs."

The number sank in. Bruce felt a sudden pang as he realized how little time they had left together.

The three of them reached the park, and the topic of their future was dropped as they hunted for a good spot to sit. They finally settled on a clear patch of grass and waited for the band to come onstage. While Dianne argued with Harvey about the best song and Harvey tried to get her to sing the lyrics out loud, Bruce found his thoughts wandering to Madeleine.

Detective Draccon had warned him that Madeleine would try to manipulate him. She was probably right, too. But something about the girl's tone . . . *You have a heavy heart, for someone with everything.* She had said those words in a familiar way, as if something from her past weighed her down, too. What had she once lost? Draccon hadn't said much to him about Madeleine's past, or who her family might be. What if there was more to Madeleine's words than Draccon knew?

A cheer went up from the crowd, momentarily distracting him. The band was taking the stage, and the microphone squealed as the lead singer cleared his throat. Dianne cupped her hands around her mouth and shouted a song request, while Harvey jostled her aside to yell out his own choice. As the band began to play, the crowd joined in on the chorus.

Bruce just listened as everyone around him sang along, his gaze fixed on his friends. They made it seem so easy to get close, to take down their walls and just *be*. The feeling of aloneness came to Bruce again, the realization that he might never be able to let down his guard in the way that they could. There was Harvey—clean-cut, law-abiding, determined to do the most good from inside the system. And Dianne, the product of a large, loving family, simply had faith in the system altogether.

But what if the system just needed help? In every mystery he'd ever read, the police always stayed one step behind the hero. What if taking things into his own hands was the *only* real way to fix everything?

He clapped along to the second song, trying not to grimace at how bad it was, until he was sure that Harvey and Dianne had both turned their attention entirely to the concert. Then, when a track came on that got everyone jumping to their feet, Bruce rose and started edging through the crowd. Dianne cast him a brief glance as he went. *Bathroom*, he mouthed at her, before continuing on.

Beyond the park, the evening streets were surprisingly quiet. It seemed as if everyone within a one-mile radius of the concert had either decided to attend or completely avoided the area, leaving the sidewalks empty. A cool breeze blew past, bringing with it the scent of the ocean and a raw, pungent smell of underground sewage.

Bruce straightened his blazer and the hoodie underneath it, then pulled the hood over his head. The bats of Gotham City were out in force tonight; when he paused to look up, he could see a colony of them circling along the horizon, eager to start their evening hunt. He quickened his steps as the light faded completely from the sky, until only pools of streetlight illuminated the road.

Finally, he stopped at the corner of the intersection, right under the signs that said EASTHAM and WICKER, and studied each of the buildings.

Nothing seemed remarkable, at least at first glance. The cluster of police cruisers and blockades were long gone, the broken glass and bullet shells cleared from the streets, and it seemed almost as if nothing unusual had happened here. But the skid marks on the ground remained—deep black angry lines—and the Bellingham building still bore the charred scars from the explosion and fire. A maze of wooden scaffolding now covered up most of what had been damaged, new windows and bricks in a half-finished state, and a chain-link construction fence draped with black tarp now surrounded the property, hiding the bottom floor from view.

He walked slowly around the corner, taking in the details and remembering what had happened here. The police blockade, the speeding getaway car. The gunfire, the explosion that destroyed the building.

The Nightwalkers destroy their victims' legacies.

Bruce stopped when he made his way to the intersection, then turned. Here, he could finally see the name of the storefront painted on the brick lining the second story: BELLINGHAM INDUSTRIES & CO.

He crossed the street and made his way over to the building. Above the chain-link fence, he could see the chips in the brick that had worn away over time, the history embedded in the walls of this place. He walked quietly along the barrier, searching for something, *anything*, that might be unusual. The minutes ticked by.

Until a voice from behind startled him.

"Bruce."

CHAPTER 13

Bruce whirled to come face to face with Dianne.

He let out a breath and leaned against his knees. "For chrissakes!" he swore. "Could you have been a little quieter about following me?"

"*I'm* the one who surprised you?" she exclaimed, holding her arms out wide and answering with a swear in Tagalog that he couldn't understand. *She really is upset,* he thought. "What the hell are *you* doing here?"

Bruce sighed and ran a hand through his hair. "Is Harvey with you?"

"I made Harvey save our spots. Now, tell me what's going on with you. You're attacking Richard, you're wandering off alone to the crime scene where you got into trouble—come on, Bruce!"

"Nothing. I'm just taking a look."

He met her withering glare. Bruce could tell from the light in her eyes that she already knew he was hiding something from her—it was far past the point when he could continue keeping secrets. Besides, she'd already caught him sneaking around.

"Fine." Bruce crossed his arms. Taking a deep breath, he began telling Dianne about Madeleine. The first time she'd spoken to him. Her past crimes. Being involved in Draccon's investigation. He spoke in a rapid, hushed voice, as if someone might overhear him and send word back to Detective Draccon.

When he finished, Dianne's face had changed from brown to ashen. "I can't believe they roped you into something as crazy as this. You've got to be kidding me."

"They needed my help."

Dianne gave him a pointed look. "Listen, let's say that this girl—who is an *unhinged murderer*, I'd like to remind us both—*was* telling the truth. How have the police not found any evidence yet? They combed this street corner for weeks without finding so much as a hint of what the Nightwalkers might have been up to."

Bruce held up a hand. "And if there's nothing to find, then all I've wasted is a night of my time. But what if Madeleine gave me an honest hint? She told me to pay attention to the north wall. Maybe there's something the cops missed."

Dianne leaned forward and squinted at Bruce carefully. "Oh, I get it," she declared after a moment. "I've figured it out."

"Figured what out?"

"*You*. What's up with you—I've figured it out." She crossed her arms and peered at him. "You like Madeleine. You're all hung up on her."

"What?" Bruce leaned away from her. "*That's* what you got from what I told you?"

"It's obvious, Bruce. Remember Cindie Patel from seventh grade? You were wild about her—remember when she lost her grandmother's bangle during lunch, and you skipped five lunches after that just to look for it?"

"Hey, I found that bangle."

Dianne clapped her hands twice. "Focus, Bruce! You always need to be the white knight, and now you're obsessing over a random hint from this girl to the point where you're willing to risk your probation. It's the exact same thing."

Bruce gave her a wry look. "Except I knew Cindie Patel because she sat next to me in Biology, and I know Madeleine because she's in jail for three murders."

Dianne waved a hand in the air. "Details. You know what I mean."

Madeleine materialized again in Bruce's thoughts. *Maybe she's right.* But that made no sense at all. "Look, I'm here because *I* want to be," he said, firmly this time. "That's it."

"Whatever. You know, Harvey would be pissed at you if he found out this is what you're up to right now. And he's got a point, Bruce. Sometimes you should trust the police to do the right thing. If Draccon finds out you're snooping around like this, they might even extend your sentence."

Always curious, aren't you? He shook his head, trying to shake Madeleine's words out of his head. "How about this: if I find nothing—"

"If *we* find nothing." Dianne shrugged at him. "I'm involved now. I can't just leave you here."

Bruce glared at her, but she didn't look away. "Fine. If *we* find nothing, I promise I'll never do this again. Ever. But you can't tell anyone else about this. I'm serious."

Dianne scowled at him. "You owe me one, for making sure you don't get yourself killed."

At that, Bruce gave her a wry smile. "All right, all right. I owe you one. Thanks for looking out for me. And hey—Lucius is throwing a huge gala in a couple of weeks, to demonstrate some of WayneTech's drone security technology. Do you want to come with me and make sure I don't get myself killed?"

Dianne gave him a sideways look. "Really?"

"It's pretty fancy."

"Will they be serving good food?"

"The best," Bruce promised.

She considered for a moment with pursed lips. "Okay," she said. "Sounds like a plan."

Bruce gestured to the corner of the block. "Stay over here, by the frame of that doorway. There. You're not so conspicuous now. Keep a lookout for me. If I'm not back in thirty minutes, call someone."

"Fine. But only if you stay on the phone with me the entire time." Dianne took out her phone and tapped it twice. "And if it actually takes you longer than thirty minutes, I'm sending every cop in Gotham City after you."

"Fair enough."

Bruce headed away from Dianne and back along the fence. It wrapped all the way around the building without a single break, leading him right back to where he had started. He paused after another round, rubbing his eyes from staring so hard at the building.

What was he looking for, anyway?

Something in the corner of his eyes caught his attention. He looked down at the chain-link fence. He frowned, looking harder.

The fence was unbroken, sure . . . but along the chain link was a series of metal bumps, what looked like former breaks in the fence that were then welded back into place. It was a subtle detail, one that Bruce had nearly overlooked. But there was no question about it. The fence was welded shut. Which meant someone else had cut through it at some point, then carefully hid any tracks.

Construction workers. GCPD investigators. Private detectives. Bruce ran the series of noncriminal possibilities through his mind. It could mean nothing at all, of course . . . but this was a former crime scene, and an *unsolved* one. What if the Nightwalkers had been up to more here than just destroying the Bellingham legacy? Bruce looked back up at the facade of the building. Something had made someone return here, without wanting anyone else to know.

He swung his backpack around and unzipped it, took out his

ski mask and gloves, and pulled them both on tightly until his face and hands were hidden from view. He held up the bolt cutters, carefully placing each bolt between the metal teeth. *Clink. Clink.* One by one, they popped off, dropping soundlessly into his waiting palm. He tossed the broken bolts into his backpack and zipped it up. The overlapping fence swung open a hair. Bruce pushed it open wider, until there was just enough space to slide through, and then he inched his way in, disappearing past the black tarp.

Wooden boards were nailed all along the side of the building, but enough gaps existed for him to climb through. Inside, the space smelled musty, claustrophobic, the air reeking of dust and the tang of metal. Bruce waited for a moment, letting his eyes adjust. He felt comfortable here in the darkness. Immediately after his parents' deaths, he had spent many nights tucked in the safe black space of his closet, or in an empty pantry in the mansion, or up in the attic, where a cold draft blew. So many of his classmates had been afraid of the dark, as if it could hurt them. But Bruce knew the darkness hid *him* as well as it hid anything or anyone else. The darkness was an advantage.

His reflexes were on alert now, honed by all the hours spent at the training gym. As things gradually started to take shape in the dim light, he realized that he was standing in a single open room. Edison bulbs dangled from the ceiling's exposed beams, half of them burst open and broken, leaving shards of glass strewn across the floor. Everything had been draped in sheets—tables, chairs, machines. The dust on the floorboards was marked with shoe prints, perhaps from the police who must have passed through here. *Perhaps from others, too.*

"This place is a mess," Bruce whispered into his phone.

"What did Madeleine say to you?" Dianne answered.

"The north wall," Bruce murmured back, orienting himself. "The bricks that line it. She said to look there."

He turned to the north wall. It stretched unbroken from one

end of the room to the other—and sure enough, lining the bottom third of the wall was a layer of old brick, dark against the white paint above it. Bruce headed toward the closest end of the room, stopped right in front of the wall, and bent down. He ran a hand along the bricks. They were all covered in a fine layer of dust, just like everything else here.

So, Madeleine was right about this, had known the north wall would have bricks lining it. She must have been here before.

"Anything? What exactly are you looking for?" came Dianne's voice.

"Something unusual," Bruce replied. He suddenly felt foolish as he ran one hand along the bricks, slowly making his way down the room. He had no idea what would count as unusual, either—only that if he found it, he would know.

He had made his way across almost the entire length of the room before his hands paused on one of the bricks. Something felt odd about the texture of this brick—slightly smoother than the rest, as if it were handled more than the others. Bruce frowned and leaned down to get a closer look.

"Hang on," he whispered. "I think I found something."

"What is it?" Dianne asked.

"This brick feels weird." He gingerly pushed on it. "It's not sealed in like the rest. The edges don't quite meet the mortar holding it to the others."

Bruce pressed harder. Nothing gave, at first. Then—all of a sudden, the brick pushed inward by an inch, and the wall shuddered. He jumped back, nearly dropping his phone. When he looked up, he saw that a part of the brick wall had slid sideways by half a foot, revealing a gap of darkness.

Bruce stared numbly for a moment. Then he took a tentative step into the black and felt with his shoe for a foothold. *Stairs.* There were metal steps behind this wall, leading down a narrow shaft to somewhere beyond view.

"Dianne," he whispered, eyes wide. "There are stairs behind this wall."

Dianne uttered a curse over the phone.

Madeleine actually told the truth. Bruce shivered, wondering why she would help him—wondering if perhaps she was *trapping* him instead.

"Don't go down there." Dianne echoed his thoughts. Bruce could hear fear in her voice now. "Whatever you find won't be good."

He shook his head. "I'm going. Keep an eye out up there. Let me know if you see anything suspicious."

"*You'd* better find something suspicious down there," she retorted, "with all the trouble you're going to. You owe me big-time— you owe me so much you'll be paying off loans for years."

Bruce chuckled, then turned back around and wedged himself through the narrow opening. Down into the gloom. It was slow going—the steps were narrow and high, and wound down in a spiral. He stopped and tested his foothold at each step before putting his weight on it. Gradually, he descended through the darkness, one stair after another, until his foot finally hit what felt like a concrete floor. He was in a narrow space, and the air here was tight, full of dust. He forced down a cough.

"I'm at the bottom," he whispered, hoarse. Nearby, he could make out the dim outline of an abandoned construction barrier.

"Where the hell are you?"

"I have no idea," Bruce whispered back. He stood up and lifted one arm slightly above his head, trying not to bump anything. His hand hit the ceiling. It felt rough, like unfinished concrete. He held out his phone in front of him and turned on its flashlight.

The phone illuminated the space several feet ahead of him. It was a tunnel that led into pitch black. To Bruce, the tunnel reminded him of the narrow passageways in the cave near his family's estate, and the bats that sometimes poured out. He half expected them to come barreling toward him now.

What are you so curious about? The thought raised goose bumps on his skin, but he tightened his jaw and stepped forward. He kept his footsteps completely silent. "I'm heading in," he murmured.

The tunnel went on longer than Bruce expected, and the ceiling grew lower and lower. Why would Madeleine send him down here? What did she know about this place? What if the tunnel collapsed?

What if someone else is also down here? Bruce suddenly pictured an armed man waiting for him at the end of the tunnel, gun pointed straight at him.

He kept going.

Finally, the tunnel before him opened up into a larger space. He stumbled as the ground fell a half step.

The ground was different here—polished, finished. His phone's flashlight cast a small glowing circle on the wall. He shone the light farther until he saw a switch. There.

He flipped it on.

Fluorescent light blinded him. Bruce's eyes squinted shut, and he shielded his face instinctively. When he opened his eyes again, he sucked in a gasp of air.

"Shit," he whispered.

"What?" Dianne said, her voice pulled tight like a string. "What is it?"

Bruce stood staring at a room stocked half full of ammunition. Guns, bullets, extra clips. There must have been at least a hundred weapons of all shapes and sizes here, laid out on tables and hanging on the walls. He gaped. This looked like a military arsenal.

"Bruce," Dianne murmured over the phone. Even though she couldn't see what he was seeing, she could hear the tension in his silence. "Get out of there. I'm coming for you."

A faint sound drifted toward Bruce. He froze. It came from the other end of the room, where a second door led out. It was a voice, male and deep, frustrated. He sounded like he was talking to someone. Immediately, Bruce flipped the light switch and turned off his phone, shrouding the room in darkness again. He started to back up.

Too late.

The second door opened—and a man's silhouette stepped in, still talking loudly as he switched on the light. Bruce glimpsed a pale worn face, a beard. "Look, I don't have time to babysit this storage anymore. Tell them to bring the truck tomorrow night so we can move the rest—"

His words cut off as his gaze fell on Bruce. The two of them stared at each other for an instant, both stunned into silence.

The man squinted at Bruce's mask. "Hey—you're not—did the boss—"

Bruce started sprinting away, but the man bolted after him. Right as Bruce reached the narrower part of the tunnel, he felt rough hands grab him by his shoulders. His fighting instincts went on autopilot. Bruce twisted free of the man's grip and brought his fist up to punch the man's face in the same motion.

His opponent blocked his blow, barely, and threw his own jab at Bruce. Bruce ducked down. He swung a leg out, catching the man hard enough in his calves to send him toppling. Bruce turned to run again, but the man's fingers hooked onto his pant leg, dragging him down, too. Both hands grabbed at the mask on his face.

It left the man defenseless for a moment. Bruce swung up with every ounce of desperation inside him. His fist connected with the man's chin, landing exactly where it needed to—his opponent's head rocketed back. His body flopped, suddenly limp, and he collapsed on the floor.

Shaking from head to toe, Bruce stared down at the unconscious man lying at his feet. His limbs burned. Were there more people down here with this guy? *Stockpiling weapons.* Madeleine had led him straight to it. She had helped Bruce, when the police had failed for months to get her to talk.

Draccon's going to kill me for this.

But what were they stockpiling weapons *for?* There was so much ammunition down here that it seemed excessive for anything less than a full-on raid. And what if this wasn't the only hideout? An ominous premonition weighed on him. What were the Nightwalkers planning that would require so many weapons?

I should tell the police that I was here.

But what would he tell them? That he acted on a hunch based on the words of a murderer? That he was trespassing? He might get into even more trouble this time around—and he was in no mood for that. *Let the police piece it together from here. They'll find the cut fence and the opened wall.*

Bruce switched his phone back on, his hands still trembling. A call from Dianne rang immediately, and when he picked up, she was shouting something in a thin, high voice, a sound of near panic. "Bruce? Bruce! Where the hell are you? I called the police. Get out of there!"

"I'm okay. I'm heading up," Bruce said to Dianne as he hurried back the way he'd come, the mystery of the hideout still hanging over him.

CHAPTER 14

The next day, Bruce sat quietly in Draccon's office, staring out at the wet streets of Gotham City while the detective sat across from him, reading the front-page news. Madeleine's manila folder was open on the table, the documents stacked in a neat pile. Finally, Draccon threw the newspaper down and leaned forward on the desk onto her elbows.

"What happened?" Bruce asked.

Draccon pushed the paper toward him so that he could read the top headline.

POLICE UNCOVER NIGHTWALKER HIDEOUT

"There was an unfinished underground path," she muttered.

"Like the ones that connect the buildings downtown?" Bruce asked, careful about how he was wording each sentence. As far as anyone was concerned, he knew nothing about the incident.

Draccon nodded. "You know the tunnel running underneath Wayne Tower, right?"

"Yeah," Bruce replied. Wayne Tower had one of those underground pathways, as did the Seco Financial Building and every other skyscraper. On hot summer days, when commuting on the surface of the city felt like walking in an oven, or on days when freezing snowstorms rolled in, people could take the subterranean routes and never have to set foot outside.

"Well," Draccon continued, "it was part of a subterranean route that had been defunded by the city. The Nightwalkers apparently turned the section underneath the Bellingham building into a storage facility for weapons."

The previous night replayed itself over and over in Bruce's mind. He and Dianne had headed back to the concert in silence, had managed to convince Harvey that they'd been questioned by police. *Something crazy going on down the street*, Bruce had said to Harvey, and Dianne had agreed. *Cops are investigating that corner again and have been questioning people all the way up these blocks.*

Barely minutes later, they'd heard sirens reach the corner of the Bellingham building. It seemed to verify their story, and Harvey had let it drop.

Dianne hadn't said a word about what happened, and neither had he. The potential for a longer probation sentence for Bruce— but also the possibility of putting Harvey in harm's way—kept them both mute. And although he kept expecting the police to call him, or Draccon to question him—no one seemed to know they'd been there.

"How did the police find the hideout?" Bruce asked.

Draccon rubbed her neck in weariness and nodded. "Officers got an anonymous call," she said with a sigh. "Who knew someone had opened up that unfinished tunnel? There was an unconscious man down in the bunker room, a supposed supply runner for the Nightwalkers. He was low in the ranks and had been assigned to move their weapons to a new location."

Bruce kept his expression curious and ignorant. "Did he say why they were doing this?"

"I don't think he was ranked high enough within the Night-walkers to know," she replied. "He revealed the location he was going to move the stuff to, but when the police checked it out, everything was already gone. Another Nightwalker had already moved the weapons out, cleared the place clean. He didn't say anything else. In fact, the poor bastard was so terrified yesterday that he tried hanging himself with his shirt." Draccon hesitated. "Kept saying something about a masked robber or someone who attacked him, kept saying it must've been an undercover cop. Couldn't give any more details than that. The Nightwalkers might have made some enemies in the local gang scene by encroaching on their space."

"Maybe I can get something out of Madeleine," Bruce said.

Draccon laced her fingers together and gave him an uncertain frown. "I'm not sure about this, Bruce."

"She might know the reason behind all the stockpiling."

Draccon sighed again and took a swig of her coffee. "I don't like keeping this up. You're not supposed to be this deeply involved, and the fact that she keeps talking to you unsettles me. Also, I don't want to get on your guardian's bad side."

Alfred. Bruce hadn't mentioned any of this to him yet, nor explained why his nightmares had been getting steadily worse, haunted by shadows or dark halls or a girl with long black hair. "But I'm still sitting here in your office," Bruce replied, pushing his other thoughts away. "You're still briefing me on what's happening with the Nightwalkers. Right? That must mean you still want me to help in any way I can—that you think I can get something out of Madeleine."

Draccon looked at Bruce with serious eyes. "Remember who her past victims were. Philanthropists with a lot of money. She targeted them for their money, stole vast amounts before killing them in their own homes. You saw their deaths." She hesitated. "You already know that you match the description for her victim of choice."

"I'll be okay," Bruce replied. "She's locked away at Arkham. But we're close now. We can find a way to unearth the Nightwalkers, all the way up to their boss."

Draccon stared into her coffee for a long moment.

"Don't put a wire on me," Bruce added. "She'll be able to tell. Just let me keep talking to her."

Finally, Draccon leaned back in her chair. "You get another conversation with her," she replied, holding up a finger. "One. We'll see how it goes from there."

A thunderstorm swept through Gotham City, and by the following morning the sky outside the asylum's windows still looked black as night.

When Bruce went downstairs for his shift and stopped by Madeleine's cell, he didn't see her sitting upright in bed. For an instant, he thought that perhaps she had been taken out of her cell—before he noticed her curled up in a tight ball on her bed. All he could see were her white prison jumpsuit and the spill of her black hair around her body.

"You were right," he said after a long pause.

She didn't move. She seemed to be staring off into space, her eyes concentrating on a spot somewhere on the floor. Her meal tray was on the other side of the room, and her napkin—usually folded into an intricate origami shape—was crumpled near the edge of her bed. An unsettling feeling weighed on Bruce. *Something is wrong.*

"Madeleine?" Bruce said. "Can you hear me?"

Another pause. For a moment, Bruce thought that the guards had changed the windows on her cell door to be soundproof, or that she was lost deep in thought. Or maybe she was ignoring him in the way she sometimes did. It made him feel silly for being here, and he was about to turn around and step away from the door when her answer finally came.

"What do you want, Bruce Wayne?" she asked. Her voice was quieter today, not as full of its usual bravado, and irritated. The feeling of unease in Bruce's stomach grew.

"I don't know if you heard the news," he replied, although a part of him knew that she must, somehow, have heard. She seemed to know everything, after all. "But the police uncovered one of the Nightwalkers' underground weapons rooms at the Bellingham buil—"

"Congratulations," she replied before he could finish. She shifted a little, loosening out of her tight ball so that he could see her face more clearly. She looked at him without lifting her head. "You can follow directions after all."

Gone today was her playful nature, the teasing smirk she usually gave him, and in its place was someone cold. Bruce blinked, confused. He didn't know why it bothered him that she seemed upset today. "Why are you doing this?" he asked. "Why did you wait until I came along before you started feeding information to the police? You clearly knew about that room—you knew about the brick wall. You've obviously been involved with the Nightwalkers this whole time. So, why now? What do you get out of this?"

"Maybe I've decided to turn over a new leaf," Madeleine replied, her voice dripping bitter sarcasm.

The hall fell silent again. Bruce looked closer at her. When his gaze traveled to her arms, he noticed something new—a blue-black bruise on her upper arm. Four bruises, to be exact, as if left there by someone's hand. He studied her other arm. Now he could see red scratch marks near her wrist, as if someone had tried to restrain her.

Madeleine Wallace was a criminal, a notorious killer jailed for three brutal murders—but in this moment, Bruce forgot that. All he saw before him was a girl his age, curled into a tight, protective ball, her usual arrogance replaced with something vulnerable.

Muffled thunder rumbled from outside. Madeleine spat out a curse. "I hate thunderstorms," she said. "If the lightning causes power issues in here, the hall doors will seal us all in like rats."

Bruce looked toward the doors. "Nothing's going to happen to you," he said. Was he really trying to reassure her? "And even if it did, I'm sure they'd evacuate all of you."

Madeleine ignored him and continued looking down. "Just rats in cages," she said, even quieter now. She shuddered and made herself smaller. *She's claustrophobic*, Bruce thought.

"Are you all right?" he asked. "What happened to you?"

She took another long moment to respond. "I refused to take my IV today," she finally said. "We had a little fight in the clinic."

An IV. Draccon hadn't mentioned that Madeleine was receiving medicine. "They hurt you?" he said.

"Is it obvious?" Madeleine lifted her head up at that and gave him a wry look. Then she put her head down on the bed again and sighed. "Don't tell Draccon you know," she said. "I'd like her to keep thinking I'm difficult."

"I'm sorry," Bruce said. And to his surprise, he actually *was*. Whoever had gripped her arm had done it roughly, hardly the work of trained professionals. A rush of anger welled up in his chest at that. He thought of the inmate James had shoved against the wall on Bruce's first day. The inmate had attacked him, sure, but the warden also didn't seem to have a problem with treating the prisoners roughly. Bruce hadn't thought they'd do it to someone as young as Madeleine. Did Draccon not know about this?

"It's not your fault," Madeleine muttered. She leaned over and dangled her legs over the side of the bed. Then she looked at him. "You asked me why I decided to tell you about the underground room."

Bruce nodded quietly, waiting for her to continue.

"After your parents died, how did you cope?"

A weight hit Bruce. *Be careful.* "What does that have to do with anything?"

She brought her shoulders in until she looked even smaller. "People always expect you to move on so quickly after you experience loss, don't they?" Madeleine looked away. "For the first few months, the sympathy pours on you. Then, gradually, it dwindles down, and one day you find yourself standing alone at the grave site, wondering why everyone else has moved on to caring about something else while you still stay right here, silently carrying the same hurt. People get bored with your grief. They want something new to talk about. So you stop bringing it up, because you don't want to bore anyone."

Bruce felt himself nod. And then the words came. He heard himself recount the days before and the days after the theater. Every word infused with anger directed toward her, toward any criminal who killed the innocent and left others to pick up the pieces.

When he finished, he half expected her to be smiling, taunting him again, gloating in getting this information out of him. But she had turned on the bed to face him directly, her dark eyes grave.

Why had he said all that? Did he want her to understand the pain she'd inflicted on others? Or because he wanted to hear *her* pain, to try to understand her?

"My mother was sent to prison for killing someone," she replied after a while. "She did it out of love for my brother."

This was a surprise. Bruce hadn't known *why* her mother was jailed, nor anything else about her family. "Your brother?" he asked.

Madeleine nodded. "I had an older brother. When he was young, a rare bacteria attacked his joints and made him violently sick. He suffered extraordinary pain as the infection ate away at him." She paused, her brows furrowing deeply at the memory. Bruce had never seen her look like this—her face dark with an expression that reminded him of his first months as an orphan. "My mother poured all of her energy into trying to save him—taking him from one clinic to another, being turned down at all of them. She was a professor, but she wasn't rich by any means. Our insurance was a joke. It didn't even come close to covering it. My mother worked extra jobs." She took a deep breath. Bruce felt a twinge of guilt at the reminder of his own fortune, and others' lack of it. "Finally, she found a doctor willing to take my brother on. We were thrilled."

As she spoke, Bruce could picture the scenes playing out before him—a woman sitting by her son's bedside, head in her hands. One run after another to various clinics, each time more desperate. "What happened?"

"My brother died under that doctor's watch. She claimed that there'd been nothing she could do, that it was his time and that he had finally succumbed to the disease. But my mother didn't believe her. Something seemed wrong. So she broke into the office one evening, sifted through the papers, and found out that the doctor hadn't been caring for my brother at all. She'd just been taking our money and feeding him placebos and sugar water." Madeleine looked back up at Bruce. "The doctor walked in while my mother was still there. My mother didn't even hit her hard—just hard enough to kill her. It was an accident."

Madeleine stopped, and the silence suddenly seemed overwhelming. "I'm sorry," Bruce managed to say. What words could he offer other than those? What other words had anyone else offered *him* when his own parents had died?

"She died in prison. No one can tell me exactly what happened to her, although I've seen how they treat their prisoners." Madeleine shrugged as if she were wholly accustomed to living with this information. Bruce's eyes went back to her own bruises. "During her time here, I watched the rich waltz out of jail. I hacked the prison system, and it turns out *they* always got released on house arrest.

Meanwhile, I watched my mother rot away. We had no money. I was ten years old at the time."

Ten. The number hit Bruce hard, and suddenly he saw himself at that age, walking alone for the first time to school, facing every afternoon knowing that Alfred—not his mother or father—would pick him up from the academy. What had Madeleine looked like? A small, delicately framed child with long hair and grave eyes? Had she walked alone, too? Where did she go, with no guardian or money to protect her? How had she ended up here, another murderer, taking her mother's crime to the next level?

Did Draccon know all of this about Madeleine? Bruce doubted it—she was stern, but she wasn't cruel.

"You once asked me why I committed those murders," she finished. "Tell me, *Bruce Wayne*, do you think of me as the same cold-blooded criminal who killed your parents? Do you think I deserve to rot in hell, to die with poison injected into my arm?" She sneered. "You're a billionaire. What do you *really* know about me? Would someone like you ever understand desperation?"

Trust nothing, suspect everything. His thoughts grew muddled, the images of his parents lying on wet pavement contrasted with the image of a lonely little girl, lost without her mother and brother. Bruce shook his head and frowned. "If Draccon knew this was happening to you, she wouldn't approve of it. I don't even think Dr. James would."

Madeleine made a disgusted sound in her throat. She rose from the bed and walked over to the window, until Bruce was separated from her by inches and a glass barrier. "Still so trusting. No one cares what happens to me," she said. "They just want the information I can offer them. They'll probably stop allowing you down here." She hesitated, then continued, "I don't want to see Gotham City burning. But I'd rather die before giving up what I know directly to them."

Madeleine's eyes had turned soft now, and Bruce could see that they weren't fully dark after all—now and then, when the light hit right, there were slashes of hazel and chestnut brown. If they weren't separated by glass, if she weren't being held in a facility like this, he would find their nearness awkward, even intimate.

"And that's why you've decided to talk to me?" Bruce said. "Because you feel like we have some sort of shared history?"

She furrowed her brows at him, her expression puzzled. "I'm telling you this because . . . it's hard to figure you out. Maybe I'm telling you to be careful." She said these last words with such finality that Bruce felt a deep chill in his chest. *She's giving me a warning.* Her expression shifted again, and she turned her eyes down. She frowned, as if unsure of herself for the first time. "Or maybe I just like you," she muttered.

"They're not going to let me talk to you again," Bruce replied, resting his hand against the glass. "Draccon said this would be my last time down here."

She eyed him, untrusting. "They can't stop you if they can't see you." She paused to nod up at the cams again. "If you want to come down here again, you'll have to use the right scrambler at the right frequency."

She's tricking you, Bruce told himself, torn between a tide of unease and a well of confusion. "Are you seriously telling me to mess with Arkham's security system? Why would I do that?"

"I'm not telling you to do anything," she replied. "I'm just telling you what it would take for you to see me again. If you wanted to." She hesitated. "If you *needed* to."

Tricks. Cons. Lies. But there was a strange, silent plea in her words, in the way she said that last phrase. *If you needed to.* Something in her tone sounded like a warning. Something urgent. There must be so much more that she wasn't telling him.

Then she shook her head, as if changing her own mind. "You

don't believe me," she said. "Then just don't come back. Tell Draccon what I said, if you feel like it. None of it will change what happens to me down here anyway."

Bruce opened his mouth to reply—but a deafening clap of thunder shook the hall. The lights along the corridor all went out in unison. His words froze unanswered on his tongue.

At first, the darkness was all-consuming, so that he felt like he was adrift in a vacuum. Around him came shouts from the other inmates in the hall—some whooping, others howling for the guards to come fix the lights, still others tapping against the glass windows of their cells, pushing against their doors as if testing them. He couldn't hear Madeleine's voice in the mix anymore, couldn't even see her face directly in front of him. But another sound made every hair on his neck rise.

The creak of an opening cell door.

A scarlet-red light came on, bathing the hall in blood. Through the light, Bruce saw two of the inmates stepping out of their cells while an urgent voice came on over the speaker system. An alarm began to scream.

Jailbreak.

CHAPTER 15

The inmates who had just stepped out of their cells blinked in the blood-red light. One stared up at the nearest security cam in confusion. The other looked at Bruce in disbelief, as if still not quite sure he himself had escaped from his confinement. From somewhere above, Bruce could hear the alarms blaring on the higher floors and feel the tremble of footsteps thundering.

"System lockdown!" a voice over the speakers shouted. *"System lockdown!"*

Bruce glanced toward the exit door as a loud buzz echoed throughout the hall. The light over the exit door flashed green, indicating it was open. *Run*, he thought. *Get out of here.* His eyes darted to Madeleine's cell for an instant. She hadn't opened her door, but she was also nowhere in sight, out of her window's view.

The first freed inmate charged toward the exit. Before Bruce could stop himself, he ran to block the door.

The man bared his teeth at Bruce and lunged, aiming to bite him. Bruce darted back, protecting his neck. He swung a fist at the man's jaw, catching him in a clean blow. The man stumbled backward, shrieking a curse. Then he lunged toward Bruce again. There was a wildness in his eyes, a searing desperation, and his voice sent a shudder through Bruce.

"*Let me out,*" he hissed. "*Get out of my way—*"

Bruce winced as the man's clawing fingers raked across his shoulder. He ducked, then threw his full weight at the inmate, sending him careening backward and off his feet. Bruce collapsed to the floor with him and grabbed for the mop handle lying nearby—his hands found it right as the inmate scrambled back to his feet. Bruce whipped the mop handle out, catching the man hard in the shins. He let out a yelp. Bruce leaped to his feet and hit the inmate again with the handle, this time jabbing him hard in the stomach. The man doubled over, his eyes bulging, and collapsed onto his side. The alarm continued to scream around them; everything had become a blur of scarlet.

Bruce lifted his head to see the second inmate. It was the man who'd threatened to cut Bruce. The inmate wasn't focused on the exit. Instead, he had wandered to Madeleine's cell and put his hand on the door. Fear shuddered through Bruce.

As the man pulled Madeleine's door open, Bruce shoved him away. But the prisoner towered over Bruce by at least an extra foot. A dark grin appeared on his face. *I'm going to die here.* The sudden thought sent adrenaline surging through Bruce's veins. The man swung. Bruce ducked to the ground, narrowly avoiding the blow, then darted away and toward Madeleine's door.

The inmate turned on him and prepared to strike.

Guards burst through the hall door, shields up, guns drawn, helmets on—blurs of black as they shouted at the inmates to get down on the ground. The enormous man facing Bruce looked away as the guards surrounded him. He opened his mouth in a snarl, then shuddered as one of the guards fired a Taser at him, forcing him to collapse. Bruce looked on as the guards dragged the inmate, still struggling and shouting, back to his cell. The alarm blaring overhead finally quieted. The doors on each cell locked once more.

James appeared. Her eyes settled on Bruce, and for the first time since he'd known her, she looked shocked. Maybe even guilty. "You okay?" she asked as he picked himself up. Strands of her hair had loosened from her braid, and she was breathing heavily. "Damn storm. You shouldn't have stayed down here. I—" She sighed, shaking her head as she put a hand on his shoulder. "I'm sorry. Let's get you out."

Bruce turned to look into Madeleine's cell as he went. She was back on her bed now, leaning forward on her knees, her hair a river over her right shoulder. She looked like she was trembling slightly. As he left, she lifted her head to look at him. A brief smile appeared on her lips, one that flickered in and out like a candle, so brief that no one else must have seen it.

Bruce found himself thinking about Madeleine's words again. *Just rats in cages*, she had said. And he had leaped to protect her.

Bruce's hands were still shaking as he turned away and followed James out of the hall, the shouts of the other inmates still echoing behind him.

Bruce didn't return to the asylum until the following week, needing some time off after the brief jailbreak was mentioned in the news and reporters swarmed the front gates.

James seemed subdued when she saw him again, and her usual sarcasm was replaced with concern. She even informed him that she would put in a word with Draccon and the court to shorten his remaining hours, due to what had happened. His duties cleaning the intensive-treatment level were done away with altogether.

Except Bruce didn't want to shorten his time at Arkham, or stop visiting the lowest floor. He had too many questions, too much about Madeleine still to figure out. He went to go find Draccon at the precinct and see what she could tell him.

"I'm glad you were unharmed," Draccon said to Bruce as she flipped through folders of court documents in her office. Bruce watched her work from his chair across her desk. "I'll put in a word with the court. I've never heard of a malfunction before at Arkham Asylum, but the storm had apparently initiated a perfect chain reaction of faults in the security system. It shouldn't happen again."

"Madeleine never even tried to escape, you know," Bruce replied, frowning. "Why would she just stay put like that, when she had a chance to run for it?"

"I have no idea. Did she say anything about the underground discovery?"

Maybe I'm telling you to be careful. Or maybe I just like you.

Bruce pushed her words out of his head. "She didn't say anything else, but she didn't seem surprised when I told her about it, either," he said. "Anything else useful that she might have said, I've already mentioned to you." Bruce studied the detective. Madeleine had asked him not to, but he wondered if he should bring up the issue of the bruises he'd seen on her, to ask about her medications. But if he sounded like he was criticizing the police's handling of her, it might also start to sound like he felt pity for her, even affection.

The thought of not talking to Madeleine again brought up a strange, unpleasant feeling in his chest. Why had he protected her?

Don't tell Draccon, Madeleine had whispered.

Maybe it would be better, Bruce thought, if he went off on his own again. There had to be something out there about Madeleine's mother and her time in prison. He would figure it out himself. His eyes settled on the neat stack of folders sitting on the edge of Draccon's desk, all of Madeleine's documentation to date.

"And the rest of the conversation?" Draccon asked over her shoulder as she grabbed a thick black binder from her top shelf and pulled out a form.

Bruce opened his mouth, still torn about how to tell Draccon about Madeleine's recounting of her mother's arrest—but what came out instead was "She asked me about my parents. So I told her."

"Then I'm glad we're no longer sending you down there," Draccon said, shaking her head. "It isn't worth endangering you to risk getting some potential information out of her." She sighed, then knelt to pull a container of folders from her bottom shelf. "Ah, here are your court papers." For a moment, she disappeared from sight.

Bruce thanked Detective Draccon for her concern, but a rumble of doubt lingered in the back of his mind.

What if Madeleine *was* confiding in him?

And as Draccon searched for his paperwork, Bruce reached for the document showing Madeleine's profile. He quietly rolled it up and tucked it into the inner pocket of his jacket. He needed to get to the bottom of this girl's mysteries; he needed to get all the information he could. And he needed to do it without the police looking over his shoulder.

CHAPTER 16

The next day, when Alfred dropped Bruce off at the entrance circle of WayneTech's new labs, Bruce felt exhausted. His dreams had been a mess—prison halls bathed in bloody light, stairs that led down into darkness, a girl curled up tight in her inmate uniform, a menacing figure looming over him. He had dreamed of his hand against the glass, of Madeleine's hand pressed against the opposite side, and of her telling him to be careful.

"You seem tired," Lucius said as he greeted him by the entrance. He was dressed all in white today, the color a striking contrast against his black skin.

Bruce gave his mentor a smile as he fell into step with him. "Thanks. You look great, too," he replied.

Lucius let out a chuckle. "Glad your time at Arkham's coming to an end soon."

Had Bruce already been at Arkham for so long? The dirty buckets of water and the menial labor would soon be far behind him, but so would the strange, secretive, brilliant girl locked away in the basement level, the seeming holder of information on the Night-walkers.

"We've been hard at work perfecting the smallest details," Lucius was saying as they cut through the main lobby. The mention of Bruce's name snapped him out of his reprieve. He looked at Lucius as the man pressed a hand against the monitor at one end of a set of sliding glass doors, then waited as Bruce did the same. Two researchers offered them each a white coat and a pair of goggles. "If Gotham City is to use our technology as a part of their security and justice system, we'll need to make sure everything feels foolproof. The citizens need to have full faith in us, as does the city council." He looked at Bruce. "As do *you*."

Heading down one of the lab's corridors, Bruce felt a sense of déjà vu. He had walked these halls with his father back when Lucius was still an intern; now it felt oddly natural that Lucius would do the same with Bruce to help him learn the ropes. Thomas Wayne's work could be seen everywhere in Wayne Industries—and especially here, in the experimental labs, Bruce could tell that the sleek lines of the halls and architecture were directly influenced by the discerning eye of his father.

At last, they stopped before a set of metal double doors stretching from the floor right up to the ceiling. Bruce straightened in anticipation. He had been to other parts of the building dozens of times—but *these* doors led into the prototype factory. The last time he was in here, he was a child, and his father was still alive.

Lucius grinned over his shoulder at Bruce while one of the other researchers typed a code into a panel beside the doorway. The panel beeped, turning green, and they walked inside.

The room looked even larger than Bruce remembered. A metal lattice of beams crisscrossed the ceiling, the space lit up by hundreds—thousands—of lights. Around them loomed objects of all shapes and sizes: several remodeled and fully customized

Humvees, encased with dark metal plates and shielded tires; sheets of razor-thin metal erected one after another in a grid; an entire row of metal racks, each one holding what looked like arm cannons that belonged in science fiction. While one of the researchers asked Lucius a question, Bruce browsed the racks, picking up a few items and inspecting them.

He paused on a small, square device, its entire top surface a screen. When he turned it over, he saw a series of frequencies printed in the plastic.

"Oh, that," Lucius called out from the end of the rack, shrugging as he caught sight of Bruce analyzing the item. "It's just a repair device. You might want that for your system at home. Its frequencies will reset your electronics if they're on the fritz."

Bruce nodded casually back at Lucius, but when the man returned to talking with the researchers, Bruce popped open the back cover of the device. Madeleine's words now came back to him, as did the memory of her staring up at her ceiling. If he could redo some of the settings on this device, he could fool it into temporarily scrambling the security cams at Arkham. With this, he could at least get to Madeleine if there was an emergency or if the Nightwalkers attacked again and he needed more information from her.

Bruce deactivated the device's alarm so that he could take it out of the room. Then he slipped it into his pocket and headed back to join Lucius, who was standing in front of a display.

"What's this?" Bruce asked.

Lucius grinned. "Something you'll find impressive, I think."

The display showcased an opaque black helmet and a black armored body suit made of latticed fabric. It gleamed under the light as if entirely made of metal, but its texture made it clear that it was as foldable and bendable as silk, armor that seemed capable of molding to fit its wearer. Bruce leaned down to study its surface closely, admiring the light reflecting off it.

"We've been working on protective gear," Lucius went on. "This is our latest experiment in wearable, bulletproof fabric, with reinforced links like microscopic chain mail, strong as steel, comfortable enough for the wearer to make full leaps and twists. Still in beta testing, of course, and not ready for prime time yet. But it can double the strength of a human. The navy commissioned it two years ago. It's been quite a lucrative contract for us."

Bruce nodded along. This suit would have come in handy when he headed into the tunnel below the Bellingham building.

They walked down several more rows before Lucius stopped them. An open row yawned to either side, dividing the lab in half, and on the other side, Bruce saw a series of cyborg-like machines, each of their metallic legs and arms as thick as his waist. Double rotors attached to their backs seemed to give them flight capabilities, and two thin lines of blue-gray light shone on their heads like a pair of narrowed eyes.

Lucius stopped beside one of the machines and held out a hand in its direction. "Now, this! This is what you've been waiting to see."

Bruce stared up at the machine's eyelike lights. *These are the drones.* It appeared to stare back at him, as if it were eerily *aware* of him. If Lucius was going for intimidation, he succeeded. "How do they work?" he asked, trying to tear his eyes away from the piercing gaze.

"Well," Lucius said, "let's bring one out and demonstrate."

The drone nearest to them stirred to life, and its eyes began to glow a steady blue. Immediately, it seemed to detect them standing in front of it.

"Ada," Lucius said, nodding at the bot. No sooner than he said this name, the robot's head swiveled in his direction.

"Mr. Fox," it replied.

"Now," Lucius went on, turning back to Bruce, "Ada—or our Advanced Defense Armament—has already decided, based on our heart rates, the electric signals our bodies give off, and the body language that we are all using, that you and I are friends. It has also swept the Internet to gather information about us both. Hand me your phone."

Bruce did as he asked. Lucius took it, held it up to his own so that the two devices were touching, and installed something on Bruce's phone. Bruce watched carefully. Lucius returned the phone a moment later. On its screen, Bruce saw an app displaying blue-and-white silhouettes of himself and Lucius, color-coding them both into a FRIENDSHIP category.

"Now, if it were to detect someone as hostile," Lucius went on, "it would immediately react in an appropriate manner."

"And how does it know if someone's hostile?"

"Body language. An aggressive stance. It can also understand what the person is saying, and certain words will trigger its hostility detector." Lucius hunched his shoulders forward at the bot, then narrowed his eyes and held up his fists. "Allow me to demonstrate," he called to Bruce without shifting his eyes away from the machine.

Ada's stance instantly became rigid, and the limbs unfurled, revealing two embedded sets of weapons attached to each side. It straightened, towering momentarily over Lucius. *"Stand down, or you will face arrest."* At the same time, a metallic shield unfurled from one of its arms and stretched out before Bruce and the others, so fast that he barely had time to see it happen. Bruce instantly sprang back, his hands going up in defense. When Lucius put his arms up as if surrendering, the bot detected the movement and spoke again.

"Thank you for cooperating, Mr. Fox," the drone said. Even in Bruce's excitement, the words sent a chill down his spine.

"What does it do if you don't cooperate?" he asked.

Lucius tapped the button on his phone again, and the drone immediately went back into a passive stance. "Ada's number one objective is to protect the officers under its charge. It will be in defensive mode at all times, and will reserve offensive modes as a last resort, when it can sense that a dangerous perpetrator is about to attack." As Lucius delved further into the detailed inner workings, Bruce stepped forward to inspect the drone's joints. Lucius popped open a panel on the drone's side, pointing out a series of circuits. "Had I run away or struggled, for instance, Ada would reach out and restrain me calmly. It's also programmed not to attack its fellow drones. They won't open fire on each other."

"Impressive," Bruce said, watching intently as Lucius showed off the wiring behind a second panel on the drone.

"We are proposing that one of these drones accompany each police squad, and several join each SWAT team in the city. They can offer an image of assurance, boost the morale and confidence of their human counterparts, as well as act as a lightning-fast defense, protecting the lives of our city's officers on even the most dangerous streets."

Bruce kept his eyes fixed on the drone's. He had never seen AI this responsive before. His mind whirled, trying to piece together how Lucius had accomplished this. There had been an earlier drone, he remembered, a flying one that Lucius had conceptualized and scrapped years ago. Bruce thought back through the code and hardware he'd seen working in that. Had Lucius expanded on it into this?

Madeleine would like this.

The thought flashed through his head, here and gone in an instant. He blinked, embarrassed. She was a criminal, the type of person this drone was designed to arrest in the first place. Why would he care if she could understand enough about this technology to find it interesting?

"Ada can fold itself into several different sizes," Lucius went on, nodding to the bot and tapping a few more buttons on his app. As they looked on, the bot's metal legs elongated until it stood nearly twice as tall as it originally did—and then it furled itself back down, farther and farther, limbs contracting until it stood at almost exactly the same height as Bruce. "This allows it to have a stunning degree of mobility as it goes about its protective duties."

"When will this roll out as a beta?" Bruce asked.

"During the gala," Lucius replied, folding his hands behind his back. "We'll have it there in place of a human security detail, to impress our guests."

"Nice," Bruce replied, but his thoughts were already returning to the Nightwalkers. He still didn't know why they were stockpiling so many weapons, nor when they might strike next. His hand brushed against the frequency device he had stashed in his pocket. If he needed to talk to Madeleine again, he would need that, and if he had another confrontation like the one at the Bellingham building, he would desperately need the protection offered by the tech in this room.

He turned to Lucius. "Can you add me into the system so that I can come in here on my own? We won't get a chance to meet like this very often for the next few months." He cleared his throat and gave Lucius as earnest a look as he could. "I would love to study the drones a little more."

"Of course." Lucius bowed his head respectfully, a gesture he used to make to Bruce's father. "This is your corporation, after all."

CHAPTER 17

That night, Bruce found himself lost in another nightmare. He was wandering the dark halls of his home again. The mansion seemed to stretch endlessly in all directions, halls turning into study rooms turning into balconies overlooking nothing but shadows. Alfred was nowhere to be seen. Bruce stopped in the dining room. Someone was lounging on the couch.

The storm raged—in Bruce's dream, one of the large windows in the parlor shattered, scattering glass everywhere. A cold wind blew in, putting out the fire in a puff of smoke. Bruce cringed, throwing up an arm instinctively to shield his face—but when he looked again at the darkened parlor, the mysterious silhouette was no longer there. A hint of fear hummed underneath his skin, and he felt a sudden urge to run.

A hand touched his arm. He whirled around.

It was Madeleine.

She looked ghostly pale in the night, an apparition, beautiful. Her dark hair hung straight and shining over her shoulders, glinting blue underneath the slivers of light slicing the floors and walls.

She smiled at him as if she had been expecting him, and Bruce felt himself smile back even as his skin prickled where her hand had rested. She wasn't supposed to be here, was she? Had he forgotten something? She was a criminal, sitting behind a thick glass barrier at Arkham Asylum. So what was she doing here? It was difficult to understand things when he was around her, as if everything that would have seemed logical only a moment ago had now turned upside down, inside out.

"Don't you remember?" she murmured, drawing close to him. "You got me out and brought me here." Her voice was very quiet, raw with pain, and Bruce felt a tug on his heart at the sound. Her hands were small and cold against his chest.

Bruce leaned toward her until they were both against the wall. It took him a moment to realize that there was blood on her hands, and it left dark streaks on his skin.

"Do you think my brother deserved to suffer like he did?" she asked.

No. Of course not. Bruce winced as her words brought up the familiar feelings of his parents' absence, and as he looked away, Madeleine's arms came up to wrap around his neck. She touched his chin, gently guiding his face back toward her.

"Tell me the truth," she murmured. Her eyes were so dark, the pupils black and indistinguishable from the irises. "You can't stop thinking about me."

I can't.

She smiled. "And what exactly do you think of me, Bruce?"

Your lips. Your eyes. The twist of your smile. The blood on your hands. I want you. I'm afraid of you.

Bruce started to shake his head and step away—he knew she shouldn't be here, that every fiber of his being told him that he was in grave danger—but she pulled him back toward her, tugging him down until his lips hovered over hers. Then he was kissing her, and her soft body was against his, and this—*this*—was everything he ever wanted. Why did he want to leave? She returned his kiss desperately. He felt light-headed—every muscle in his body had tensed in desire and in terror. He had never been with someone like her before, never been in the arms of a girl who genuinely scared him. It felt *wrong*, sickening . . . and yet, it was the greatest feeling in the world. He couldn't pull away. He could only continue kissing her lips, then the line of her jaw, then her neck. He wanted to hear her sharp intake of breath, her whispering his name over and over. She wanted to be here, in his arms.

Run, Bruce. She is here to kill you.

Somewhere behind him came the unmistakable click of a gun barrel. Bruce flinched away from Madeleine and swung around. He was staring at a dark, blank wall. He whirled back—but Madeleine had vanished. The halls seemed to warp around him, closing in and then stretching out, and he shook his head, still dizzy from the heat of her lips on his. A sudden, bone-deep fear crept into his stomach. They were not alone here.

Nightwalkers. They're going to seal me in. He had to get out of the house.

Bruce turned and ran. His steps seemed to drag through the air. He reached the front door and yanked it open, but instead of leading him outside, it only opened back into the same hall he'd just escaped from. *Impossible.* The broken window in the foyer was now intact. What little light there had been streaming through the windows now darkened, encasing Bruce in shadows. Somewhere in the darkness, he saw a silhouette run by. More footsteps. Whispers. The sound of a sharp object against metal.

"Madeleine!" he called out.

"I'm right here," she replied behind him.

Bruce bolted out of his dream with a rasping gasp. A roll of thunder echoed from outside, and tree branches were slapping hard against the glass of his windowpane. He sat upright in bed for a few seconds, breathing heavily, his eyes still wide and darting around his room.

Had it really been a dream? Were the Nightwalkers here, in his home, sealing him in like Madeleine's former victims, and hunting him down? He could still feel the burn of Madeleine's lips, the warmth of her arms around his neck. His chest was slick with a sheen of cold sweat. Bruce stayed where he was until his breathing finally calmed down and the memory of his dream had started to fade, taking his terror with it. The storm continued to rage.

It was just a dream. And yet, somewhere in his subconscious, he could sense Madeleine there, was both terrified of her and filled with the desire for her in his arms.

Bruce glanced at the time on his phone. It was just past dawn, but the black clouds made it look like the dead of night outside. He tilted his head back and closed his eyes for a moment. Then he swung his legs over the side of the bed and rose. Weak light illuminated his naked chest and the pants that hung low on his hips. He walked barefoot out of his room and stared down the hall for a moment, watching where it disappeared into the shadows, imagining Madeleine materializing there, a ghostly figure in the dark. Only silence and storm greeted him. Alfred hadn't even gotten up yet. Speckled light trembled in patches on the floor. After another long moment, he ventured out in the hall, his feet making no sound as he made his way to his study.

The air seemed stale in this room, and the rain lashing against the windows smeared the outside world into streaks. Bruce paused to stare at the old grandfather clock against one wall. The hands were stuck, and he had never bothered to force them to work again. He ran a hand through his hair in exhaustion, then made his way to his desk. There, he sat down and turned his computer on.

The machine—nothing but a thin, transparent glass panel as

long as the desk itself, a piece of technology he had built himself—came to life, and cold, artificial light illuminated him. He stared at the icons that popped up, hovering seemingly in the middle of the air, and then leaned over to type in a new search.

Madeleine Wallace mother

Several familiar links showed up from his previous searches about Madeleine—her original arrest, the details about the murders she'd committed that had been released to the public. He scrolled through two pages of entries. Finally, at the top of the third page, he found a brief mention in an article about Madeleine.

It was an opinion piece, going into the murky details of Madeleine's youth. A faded photo of the family. *Madeleine Wallace. Cameron Wallace. Eliza Eto.* Even though her brother was older than she was, he looked thinner and frailer, with hollow eyes and sloped shoulders, his hair buzzed short. Bruce's attention went to Eliza Eto. There was no doubt that Madeleine had inherited her beauty from her mother; the two had the same long, straight blue-black hair, the same pale complexion and full lips. Bruce went back to reading the article, murmuring aloud as he went.

"'The consequence of such negligent malpractice was tragic. One week after her son's death, Dr. Eliza Eto broke into the office of Dr. Kincaid and lay in wait until Kincaid entered the room, then proceeded to stab Kincaid over a dozen times with a kitchen knife.'"

Bruce swallowed hard at the words. The story was similar to what Madeleine had told him—but it was not the *same*. In Madeleine's version, her mother had hit the doctor once, accidentally, and too hard. In *this* version, Eliza had stabbed the doctor a dozen times with a kitchen knife, had committed a gruesome, premeditated murder, and had as a result been given the death penalty. She died in jail before the sentence was carried out.

Bruce leaned back in his chair with a frustrated sigh. Everything Madeleine said seemed to be a half truth. What about other things she had told him?

A chat bubble appeared in the corner of his screen. It was from Dianne. *You're up already?* she said.

Crazy storm, Bruce typed back. *Didn't sleep much.*

Same, she replied.

Are you ok? How are you feeling?

I'm fine, Bruce. Q is, are you fine?

Bruce sighed. *Not really*, he replied. But as much as he hated that Dianne was now somewhat involved in the case, too, he still felt relieved to have someone besides Draccon and Dr. James to talk to about everything. He cleared his search and tried another one. This time he looked up Cameron Wallace.

So—Madeleine told me some more about her past, Bruce typed back to Dianne. *At least Draccon was right about her coming from a criminal family, although I still can't tell how much of what Madeleine said is true.*

Bruce. He thought he could almost hear Dianne's sigh. *You're still on this case? The one that almost killed you?*

Just listen. Please, Di.

Fine. Fine. What else?

Her mom was on death row for murder, too.

A pause. *Damn.*

I feel for her, though. She was ten at the time. And it was over her brother.

Oh, Bruce, I'm sorry. Also I didn't know she had a brother?

Bruce stared at the screen's search results. The top one was an obituary for Cameron Wallace, age twelve. Up popped a photo of the same weak, smiling boy.

Her brother died of some kind of bacterial infection. He sent Dianne the link.

How had that led Madeleine to the Nightwalkers?

Revenge. Bruce knew this instinctively, without a doubt—he could hear it in the way she talked about the death of her mother and the callous way the justice system had treated her, in the way she talked about her brother. Bruce might have even done the same, in her shoes. But his thoughts lingered on the doctor who had been murdered, and then on the three philanthropists killed in cold blood.

Whatever the reason, Bruce replied, *she didn't do it alone.* A ten-year-old girl simply didn't become an assassin in eight years without someone else's help.

Bruce frowned, then leaned forward in his chair and reached for Madeleine's profile that he'd taken from Draccon's office. *I'll put it back the next time I'm there*, he told himself. His finger scanned her profile, her crime reports. He stopped near the bottom, where a link was printed alongside a username and password. It was to her interrogation video.

He hesitated briefly. Then he typed it into his browser. The page promptly asked for the username and password, and Bruce entered them.

GCPD Guest
GreenLightning

The prompt flashed once, and the screen refreshed. He was in the GCPD video directory.

The familiar reports on each of Madeleine's crimes popped up, followed by a series of videos and interrogations. Bruce paused at one video, where Draccon and several other officers had surrounded Madeleine in her cell. She stayed on her bed, her head turned away nonchalantly, as they asked her a slew of increasingly frustrated questions. The sight brought a cynical smile to Bruce's lips as he remembered how he'd felt whenever Madeleine ignored him in the same way.

"You're not doing a very good job of lying, Miss Wallace," Draccon was saying, the bite in her voice the same as when she'd first met Bruce. "We are well aware that you were not alone in the Grant home. In fact, we suspect that you had at least three, perhaps even four, others working with you on this murder. Who were your accomplices?"

Madeleine, as expected, stayed quiet, her gaze so calm and distant that it was as if she thought she were alone in her cell. The only thing Bruce caught was the slight movement of her hands—and when he looked closer, he realized that she was folding and refolding one of her paper creations in her lap, making the same three or four creases over and over again.

Draccon stepped forward and shook her head. "We're going to get them, whether you tell us or not," she said. "But your confession will mean the difference between a life sentence for you or the death penalty. Your choice."

Madeleine didn't deign to respond.

Bruce looked on as the interview continued, fruitless, just like every other interview conducted on Madeleine before he came along. *Her crew.* He sat in the silence of his room, listening to the storm pound away outside and the muffled sound of the ongoing interrogation, wondering about the other people Madeleine worked with. She had hacked into the prison system when she was only ten years old—sure, she was smart, but she likely had help, too. Then he thought about the murders themselves, the grisly nature of each of them—throats slashed, blood everywhere, the signs of struggle rampant throughout each house.

A ten-year-old girl simply didn't become an expert murderer in eight years without someone else's help. And with as many as four accomplices with her . . .

The video ended. Bruce hit replay, letting it cycle again.

What if *Madeleine* had been there, but not been the actual murderer? *Who else was with her?*

The video had reached the point again where Madeleine was folding the paper shape in her lap. Bruce narrowed his eyes. . . . Something, *something* about her movements made him pause the video. He replayed the segment. Sure enough, she would fold the same creases over and over, three or four times, undoing and redoing it before moving on.

Bruce had seen her do this before, of course, but never from the point of view of the security cams. From this angle, a new thought occurred to him.

He and the officers had always thought her origami was just the idle habit of a bored, intelligent mind. But what if it wasn't trivial at all? What if it was her way of communicating with the outside world? What if she was using it to send *signals* to whoever was on the other end of the cams?

Bruce sat back in his chair as a wave of nausea hit him. She was perceptive, but sometimes it did seem like she knew more about what went on beyond the walls of her cell than she should. There were others out there who had worked with Madeleine . . . who might *still* be working with her.

Hey. Hey. It was Dianne, pinging their chat box. *Hey hey hey is Bruce Wayne still awake? Hello?? What the hell is going on outside?*

With his new theory about Madeleine still swirling in his mind, it took him a while to realize what she was talking about. Out in the storm, muffled behind the roar of rain and thunder, he heard the faint sound of sirens. A *lot* of sirens.

The sirens? he typed.

Dianne sent him a video from her phone. The wails and flashing lights were coming from somewhere down her street, close enough to Dianne's home that they were deafening.

Yeah. Looks like a New Year's parade.

He rose from his chair and went to his window, then peered through to see if he could catch anything. There, on the curve of the street below his hilltop, was the glow of a mass of police lights.

Something big had happened.

He hurried back to his desk, then picked up the remote for the room's TV and turned it on. He flipped through several channels before he landed on a morning newsfeed, and there, he stopped. A giant headline was emblazoned over a frantically talking reporter, displaying the newest Nightwalker victim.

TERROR REIGN
Mayor Price Found Dead in Home

CHAPTER 18

Bruce sat frozen before the screen, his hand still hovering, trembling, over the headlines—as if he had the power to swipe it away.

Right below the headlines were photos of the mayor, smiling at the last public event he had attended, his wife and children standing beside him. His youngest, a little girl, had her arms wrapped around his leg. The sight made Bruce's heart clench. The last time he'd seen Katie, she had still been a toddler, squealing with delight as he tossed her in the air again and again.

His eyes went to Richard in the photo, who was turned in the direction of his father. Bruce remembered the way he had left things between them, the way Richard had glared at him as he wiped the blood from his nose.

He could imagine Richard standing in the foyer of his home now as the police swarmed around him, his sneer gone, his hands hanging loose at his sides. Was he sitting in the back of an ambulance, a blanket draped around himself, staring off into space? Had he witnessed his father's murder? Was he comforting his mother and little sister?

Bruce tried to call Richard, but the number went immediately to voice mail. He tried again. Same result. It made sense; the last thing his former friend probably wanted right now was to answer the phone.

The article was refreshing every few minutes with updates—the latest one announced that, this time, the Nightwalkers had left behind a note.

> *Gotham City—Blame the virus, not the fever. You are not under attack from the Nightwalkers. You are under attack from your own rich, and their corrupt system of blood money. Now they will bathe in blood. Do not try to stop us. Death to tyranny.*

The Nightwalkers' symbol was stamped below, the burning coin, further sealing their involvement.

His heart pounding, Bruce threw his clothes on and rushed downstairs. In his pocket was the frequency device he'd taken from WayneTech, the weight of it bouncing with each step. He double-checked that he had his Arkham access card. Since the jailbreak, Dr. James had gone easy on him. She'd probably agree to adjust his hours and let him sign in early today.

Without a backward glance, Bruce opened the door and stepped out into the black.

Rain splattered against Bruce's windshield as he drove Alfred's car to Arkham. In this darkness, the landscape looked even more foreboding, like a creature come alive in the night—all gnarled limbs and sharp shadows, an illusion around every corner.

The last time he'd investigated things with Madeleine's help, he'd managed to uncover an entire underground hideout that belonged to the Nightwalkers, forcing them to move their operations elsewhere. If he could talk to her now and get a clue out of her, if he could figure out *who* she was possibly communicating with, they might be able to find where this crime trail led. They might get a lead on the boss.

Of course, the question—as always—was how much he could trust Madeleine. But right now she was his only lead, and the Nightwalkers had just escalated the stakes.

He had to help the police get to the bottom of it before fate came knocking on his own door.

What if she is innocent, too? She had been arrested at the scene of the last murder with the victim's blood on her hands—but *what if* there were more to her story?

By the time Bruce reached Arkham's gates, the downpour had lightened a bit, and he could see the asylum looming clearly behind his windshield. Yellow light dotted the windows. He passed through both clearance gates and then pulled up to the entrance and stepped out, wincing at the gust of wind that hit him. Quickly, he scanned his ID at the door and hurried inside when the double doors slid open.

"Early morning, Wayne?" the security guard said as Bruce signed in at the front desk. The guard had seen Bruce so often that he didn't even bat an eye.

"Yeah," Bruce replied. "I need to talk to Dr. James."

"Urgent enough to drive through this storm?" The guard took another large bite out of his doughnut and went back to watching the weather tracker on the news. "Go ahead. She's probably in the cafeteria."

Bruce needed no second bidding as he hurried past the front desk and toward the elevator leading to the basement level.

He wasn't supposed to be on duty down here anymore, but James wouldn't notice for hours. Draccon might not show up at all, in fact, not with the mayor's murder all over the news—she was probably at the Price estate right now. She wouldn't be thinking about Bruce. He reached into his pocket and tightened his grip on the frequency device.

The two inmates who had broken out during the brief jailbreak were gone now, moved somewhere else. Replacing them were others, all similar, with haunted eyes and menacing faces. Bruce stopped at the front end of the hall, right before the first security cam on the ceiling, and then turned on the device.

It didn't make a sound—at least, none that he could hear. Bruce let it run through every frequency it could. The seconds dragged on.

Then, a match; he heard a faint click from one of the cams. The others all followed in a domino effect of sound; the red light usually shining on each cam had now gone dark. Bruce waited. When a blue light blinked on, indicating a reset, he pressed the device again and set all of the cams on the wrong band so that they were not recording footage of the hall.

He headed for Madeleine's cell.

She was awake and alert. Her face was turned up at the ceiling, as if pondering the security cameras once more, and Bruce wondered if she already knew what he'd done. Not only could their meeting be off the record, but if she really *was* using the cams as a rudimentary way to communicate with the outside world, then he'd temporarily shut that down, too.

She turned to look at him as he approached her cell window. "I thought you weren't allowed down here anymore."

"The Nightwalkers struck just a few hours ago." Bruce rested a fist against the glass. "The mayor was killed. But you might already know that, don't you?" He nodded up at the broken cams. "You have some sort of system in place to communicate?"

If Bruce weren't so used to Madeleine's enigmatically calm expression, he wouldn't have thought much of her sharp blink, the subtlest gesture showing that she was surprised. "So early this morning, Bruce, and so upset," she said. "You've been thinking about me."

Her words were so similar to what she'd said to him in his

dream that Bruce had to take a step away from the window, as if the extra distance might protect him from her. He hoped she couldn't see his flush and guess instantly what his dream had been about—that even now he couldn't help looking at her lips. It had all felt so real.

"Come on, Madeleine," he said, lowering his voice. He couldn't afford to be confrontational with her right now—he needed her to see him as vulnerable. To let down her own guard. "Haven't we talked enough to skip all the games? Look . . . the mayor was my friend's father." He looked away for a moment, then stepped forward to put his hand on the glass again. "You've helped me once before, given me a clue that uncovered one of the Nightwalkers' hideouts. If you know something, *anything* . . . please. Tell me."

Madeleine sighed. For a brief second, she even appeared angry, as if the news Bruce was delivering to her was not what she'd expected. Then she got up and walked over to the window separating them. Her nearness reminded Bruce again of his dream—her arms around his neck, pulling him down, her lips moving against his— and he swallowed hard, trying to push it away.

"I don't think you committed those murders," he went on. "I think you're involved—that you *know* who did, but that you're not coming forward for some strange reason. You're taking the fall. And I think you can help me stop the killing of more innocent people, if you would just let me in."

His words seemed to surprise her again. She studied his face, thoughtful now, and for a moment, the glint in her eyes actually seemed to belong to a teenager.

"Bruce Wayne," she said softly. Her eyes were strangely warm now, the hazel shining brightly through. "Two kinds of people come out of personal tragedy, you know? And you're the kind that comes out brighter."

"Which kind are you, then?" he asked.

Madeleine stared at him, not answering, and a chill passed through Bruce. Was he being a complete fool?

Then she stepped as close to the glass as she could, so that her breath fogged its surface. "Listen carefully," she said, her voice so quiet he could barely hear her. He leaned toward the glass, too. "The Nightwalkers had originally planned to break into the mayor's bank accounts weeks from now. They got a tip, some help from the inside."

"The inside? Who?" Bruce said, his voice hushed and urgent.

Shaking her head, Madeleine continued. "That's not important. If they've already attacked, then that means their whole schedule has been accelerated—which means the rest of their list has also sped up."

Their list? Bruce held his breath; all this time, Madeleine had *known* what would come next, had held this information hostage from all of them. "You intentionally kept this upcoming attack a secret from the police? We could have saved him, had we known."

"The mayor's *life* was never supposed to be on the table."

"So you *are* a member of the Nightwalkers?"

"I know enough to warn you."

A vise clenched around his stomach. "Warn me about what?"

"About *you*. Be careful, Bruce. You're on the list."

"What list?" he whispered, afraid to hear it.

"The list of the Nightwalkers' targets. Each one had been paying off the mayor to look the other way while they lined their pockets with government funds. You know what that means, don't you? *Millions* that should have gone to helping the poor, paying for the sick, educating the youth, protecting the streets—all waved away with the mayor's magic wand. The mayor's time had simply run out."

Corrupt officials. Philanthropists in dark dealings. The mayor himself, taking bribes and participating in fraud. "And me?" Bruce snapped. "Why am *I* on that list? I've done none of those things. My parents were good people—they enacted *real* change with their wealth. All I've done is try to continue their legacy."

"WayneTech is going to make millions on that contract to improve Gotham City's police forces. Isn't it?" Madeleine's expression was grave now. "The Nightwalkers fight against obscene wealth that controls the hands of government, the shackles that imprison those too weak to defend themselves. They don't believe anyone should have the right to that much money and power. *Death to tyranny.*" She said it like it was a slogan, and Bruce felt a chill sweep through him again as he recognized it from the note left by the Nightwalkers at the mayor's murder scene. "They fight against people like *you*, regardless of whether or not you've been lumped in with the wrong crowd. They hadn't targeted you before because you had yet to turn eighteen and come into possession of your funds. But now you're on the radar. You have the wealth they want." She paused. "You're next, Bruce."

Her words sounded more like a threat than a warning. "And what do you suggest I do?" he said.

"Leave Gotham City," Madeleine replied immediately. "Go take a trip somewhere; fly to Tahiti and spend the rest of the summer there. You're done with your time here at Arkham soon anyway, right? That'll be the end of our conversations. Stay out of the Nightwalkers' way."

Bruce shook his head in confusion. "Why are you doing this?" he asked. "You seem like you want to stop them; you're trying to protect me. But now you don't want to get in the Nightwalkers' way. Do you support them or not? What are you doing, Madeleine? *Who are you protecting?*"

Madeleine just looked at him as if she wished there were some other way. He could feel something invisible pulling him toward her just as she leaned toward him. Then she turned away. "I'm sorry," she said with a glance over her shoulder.

And that was it.

"Wait," he called after her, but she didn't turn back around. He was in danger? He was on the hit list? "You have to tell me more. You know what they're—"

"Bruce."

He whirled to see Detective Draccon storming down the end of the hall, her long coat flapping behind her and Dr. James close at her side.

"What the hell are you doing down here?" Dr. James blurted out at the sight of him. Her eyes darted up to the security cams, which were once again blinking red.

"You're off the case," Draccon added. *"Done."*

Bruce glanced back into Madeleine's cell. She wasn't facing him, but her stillness told him that she was listening to what was happening. As the detective and warden reached him, Madeleine turned her head enough for him to glimpse the profile of her face. She was smiling slightly.

"You don't understand," he said to them, pointing at Madeleine. "She knows more about the mayor's murder. She said that I—"

"You're coming with me." Draccon cut him off. Her hand clamped down on Bruce's arm. "And if I so much as see you look in the direction of that girl again, I'll send you back to court myself."

CHAPTER 19

Rain dotted the windshield of Draccon's car as she drove Bruce off Arkham's premises. As they headed into the winding path framed by skeleton trees, the detective's dark eyes flashed with fury in the dim light.

"What about my car?" Bruce glanced over his shoulder toward the asylum.

"GCPD will have it back to you in a couple of hours," Draccon snapped, handing him a folded piece of paper. "After the mayor's death and your actions this morning, it wasn't difficult to get a warrant to search your car. Besides, I want to see you actually arrive home with my own two eyes. Who knows what else you're getting up to by yourself."

"You suspect me of something?"

"Am I being unreasonable, after your display today?" She glanced at him. "I specifically told you not to go back down there. Why'd you do it?"

"I had to ask Madeleine one last question," Bruce insisted.

"Detective, Madeleine can point us to who killed the mayor. *She knows.* I think the Nightwalkers are up to something big, and I—"

"Know what I think? I think you're sad to leave her. Tell me, Bruce, was it a coincidence that the security cams down there reset at the same time you decided to talk to Madeleine without my consent?"

"I don't know what you're talking about."

"You can cut the act with me. You think I've never seen a boy in love?" She sniffed once as she made a sharper turn than she needed to, sending her bag and papers sliding across the car's back seat. "I've fallen in and out of love more times than I can count, and let me tell you—you've made a little room for her in that heart of yours. I hate to be the one to break it to you, but this one's probably not going to work out."

Bruce tried to imagine the detective in love, letting down the authoritative shell she operated behind. "That's ridiculous."

"Is it?" she said. "Why do you keep talking to her, then?"

Draccon had been watching the security tapes closely. Bruce looked over at her to see that her expression had turned clinical, that she was fishing for more. He took a deep breath. "I don't think Madeleine killed those three people."

Draccon shot Bruce a hard glance. "And what makes you think that?"

"I was reading about the details of her crimes, and of her mother's crimes. She seems like she's protecting someone out there who's still at large. You know those napkins she's always folding? I don't think she's just doing them for fun—I think she folds them to send messages with her gestures via the security cams. And the mayor was murdered this morning. Someone else is still out there, committing the crimes that we *thought* Madeleine was responsible for. It just doesn't add up."

Draccon leaned forward against the steering wheel. "Wow— you've got it worse than I thought."

"I'm saying this objectively," Bruce snapped. "I'm not stupid."

"No. You're just naive." Draccon's fingers tightened on the steering wheel. "When we arrested her, it was at the scene of the final murder. I was one of the officers shining the spotlight on her. She was covered in blood, Bruce, with cuts in her gloves and knives strapped to her legs. Her fingerprints were all over the house. When the police questioned her afterward, asking if she'd done it, she nodded for each of the murders."

"She's far too smart to leave fingerprints all over the house," Bruce replied. "You haven't stood there and had a conversation with her. You haven't *heard* her. If you did, you'd understand what I mean."

"I haven't talked to her because she *chooses* to talk to you. Why do you think that is? You're questioning my work, Bruce, the work of the entire police department," Draccon said. "She killed those people. Now she's giving us—*you*—some information that's slightly useful to us, because she's finally realized that it might help her avoid the death penalty. It doesn't do her any good to keep holding information back."

"And what have you all done to try getting more information out of her?"

"What do you mean?"

"I mean, do you and Dr. James also authorize Arkham to treat her roughly?"

"What are you *talking* about?" Draccon's irritation turned into bewilderment.

"Her *bruises*. You must have seen them before, too. A while ago, when I spoke to her, she had deep scratch marks below her wrist, and her arm was black and blue."

Draccon stayed silent. "That's absurd," she finally said. "No one has ever touched her."

"It happened on the same day she said she got her IV medication. Did she get those bruises while she was in the medical wing?"

"Bruce, she *doesn't* need IV medication. And even if she did, we'd administer it in her cell. She's not meant to go anywhere outside her confines."

Bruce hesitated at that. He turned to look at the detective. "She told me she got into a fight with the nurse when they tried to inject her with medicine." But even as he said it, the words came out weak.

Draccon shook her head. "She was lying," she replied.

"Then . . ." Bruce frowned, trying to understand. Did she bruise *herself* as a ruse?

"Maybe you should check the security tapes," he said. "Send someone in there to check on her. If she really has bruises, then you probably need to make sure some employee isn't going in there to hurt her. She's still a valuable asset to you, isn't she?"

Draccon hesitated, making an annoyed sound in her throat. "I'll call the warden," she replied. Then she glanced at Bruce. "I told you early on to be careful around this girl. She's not normal, Bruce. She's not someone you can open up to and expect her to do the same back. She's not someone you can have a conversation with and then come away thinking you understand her better." The detective looked sidelong at him. "Now. What else has she told you that you've decided not to pass along to me?"

Bruce hesitated. *Leave Gotham City,* she'd told him. But maybe she'd been lying about that, too.

Draccon slowed to a stop at a light, then turned to Bruce. "Listen carefully, kid," she said. "If there's something she told you that I should know, you need to tell me now. Got it?"

She needs to know. Bruce looked back at the detective. "She said I was on a hit list," he replied. "She told me to get out of Gotham City, for my own safety."

At that, the detective whirled on him. "A hit list?"

"She told me to get out of Gotham City, for my own safety."

Draccon considered him for a moment. Then she let out a curse and picked up her phone. "Send a security detail to Wayne Manor."

* * *

By the time they reached the front gates to Bruce's estate, the rain had stopped altogether.

The path leading up to the main gates was still empty—the security detail had yet to arrive. Immediately, Bruce felt like something was wrong. *Off.*

Detective Draccon slowed to a stop in front of the gates' intercom and was about to speak into the glass surface when Bruce reached a hand out to stop her. "Wait," he said. His eyes focused on the gates.

"Are your gates typically unlocked?" Draccon said, now seeing what had caught Bruce's attention.

"No," Bruce replied. In fact, *never.* Alfred did not have a habit of leaving gates unlocked, even if he was expecting Bruce to come home. But there was no denying that the gates *were* open right now—the two sides pulled so slightly apart that at first glance it seemed like they were still closed. There was just enough room between them for a single person to slip through.

Bruce felt a wave of uneasiness. The gates were supposed to sound an alarm if left ajar like this. But now they sat silent, disabled.

"Wait here," Draccon said, her hand already on the hilt of her gun.

"But I—"

"*Stay in the car, Bruce.* That's an order." Draccon stepped out of the vehicle, drew her gun, and crept forward, her coat draped loosely across her shoulders. She slid through the subtle opening between the gates. Madeleine had warned him only an hour earlier. Had someone . . . ? His attention turned to the mansion itself. None of the lights were on, leaving every window plunged in gloom.

A sickening feeling hit Bruce in the chest. *Alfred.*

Draccon had made her way to the front steps of the house now and was slowly heading up the stairs, her back turned to one side and her gun pointed down. She was muttering something into the radio clipped near her collar. Bruce looked in the rear window. Still no security detail yet. He looked back toward the house, where Draccon was shouting for someone to open the door. A wave of dread washed over Bruce as Draccon called out again, but Alfred still didn't show up to let her in. A moment later, Bruce heard the door creak open as Draccon nudged it ajar. *It was unlocked.*

The details of the murders came back to him in a flash. *Trapped within their own homes.* The Nightwalkers were here, and they *wanted* him to go inside.

Draccon's tan coat had already disappeared behind the front pillars, and she had made her way into the house.

Bruce looked around in the car for anything he could use as a weapon but came away with nothing. If Madeleine was right about this—if they were here for *him*—they'd come to find him out here soon enough.

Bruce narrowed his eyes. *Let them come to me, then.* It would distract them from hurting Alfred—if they hadn't already done so. He opened the car door, stepped out, and closed it behind him with a quiet snap. Then he hurried through the gap in the gates.

The house sat eerily silent as he approached. Bruce crept forward, imitating the detective's stance, keeping his back against the pillars and his gaze constantly moving. He inched inside the door to the parlor. The house greeted him with shadows. As he closed the door behind him, it made a soft click. He paused, his hand still on the knob, and then gave it a tug. A harder tug. The door refused to budge.

He was locked in with the killers.

Bruce could hear the roar of blood in his ears. Draccon was nowhere to be seen.

Dark streaks against one wall made him freeze in his tracks. *Blood? Paint?* He peered closer, unsure of what he was seeing— then leaned away hastily when he realized what it was. A symbol had been spray-painted on the wall, a crude shape of a coin consumed by flames.

The Nightwalkers were here, waiting for him.

Bruce's nightmares came back to him, full force—walking down the dim corridors of his own home, running across Madeleine in the halls, being hunted.

No. He forced himself to close his eyes and steady his thinking. He had the advantage here—this was *his* house, and he knew it like the back of his hand, could walk the grounds blindfolded if he had to.

The darkness was his ally, not his enemy.

Bruce moved forward with soft steps, aiming for the kitchen. He needed a weapon.

From somewhere in the house came the sound of footsteps. They were not Alfred's familiar tread. The hairs rose on the back of Bruce's neck. He kept going. The white drapes over the dining and living room furniture looked ghostly in the darkness; the door to his study was thrown wide open. His eyes locked, as always, on the unused grandfather clock in there. And as he stared—he saw a silhouette pass before it.

His heart froze.

Standing still would mean death. He swiftly crossed the hallway into the kitchen, illuminated dimly by light from the window over the sink. Next to that window, he saw the row of knives displayed over the large wooden cutting board, magnetically locked onto a metal bar.

Footsteps out in the main foyer. If it was Draccon out there, she could easily shoot Bruce by mistake if he wasn't careful. He needed to hide. Bruce grabbed one of the knives from the metal bar, clutched it tight in his fist, and then felt his way through the shadows toward a large, empty cabinet that had once contained a wine fridge.

Suddenly, he heard a shout coming from the direction of the

garage. "Halt!" It was Draccon. "Police! Put your hands up or *I will shoot*!" A rush of adrenaline flooded into Bruce's veins, and the world around him seemed to sharpen. It reminded him of being trapped as a child in the caves underneath the manor, the water and blackness and creatures that seemed to close in from all sides. He shut his eyes for an instant.

Fear clears the mind. Panic clouds it.

Bruce opened his eyes and forced himself to concentrate.

A door slammed, followed by the beep of an alarm. His mind raced as he plotted out the mansion's floor plan. Someone had locked the garage door with the house's automated security. It couldn't have been Draccon. *The Nightwalkers had locked the detective away in the garage, isolating her.*

He couldn't hide here for long, not if Draccon was trapped, not if Alfred was hurt. The intruders had come for *him*, and they would stay until they found him.

The balcony overlooking the living room. The weak railing. Bruce turned to the staircase leading up to the second floor, waiting to see if the path was clear.

Taking a deep breath, Bruce darted out of the kitchen and up the staircase, avoiding the squeaky spots.

A stranger's deep voice, amused and taunting, called out from downstairs. "Bruce."

Every hair on Bruce's neck rose at the sound. A cold sweat broke out on his forehead. *Don't panic*, he reminded himself grimly. *Think.* He tucked himself into the shadows cast by a series of marble busts and waited.

Sure enough, the sound of footsteps echoed from the stairs as someone followed him up. The steps were heavy, distinctly a stranger's, and Bruce could hear the faint breathing of someone unfamiliar creeping up the stairs.

Bruce tensed in the darkness, gripping his knife so hard that his hand hurt. His knuckles had turned white against the hilt. He could strike out with it right now, surprise the person—but the thought of stabbing someone, even someone who'd broken into his home, made his chest tighten. In the darkness, Bruce could make out part of the stranger's silhouette—large, his shoulders hunched—and hear the slight mismatch of his footsteps' timing, a slight limp in his gait. His balance was poor.

He passed near the balcony's weak railing, scanning ahead, searching. *Now.* Bruce lunged out of the darkness. The man's head snapped toward him. For an instant, Bruce caught sight of his face: lined, menacing, shocked.

Bruce barreled into him. For a second, it didn't feel like enough—but the intruder stepped back to brace against the railing. It trembled, then gave way with a crack as it buckled from the man's weight. He tried in vain to stop his fall, but it was too late, and with a hoarse yell, he fell from the second story. His head hit the side of the couch below.

He twitched, moaning, on the floor.

Move, Bruce told himself. He'd given away his location with his attack, and if others were in the house, they'd know where he was now. His knife had dropped somewhere in the hall behind him, but he had no time to turn around and find it. He darted back down the stairs. Footsteps and a dragging sound came from the kitchen. A muffled voice. He curled deeper into the shadows of the dining room. Beside him, the white drapes fluttered. He looked at them, then pulled one over a chair.

"We know you're in here, Bruce Wayne," a different voice now called out, this time much closer. "That cop car out by the gates is awfully empty."

How many Nightwalkers had invaded the manor?

Bruce saw dark silhouettes outlined in the kitchen. Two men, with a third dragging between them. His eyes settled on the third person, who had a white cloth shoved into his mouth. *Alfred.*

He looked alert enough, but a bloody gash was on his forehead, and most of his weight seemed supported by the two men, both of them with masks pulled over their heads.

Every muscle in Bruce's body tightened with rage. Alfred, his guardian, who had never looked weak in his life—now at the mercy of these monsters.

"What if he already escaped?" one of the men muttered. They were drawing closer.

"No," the other replied. "House's rigged for that. We'll know if he tries to make a run for it."

"Are you sure?"

"Mads laid out the details of this house's security system herself. I'm sure."

Mads? Madeleine.

The name lodged in Bruce's thoughts, turning his stomach. How strange to hear her nickname. Maybe it fit her better, revealed her true side. Madeleine had genuinely seemed to like him—she had even *warned* him to get out of Gotham City. But what if she had targeted him this entire time?

Draccon was right about everything.

Bruce's anger burned, and it fueled him. Her other three victims had died because they'd been trying to *escape* the house. That was their first mistake, acting like the prey before they were even caught. But this was Bruce's home—his *parents'* home. They were on his turf now.

And on his turf, he was the predator.

Bruce crept soundlessly from his hiding place, then made his way around the kitchen counter. There was a remote trigger for the kitchen sink's grinder on this side of the island, and he inched toward it now. On the island's other side, the men were looking down, focused on dragging Alfred between them.

Bruce reached the island, held his breath, and flipped the switch.

The grinder burst to life, deafening in the silence. The two men jumped, swearing, and in the darkness, Bruce saw the outline of their guns as they whirled to look at the sink. Only Alfred looked the other way—toward the other side of the island, where Bruce crouched.

Before the two men could turn back around, Bruce wrenched Alfred out of their grasps. One man turned and Bruce's fist connected with his jaw, then with his stomach. The man hunched over with a wheezing gasp. Alfred kicked out, catching the second man off balance. Bruce wasted no time. In the blink of an eye, he brought his fist up and hit him squarely in the chin. Throwing himself at the second man, Bruce knocked him to the ground.

"Duck!" he shouted, and Alfred dropped to the floor.

"You little f—" the second man growled. His hand shot out, and his gun glinted in the darkness.

Bruce's eyes darted toward the dining room. "Detective!" he called out.

The second man instinctively glanced over his shoulder and mistook the white sheet that Bruce had draped against the back of a chair as Draccon's long tan coat. He startled, swinging his body and gun toward what he thought was the detective.

It was all the distraction Bruce needed. He aimed a punch straight at the man's neck. Sparring lessons from his coach flew through his mind.

Before he could land a second hit, though, a rough hand yanked Bruce backward. The first Nightwalker had staggered back to his feet and thrown his arm around Bruce's neck. The blow to his jaw had unsteadied him enough to make him sway on his feet, but he was heavy, far heavier than Bruce. Bruce twisted in vain, trying to reach his attacker, but his angle was wrong, and the man only held on tighter. Bruce choked as air lodged in his throat, blocked. He stumbled.

"Boss gonna be happy to see you, rich boy," the second man spat.

Someone barreled into Bruce's captor. It was Alfred—he kicked the man hard in the side, right in the liver, and the man keeled over with a yell of agony. Bruce dragged in a breath, hit the man squarely in the jaw, and watched him go limp.

"Bruce Wayne."

Bruce spun around to see a tall figure standing in the kitchen entrance. A pair of goggles shone silver in the night. Metal glinted on his arms and legs, like armor, and his face was concealed behind a mask, leaving only his mouth exposed. He broke into a grin that sent a chill down Bruce's spine.

The leader of the Nightwalkers.

"Well, well," he said. "All grown up and newly rich." He pointed a gun at Bruce.

The words echoed in Bruce's mind. Something seemed familiar about him, as if Bruce had once met him in another life. But he had no time to dwell on this now.

The man took aim. Bruce dropped. The bullet shattered the kitchen window behind him into a million pieces. An alarm screamed.

Bruce popped back up, yanked one of the knives off the metal bar, and flung it straight at the man.

The boss had underestimated Bruce. He made a small noise of surprise, twisting to one side, his hand flying up to his face. *Got him*, Bruce thought. He grabbed Alfred's arm and tried to drag Alfred out of the room—out of the gunfire.

Sirens blared from outside. Everyone froze. The flashing of red and blue lights could be seen through some of the windows. Draccon's security detail had finally arrived.

The boss glanced back at Bruce. Then he made up his mind—he barked out an order to his two Nightwalkers and threw something to the floor. It exploded, making the ground tremble, and a wave of black smoke rolled across them all, engulfing the room and plunging them in complete darkness. Bruce hunched over, coughing.

The boss called out a final farewell to Bruce. "See you soon."

A huge crash came from the garage where Draccon was trapped. Bruce tried to reach the other men—but they had already fled into the haze of smoke. As Draccon and the police came rushing into the house, the Nightwalkers vanished as quickly as they had come.

CHAPTER 20

The next few hours passed in a blur. Bruce remembered it as a non-stop stream of time in an ambulance, at the hospital, in the waiting room . . . doctors and nurses and police officers, all mixed together until he could scarcely tell where one ended and another began. His hand was bandaged, his knuckles bloodied from the fight, one palm cut by a knife without his having noticed, but otherwise, he'd escaped remarkably unscathed. Physically, at least. His hands were still trembling, and even though he sat in what seemed like a safe place, he half expected a Nightwalker to come lunging around every corner.

The important thing was that Alfred was alive. He'd suffered a concussion from the blow to his head—but he was going to be okay.

"Bruce!"

Bruce looked up from holding his head in his hands to see Dianne and Harvey hurrying over to him in the hospital's waiting room. When they reached him, Dianne flung her arms around

Bruce and gave him a tight hug, while Harvey put a hand on his shoulder, his eyes dark with worry.

"We came as soon as we heard," he said. "God, Bruce." He let out a long breath. "How are you?"

Bruce shrugged as they sat down beside him. "Okay enough," he replied, glancing down the hall toward Alfred's room.

"And Alfred?" Dianne asked, following Bruce's line of sight.

"He's still resting," he replied, swallowing the guilt that kept rising in him. "I'm waiting for them to let me see him."

Harvey leaned forward in his chair and lowered his voice. "Sorry," he said, patting Bruce again on his shoulder. "They're going to catch them. I'm willing to bet on it. They won't get away with this. Watch—by nightfall, the boss will be on the news, behind bars."

Dianne shook her head. "Did you really fend off three Nightwalkers on your own, and keep them from hurting Alfred?"

"It all happened so fast," Bruce replied. Even if it was true, he didn't feel much like a hero. "The Nightwalkers have a hit list, apparently, and I'm on it."

"What?" Dianne and Harvey replied in unison.

"Bruce."

The conversation paused as they all looked up to see Lucius hurrying into the waiting room. He clasped Bruce's hand in a firm shake and pulled him up for a quick hug. "You're safe, thank everything above. And Alfred?"

"Is going to make a full recovery," Bruce replied.

Lucius shook his head at Bruce in awe. "Heard you were quite a force against the Nightwalkers," he said, "but it'd be nice if we could keep you out of any more dangerous situations in the near future. You don't have to attend the gala tonight—you don't have to do anything. Just rest. Trust me, no one will be shocked if you decide it's safer to stay away. Your life was—"

"I'll be fine, Lucius, thank you." Bruce gave him a firm nod. "I'll be as safe at the gala as I will be anywhere else, and it'll be a good distraction. Our drones will all be there, won't they?"

Lucius managed a smile. "Yes, they will," he replied.

A doctor approached and interrupted their conversation. "Mr. Pennyworth is awake now," she said. "His vital signs are all good, and you can take him home tonight."

All other thoughts flew from Bruce's mind. He jumped to his feet. "Can I see him now?"

The doctor nodded. "For a bit, Mr. Wayne. But don't overdo it. He should rest some more later."

Bruce excused himself and followed the doctor down the hall, then stepped through the door that she held open for him. Inside, Alfred sat up straighter in his bed. Bruce had always considered him to be strong and invincible, kind and fair—but now, for the first time, he also seemed *old*, his gray hairs more noticeable than ever. Mortal. Bruce didn't like the thought.

"Master Wayne," Alfred said, his usually strong, deep voice now somewhat hoarse. A large bandage covered the top of his head.

Bruce hurried to Alfred's side, took the man's hand, and squeezed it. "How are you feeling?" he said. "They told me they stitched the cut on your forehead."

Alfred waved a nonchalant hand in the air. "Oh, I'll be better than fine," he replied. "This is merely a scratch compared with what I put up with in the military. The Nightwalkers will have to do better than that—although not before the police catch up with them."

Bruce felt an enormous weight lift from his chest at Alfred's upbeat words. His shoulders relaxed, and he dropped into the chair at Alfred's bedside, letting his head sink into his hands. "I'm sorry, Alfred," he said. "I'm so sorry. I thought I'd lost you." All those times Bruce had let Alfred worry about him—driving too fast, chasing after a criminal on a whim, putting his life on the line over and over—and yet, none of that had frightened him as much as the realization that Alfred could have died today. How many times had Bruce inflicted the same fear on his guardian?

Alfred's eyes softened at Bruce's bowed head. "Steady chin, Master Wayne," he replied. "I'm right here, and aside from a bump on the head, I'm feeling rather fine. You are a man now, albeit a young one who somehow manages to find trouble . . . but you'll always be my ward, and I will always look out for you. Just as you'll do for me."

Bruce met his eyes. He remembered this look, and even though ten years had passed since the night in the alley, it was still the look that could calm Bruce in the darkest moments. Bruce nodded, trying not to imagine life without him.

Alfred smiled. "We make a good team, Master Wayne," he said. "Especially with those punches you throw."

Alfred's familiar humor loosened the knot in Bruce's stomach. He reached over to clap his guardian once on his shoulder. "Not too shabby yourself, Alfred."

Alfred gave him a wink. Then his expression turned serious. "The Nightwalkers pegged you as one of their targets. You are similar to Madeleine's former targets, too, aren't you?"

"How did you know that?"

"You don't think I researched this girl you keep mentioning?" He leaned forward with a grimace. "She's dangerous."

Bruce nodded, then frowned. "I know. And I can't understand any of it." He lowered his voice. "Alfred—she warned me. That last conversation I had with her? She spent it telling me to get out of Gotham City, that I might be next on the Nightwalkers' list. She *knew* this was going to happen, and she wanted me to know."

Alfred narrowed his eyes. "Perhaps she set it all up as a trap."

The door behind Bruce opened then, and Draccon stepped into the room. The detective sported a nasty bruised eye, and one of her arms was in a sling. A wave of relief washed over Bruce at the sight of her, and he half rose from his chair to greet her. "Detective," he said. "You're—"

She smiled warily at him, but she didn't move from the door, and Bruce's reply faded on his tongue. "Detective?" Bruce said again, hesitant this time.

"What is it?" Alfred added.

Draccon took a deep breath before she nodded at Bruce. "It's Madeleine."

The happiness at seeing Alfred recovering, at knowing Draccon was well—all made way in an instant for a cold blanket of dread. Bruce eyed the detective. "What about her?"

"She escaped."

Escaped.

Bruce sat there for a while longer, unable to comprehend the thought. Escaped. *No.* How? She hadn't run during the jailbreak—why would she make her move now? "She . . . she couldn't have . . . ," he managed to say.

Draccon held a hand up at the TV in Alfred's room, which had rotated onto the news. "See for yourself."

Bruce found himself staring at a news crew's footage of the empty interior of Madeleine's former cell.

A searing jolt of nausea hit Bruce. He flashed back to Madeleine first staring up at the cams—then to her casually mentioning how they could be scrambled—then to her acting vulnerable in her cell—then to her telling him again how he could talk to her without letting anyone know. He didn't know how she did it, but somehow, Madeleine must have taken advantage of Bruce's resetting of the security cams.

Of course. It made so much sense now; why would she try to escape during the jailbreak, when the asylum was on high alert and all the guards were looking for the inmates? The place would have been swarming with guards. Instead, she chose to use that time to set things up for her real escape. It had all been a part of her grand con against him.

Now she was loose, somewhere in the city, *outside Arkham Asylum*. She may even have escaped at around the same time as Bruce's ordeal. He shook his head, numb. "Where—how?" he managed to croak out. "Any leads?"

"Yes. One." Draccon pushed the door open wider, and Bruce saw that she had several other police officers with her. One of them was holding a set of handcuffs. Behind them stood Harvey, Dianne, and Lucius, who cast confused looks his way. "You."

Bruce's vision swam in a sudden wave of dizziness. "Me?"

"We have footage showing you as the last person to enter the intensive-treatment ward, right before the cams reset. Madeleine left behind a note to you in her cell, thanking you for helping her."

"What?" Bruce exclaimed. "You can't possibly think that—especially after this morning—"

"I have no choice but to consider you a suspect. I'm sorry." Draccon sighed deeply, then motioned an officer forward.

He held up a pair of cuffs. "Bruce Wayne, you're under arrest."

CHAPTER 21

The interrogation room at the GCPD precinct was cold and spare, equipped only with several chairs and a table separating Bruce from Detective Draccon and another police officer. Draccon slid a single paper toward him, then sat back with crossed arms and scrutinized his face.

"She left you this," she said. "Security told us that, because of the camera malfunction playing the wrong footage in Madeleine's cell, she was able to attack two workers we'd sent to check on her. She knocked them out and swiped one of their IDs before any alarms were triggered, because no cams recorded her doing it."

Bruce found himself staring down at a note written in Madeleine's hand and folded into the careful, intricate shape of a flower. His head swam at the sight.

He had never seen her handwriting before, of course, but it seemed to fit her—sparse, minimal, and elegant, with the occasional surprising flourish. He thought of the security tapes he'd seen of her, of the way she seemed to send signals to the cams through her paper folding. Had she been talking to someone who worked inside Arkham, and then set Bruce up to be a part of all this? What if one of the workers had intentionally let her escape? He read the note over and over again, barely able to believe it.

> *Dear Bruce,*
>
> *We're not a very smart match, are we? I can't think of a story where the billionaire and the murderer end up happily ever after. So let's call us even: thank you for helping me get out of this place, and you're welcome for the months of entertainment. I hope you'll remember me.*
>
> *xo,*
>
> *MW*

It sounded like her. But Bruce couldn't wrap his head around why she would do this—if she wanted to escape, why leave him a note? Why do this to him after she'd also helped him work against the Nightwalkers? He read the note yet again, memories of their conversations replaying in his mind, and then folded it back along its lines. As with all her folded art, the flower could unfurl into another shape—and this time it changed into the shape of a three-dimensional diamond. Bruce stared at the two-faced paper sculpture. All those seemingly serious conversations, all her talk about sympathizing with him over the loss of his parents, pretending to help him catch the Nightwalkers, warning him to get out of Gotham City. Of her lingering looks and her final apology. *I'm sorry*, she'd said before turning her back.

Madeleine fit into only one category.

"She's a *liar*," Bruce snapped, balling up the note. The flower crumpled. "This is all part of her plan. It's too easy for her to do this. You can't possibly think I purposely wanted to help her." He looked in disbelief at the detective, then at the second policeman.

"And what about her profile that you stole from my desk?" Draccon said, her voice clipped and cold. "Is that one of her lies, too?"

Bruce hesitated. This was no time for him to start hiding things from the police. "I did take it," he admitted. "Only because I was trying to understand her better."

"And our IT security department tells us someone from outside the precinct pinged our police directories under a guest log-in. We tracked the IP address to your home."

Bruce stayed silent.

"Then you disabled the security cams," Draccon went on. "If she set *you* up to do it for her, then you gladly became her accomplice."

All you'd need to do to disable the system is to use the right scrambler, set at the right frequency. Those had been her words—*all* you'd *need to do. You, Bruce.*

She had told him exactly where her web was, and he had still walked into it.

Draccon nodded at his lack of response. "Don't make this harder for yourself, Bruce. I know this has been difficult for you, and that I sent you into her path to begin with." She tapped her pen on the table. "But you understand why I'm skeptical. *Why* would Madeleine go out of her way to thank you for her escape? If you truly had nothing to do with it, then why didn't she just escape and leave it at that?"

Bruce shook his head. "I have no idea," he answered. "But you have to believe me. She knew that by leaving this note, she would make sure that I end up in your interrogation rooms. Think. Why would she send me here?"

"Sometimes killers don't need a reason," Draccon replied. "Sometimes they just want to have fun."

"This doesn't make sense," Bruce said, his voice turning urgent again. "*Please*, Detective. You and I have worked out enough about Madeleine to know that she doesn't *ever* do something for no reason at all. I—"

He paused, realizing how he must sound. Draccon raised an eyebrow at him. Even the way he talked about her now made it sound like he knew her well, *too* well, that he had cared for her in a way beyond mere objective curiosity. And he had, hadn't he?

To Bruce's surprise, Draccon seemed tired instead of angry, and listened to Bruce with an expression of bone-deep weariness. "It's my fault," she said with a sigh. "I never should have involved you in this case. I should've left you to finish your community service sentence, and let that be it. When I thought we could rely on you to get information out of Madeleine for us, I didn't think you'd end up being her ticket to freedom."

Bruce slammed his hand down on the table. "But I didn't *help her.*"

"What would you have us believe, then, Bruce?" Draccon said. She rested her hands on the table and crossed her arms. "I've seen the surveillance tapes. I've seen your body language toward her change as time went on. Bruce—Madeleine escaped. She's on the loose now. She's probably found a way to reunite with the Night-walkers. Our police are out in force, trying to track her down . . . but she's covered her tracks well."

Bruce put his arms on the table and leaned his head into his hands. What would he need to do to work his way out of this? "How long do I have to stay here?" he muttered. "Is there bail?"

Draccon shook her head. "Sorry, Bruce," she replied. "You'll have to remain here overnight. We need as much information as we can get, and the precinct doesn't want you wandering around the city. It's as much for your protection as it is for our benefit."

"You mean you don't trust me," Bruce countered. "You think I'm a flight risk?"

Draccon's eyes didn't waver. "You're not in the best position to argue right now," she replied.

Bruce closed his eyes and let out a long breath. "Fine. My phone call, then, please."

* * *

Moments later, Bruce was inside a clear glass booth and puzzling over the details of how to dial out on a rotary phone. *When I get leave of here, I'm donating new phones to the precinct*, he thought darkly. On the other side of the glass, he could see the lines of the police cubicles, and beyond that, a series of flat-screen TVs mounted against the wall. The news was showing a journalist standing in the middle of a street, in front of a black carpet. Bruce looked away when he finally managed to dial Alfred's cell phone number. *Thank god*, he thought as the ringing began.

Alfred picked up on the first ring.

"Alfred Pennyworth speaking," he said.

"Alfred! Are you still at the hospital?"

"Master Wayne?" Alfred replied. "I was beginning to think the police wouldn't let you call. I'm doing fine—they'll discharge me tonight. How are you holding up?"

"I've had better days."

"Your friend Dianne has been calling nonstop about you," Alfred went on. "She had hoped they would release you on bail. She's already at the gala—many attendees are still going there in support of you and in honor of the mayor."

Dianne. The gala. *The black carpet on the TV.* Bruce suddenly remembered, and his eyes shot back up to focus on the TVs. Sure enough, the Ada drones from WayneTech were already out in full force, looming at the entrance leading into the Gotham City Concert Hall. The event's tone had turned somber since the mayor's death, and black draped the sides of the concert hall's walls, the cloths threaded in silver with the gala's original diamond-shaped logo. Guests arrived in black, too, treating the event as less of a celebration and more as a memorial to the mayor.

Bruce's eyes went back to the gala's diamond-shaped logo—a logo that looked almost exactly like the diamond shape that Madeleine's letter to him folded into. He froze. A fist of ice closed around his heart.

All of Gotham City's elite would be at the gala tonight. *The Nightwalkers are going to strike there, in one fell swoop.* All this time, they had been stockpiling weapons in anticipation for *this*, their biggest operation. And Madeleine had hinted it to him with the shape of her note.

"Alfred," he said urgently. "Call Dianne. Tell her to catch a cab back home right away. *Now.* She shouldn't be there tonight. Get her out of there. Tell her, *tell her*—"

"Master Wayne, calm down." There was a short pause on the other end, and then Alfred said, "I'll call her immediately. What's going on?"

Bruce opened his mouth to answer, but he noticed then that others in the police precinct offices, beyond the glass window of his phone booth, had turned their attention to the TVs, too. *No.* On the screens, he could see the journalist suddenly turn around as the sound of screams came from somewhere inside the building. Police cars pulled up to the main entrance. Among them were Ada security drones and two SWAT trucks, and Bruce looked on in horror as officers poured out of the back of the vehicles, armed with rifles and bulletproof vests. *It's too late.*

The Nightwalkers were making their move.

The faint words of the reporter now drifted over to him. "—confirmed that as many as one hundred guests, ranging from Gotham City's attorney general to the deputy mayor, from Wayne-Tech's Lucius Fox to dozens of other innocent civilians, are being held hostage by the Nightwalkers. There may be a ransom note released very soon, although we have no information yet about what it might contain."

Lucius was trapped inside. *So was Dianne.* So were a hundred other people, all of whom might die tonight. Bruce felt his heart lodge in his throat. The phone was still in his hand, and he could hear Alfred calling for him through it, but he felt far away, his mind numbed. Dianne had gone there tonight in support of him, had always been there for him throughout this entire ordeal—and now he had once again put her life in danger.

I have to get them out. I have to fix this.

The drones at the entrance suddenly turned away from facing the street. Odd.

They switched into offensive stances as police approached. Bruce blinked. *What?* The first SWAT police crouched down, pointing their rifles at the drones, but the drones stepped forward, blocking their entry into the building.

The reporter turned around with a frown. "We are just now getting word that something seems to have gone wrong with Wayne-Tech's Ada drones—what you are seeing here at the entrance to the concert hall—that they are becoming aggressive toward GCPD forces."

Madeleine. Bruce knew instantly. She had found a way to hack the drones, turning them from security forces into the Nightwalkers' own army. He shuddered as he thought back to her wry comments. *Never trust tech.* And apparently she was right—especially when she was the one behind the tech.

Bruce narrowed his eyes. He was trembling now at the thought of Lucius with his hands tied, of Dianne staring down the gun of a Nightwalker. *I'm done being your prey,* he thought, staring at the screen. *You're going to be mine now.*

"Master Wayne!" Alfred was still calling for him over the phone. "Master Wayne? What is going on?"

"We make a good team, right?" Bruce replied, keeping his voice low on the phone. "Because you have to help me, Alfred. I need to get to the gala *right away.*"

CHAPTER 22

Despite the fact that Bruce was being held without bail in a jail cell, it didn't feel like many officers were left behind to guard him. The office itself was in a chaotic state—every officer who could be deployed had been sent to the concert hall, while those forced to stay behind were either rushing around answering the flood of calls coming in or gaping in horror at the news unfolding on the TV screens.

Bruce could hear the commotion from his cell; as much as he tried, he could only see a glimpse of the side of one TV from where he was situated. It was late now, nearly midnight, and the gala would have been in full swing. Instead, what should have been a night of tribute and celebration had become the largest hostage standoff in the history of Gotham City.

Bruce paced back and forth in his cell. He didn't have much time to tell Alfred what he needed to over the phone—it had been too risky to say much with officers standing nearby. But Alfred, as always, had needed little explanation.

Bruce had no idea what he would do if he confronted

Madeleine—if she was indeed responsible for all of this, then talking to him certainly wasn't going to stop her. Still, he couldn't stop thinking about the way she had tilted her head up at him, the look on her face when she'd said, *Two kinds of people come out of personal tragedy. . . . You're the kind that comes out brighter.* Behind her confusing maze of actions and expressions, was there a part of Madeleine, however small, that actually did mean what she said?

Bruce narrowed his eyes. He needed to know why she did this to him. He needed to bring her to justice. And more than anything, he needed to stop her before the Nightwalkers hurt more people. The conviction burned in him like a dark flame.

"Get another cruiser out there!" someone exclaimed as footsteps rushed through the precinct's halls. "We don't have time— the drones have started firing—"

The drones have started firing. Bruce's heart skipped a beat. The Nightwalkers had managed to hijack every Ada drone at the gala and turn them into killing machines. If they—if *Madeleine*— could manage to find a way to access and reprogram the drones inside WayneTech, or seize control of the other weapons in there, Gotham City's police would be overwhelmed.

"Come on, Alfred," Bruce muttered under his breath.

Detective Draccon rushed past the jail door. At the sight of her, Bruce yelled, "Detective! Detective Draccon!"

She doubled back, her eyes flashing as she looked in at Bruce.

"You have to let me out," Bruce shouted. "I can help you find a way into the concert hall. I can—"

"Stay put, Bruce," she shouted back. "You'll be safe here." Bruce watched her take off down the hall after the officers, her men behind her.

As the chaos on TV continued, the scene in the back of the precinct quieted even further. Half the lights were off now, and the only people not on duty were a few guards, their attention all turned to the TVs and phones. Bruce gripped the bars hard, then closed his eyes, bowed his head, and slid slowly down into a crouch by the door of his cell. How had all of this gone so wrong? And now here he was, stuck, unable to do anything to help.

"Oh, thank you," Harvey Dent said to someone. "Yeah, I'm here to see my dad."

Bruce's eyes snapped open as his friend Harvey stepped into the holding area with an officer hurrying beside him. Harvey didn't meet Bruce's gaze right away, but when the officer pointed at a cell farther down the hall, Harvey gave the man an earnest smile. "Yes, I can go from here. Thank you, sir."

"All right, kid. You've got ten minutes." The policeman rushed off, distracted by the chaos in the office.

"Harvey?" Bruce said in a low voice as his friend's eyes locked on him.

"Bruce," Harvey hissed, then headed over toward his cell. "There you are."

"What are you doing here?" Bruce said as his friend approached him and gripped the bars. "You're here to see your dad . . . ?"

Harvey gave him a shaky smile. "I finally reported him, Bruce," he said. "The police arrested him."

At that, Bruce blinked, unable to stop a quick smile spreading across his own face. After all this time, his friend had stood up to his father. "You—you reported your dad? They're keeping him in this holding area?"

Harvey nodded. "Yeah. But I'm not here to see him. It was just a really good excuse to get the police to let me come back here." He held up a small key between them. Bruce glanced down at it, his smile fading into shock.

It was the key to Bruce's holding cell.

"Turns out," Harvey whispered, "that I have some slick hands, and that Alfred is one convincing talker."

Alfred. Bruce stared at him. "*He* put you up to this? You're helping me get out?"

"Hey, be flattered that I'm willing to break the law for you and Dianne." Harvey shoved the key into the lock. "My dad belongs in here, not you. Now, let's go."

On any other night, the holding area of the GCPD precinct would have been a near-impossible place from which to break out. Detective Draccon would have interrogated Bruce again before the night was done; there would have been two rotations of police in the back, not one; and everyone's attention wouldn't have been consumed by the screens mounted on the wall, displaying the nightmare of events going down.

But tonight, as the Nightwalkers held the city hostage, Bruce was able to creep down one of the precinct's halls at a fast clip, head down and shoulders tense, keeping his eyes on Harvey, who hurried forward in front of him. They were making a run for the building's single back door, which led out to the rain-washed parking lot behind the precinct.

Suddenly, Harvey darted to one side and wedged himself into a nook where the bathrooms were. Bruce did the same. An instant later, a young officer hurried past them, her hand on the gun at her hip. They held their breath as she rushed by. As she went, they heard her shout, "Is anybody left in here? We called for more backup!"

"The National Guard's on their way!" a voice answered her farther down the hall. Bruce heard a pair of footsteps run away from them, then fade. He let his breath out.

"Come on," Harvey snapped. They bolted back out into the hall. As they went, Bruce heard another shout go up from the holding cell area.

"I thought Draccon was keeping Wayne here!"

"She is—"

"How the hell did he get the key?"

"Get Draccon on the phone—we have a missing—"

Bruce gritted his teeth as both he and Harvey broke into a run. *I guess that officially makes me a fugitive.* They burst out the door and into the night, and the jail was behind them.

They took two steps before a black car screeched to a halt in front of them. This was not the usual, stately ride Alfred used to take Bruce around, but a car that Bruce recognized from Wayne-Tech, sleek and understated and black, its surface blending in with the night.

"Need a ride?" Alfred said.

Bruce broke into a grin. He and Harvey rushed into the car. Bruce had barely shut the passenger door when Alfred slammed his foot down on the pedal, sending them barreling out of the parking lot. In the rearview mirror, they saw the young officer stumble out of the precinct just in time to see them speed away.

"A little slower on the turns, Alfred," Bruce managed to say as they screeched around a corner and bolted into a freeway tunnel.

Alfred chuckled. He still had his hospital band wrapped around his wrist. "WayneTech cars aren't made for slow turns, Master Wayne."

"And you wonder where I get it from." Bruce felt as if his stomach could touch his spine. Even in his Aston Martin, he'd never been able to drive the way Alfred was now.

"I used to be in the Royal Air Force, Master Wayne," Alfred answered in a dry tone. "At least I have an excuse. Just because one *can* doesn't mean one *should*. I expect you not to use this against me the next time you go for a joyride."

"I'll try not to," Bruce managed to reply as he clutched the edges of his seat. In the back seat, Harvey looked green. "Why'd you agree to get me out, Alfred? I thought for sure that you would've refused. Too dangerous and all."

"Your Madeleine makes a poor friend," Alfred replied as they entered another turn.

"I'll say," Bruce muttered.

"No, I mean literally. I received an alert from your bank accounts half an hour ago. There has been some suspicious activity."

"Suspicious activity?" Bruce's words faded as Alfred handed him a phone, showing him an overview of his accounts.

"Looks like someone's organization needed a boost of funds," Alfred replied.

Bruce stared down at the zero balances in three of his older accounts, the ones that he'd had prior to turning eighteen. All three had been completely emptied. His throat turned dry. *Madeleine.*

"Holy shit," Harvey muttered as he looked on from behind Bruce's seat.

More lies, more deceit. *None of what Madeleine said to me at Arkham was true.* She had been after his funds this entire time. And when he had decided to soften and open up to her, she'd sent him to jail and taken his money in the process. Just like the Nightwalkers. Just like what they had done to every single one of their past victims before they killed them. And that meant they would target everything Wayne Industries stood for now, if the pattern of their past victims continued to hold. They would target the new accounts that had opened to Bruce, where the bulk of his family's fortune sat.

"With all due respect, Master Wayne," Alfred said politely, "hell if I'll let your parents' legacy end up in the hands of a bloody criminal mastermind."

Bruce swallowed hard and tried to channel his rage into action. *Focus. Think.* His thoughts went to Lucius, who was currently sitting among those held hostage at the gala. *Didn't he rig up a new security system for my new accounts?* Bruce thought. Then he straightened.

The security system placed on his new accounts. No wonder Madeleine hadn't touched those yet; maybe she was having trouble breaking past the shields Lucius had put up. Maybe she . . .

An idea began to brew in his head.

"I'm going to need some more help, Alfred," he said. "And from you, too, Harvey."

He half expected Harvey to hesitate, but his friend didn't even flinch. "Tell me what you need me to do. Do you have a plan?"

Bruce nodded grimly. "The start of one, at least. Harvey—I need you to alert the police. Tell them not to open fire on the drones. Tell them to stay back. I don't know what Madeleine and the Night-walkers will do to the hostages if the police try to move forward. Stall them, okay?"

"I'll throw myself at them if I have to," Harvey said, leaning forward to grip Bruce's headrest. "Just be careful, got it?"

"You too." Bruce exchanged a smile with his friend. As Alfred pulled up to the side of a street, Harvey got out of the car and, without a backward glance, headed toward the flashing lights.

Bruce watched his friend go. Then he glanced at Alfred. "We need to make a pit stop."

"Where?"

"WayneTech."

Alfred shot him a wary glance. "Lucius would warn you none of those prototypes are ready for use."

"Says the man driving *this* car. Lucius is currently being held at gunpoint at the concert hall," Bruce replied. "I think he'll for-give us."

"Not if you don't make it out of there alive."

"Come on, Alfred." Bruce cast his guardian a fleeting smile. "What's the point of being a billionaire if I can't have a little fun?" At the withering look on Alfred's face, he added, "I have to do this. I will do it with or without your help. But *with* your help, I'll have a better chance."

Alfred shook his head. "I first realized you'd be a handful when you accidentally set that old garden toolshed on fire with a blowtorch," he replied. "Do you remember that? You were thirteen.

Five years later, here we are, aiding and abetting you as a fugitive." His voice lowered. "My job is to keep you safe, Master Wayne. But if that means making sure you don't try something absurd behind my back, then so be it."

This time, there was no one to greet Bruce as they pulled up to the back entrance of WayneTech—only two streetlights illuminating the road.

Bruce hopped out of the car first. As Alfred followed, Bruce reached the door and put his palm down on the security pad. *Please open*, he begged it silently. It beeped once, then glowed green, and the door slid open. Bruce let out a breath in relief. Inside, slivers of moonlight sliced the floor into stripes, leaving the rest of the dome-roofed interior bathed in deep blue.

They reached the end of the hall, where a final set of sliding doors waited. Bruce placed his hand on the palm pad again—but this time the pad flashed red. The doors stayed shut.

"It's not working," Bruce muttered.

"Allow me," Alfred said as he came up beside Bruce. He put his own hand out and pressed it against the pad. "Lucius must not have put you in the system yet for this room."

The pad flashed green, and the doors opened, letting them in. Bruce ran down the halls, eyes scanning each row—until he finally slowed in front of a glass panel displaying the metallic silk outfit inside. *With reinforced links like microscopic chain mail*, Lucius had said. *Not ready for prime time yet*, he'd also said—but it was functional, and better than nothing. Bruce glanced at Alfred, who gave him a nod.

"Sorry, Lucius," Bruce murmured—then threw an elbow at the glass and shattered the panel. Glass rained down around them. Bruce gingerly took the outfit off its hanger, then continued down the aisles.

"This is your plan?" Alfred said incredulously as Bruce stopped before another row, where a series of laser-trained darts were arranged. "To take a whole host of your own corporation's top-secret experimental gear and head to the concert hall? On your own?"

"That's the plan," Bruce replied. He grabbed several of the metal darts from their holsters and carefully arranged them inside his backpack. "If you have a better idea, Alfred, I'm happy to hear it."

Alfred sighed as Bruce moved down the row, picking out a miniature cable launcher and what looked like a small, round sphere. Both items went into the backpack, too. "Master Wayne," Alfred finally replied as they moved on down the rows. "You might want to consider how you're going to get past the hacked drones around the concert hall. I have seen the footage. Lucius ordered enough stationed there that they can hold off nearly all of Gotham City's police force. Experimental chain mail and a few smoke bombs won't get you close enough."

Bruce nodded. "I know—I've been thinking about that. But look."

They reached the end of the block of rows. Across a path in the floor were the rest of the Ada drones, sitting dormant and awaiting commands. "Lucius told me that the drones are designed to not attack each other." He walked up to the machines. "I can use one to get past the rest. *These* aren't infected with whatever the Nightwalkers did to the others."

Alfred did not look pleased at the thought, but he didn't argue, either. Instead, he stepped closer to a drone and studied it. "How do you activate them?"

Bruce pulled out his phone, unlocked it, and brought up the app that Lucius had installed. "Give me your phone, Alfred." When his guardian handed it over, Bruce added the same app to it and tapped a button. The eyes on the nearest Ada drone lit up immediately with a blue glow and swiveled in their direction, focusing on Bruce.

"Hello, Bruce Wayne," it said. Then it moved into a steady crouch, awaiting more orders.

"Now I need a way into the building," Bruce muttered.

Alfred frowned. "Master Wayne . . ."

"You've gotten me this far, Alfred."

Alfred shook his head, but when he spoke again, he said, "The Seco Financial Building, near the concert hall. Wayne Industries is funding the construction on the building's basement level, which connects into Gotham City's downtown network of linked halls. It's unfinished, but probably passable."

Bruce nodded. "Perfect. That'll do."

"And then what, Master Wayne?" Alfred said as they watched the drone turn its head and follow their slightest movements. "Are you sure about this?"

"I'm not sure about anything," Bruce admitted. He hoisted his backpack onto his shoulders. "But I'm not about to let Madeleine get away with this. And the only way I can stop her is if I go there myself."

CHAPTER 23

On the night Bruce's parents were gunned down in the alley, Bruce had sat on the curb beside an officer and repeatedly counted the eight police cars and two ambulances on the scene. Now, as they drove as close to the edge of the concert hall blockade as they could, Bruce counted more than two dozen sets of flashing police lights, a cluster that could be seen from as far as four blocks away. A crowd of people had gathered on the outskirts of the blockade; beyond that, the streets were eerily empty as everyone holed away in their homes.

"A ransom note has come in," Alfred said. He nodded at Bruce as he brought up the news on the car's screen. "Look."

Bruce read the top headline: NIGHTWALKERS DEMAND $500 MIL-LION RANSOM, RESIGNATIONS OF CITY OFFICIALS, RELEASE OF ALL PRIS-ONERS FROM GOTHAM CITY PENITENTIARY AND ARKHAM ASYLUM.

"That's absurd." Bruce looked away, feeling ill. *And they must know it.* It was a political statement, to try to force their twisted justice. *They must know the city cannot possibly release all their inmates, and they will use it as justification for killing everyone inside that building.* His heart seized at the thought. *Dianne would be among the casualties.*

Alfred pulled the car around the corner into an alley and looked at Bruce. "Still there?" he asked.

Bruce looked down at his phone. The Ada drone had followed them on a different route through the streets and was now stopped a block away from them. Already, Bruce could see it gathering data and details about the standoff up ahead, its shields raised in defense mode and ready for possible assailants. As Bruce shifted, he could feel the cold smoothness of the protective mesh he wore, the suit of fitted black armor that secured him from head to toe. He picked up the opaque black helmet that came with the armor. In it, he could see the reflection of his face staring back at him, pale and uncertain. He took a deep breath and pulled it on.

To his surprise, sounds immediately magnified inside the helmet, and through the visor, the world looked sharper, the colors brighter and more vivid. It would be easier to distinguish people in the darkness.

"I'll go on foot from here," he said. His voice came out muffled and slightly different. "Alfred, keep an eye on our drone. Make sure it watches my back. If anything goes wrong with it, power it down immediately." He revealed a small tracker on the skin of his waist. "You'll know where I am inside the concert hall."

Alfred looked ready to argue with him one last time, to tell him how ridiculous this entire plan sounded. And it wasn't much of a plan at all. *Steal a bunch of equipment and force my way in.* What would he do if he could actually get inside? What then? How would he ever get close enough to find and rescue Dianne? Or Lucius? Or any of the others?

Bruce hesitated, heart pounding. A part of him wished that Alfred would tell him not to go. When he met his guardian's gaze, he realized that the light he saw in those eyes was not disapproval, incredulity, or skepticism. It was fear. Fear of losing him.

"I'll keep an eye on you," Alfred said. "Get Dianne and Lucius—and get *yourself* out of there safely. Do you understand me, Master Wayne?"

Bruce swallowed hard. "Yes, Alfred. I promise." He lingered for a moment, wondering if he would make it out of this alive, if this was the last time they'd get to speak.

Alfred gave him a single, steady nod. "You can do this."

Bruce found himself nodding back, trying to believe the words, feeling small again. He thought of the night when Alfred held an umbrella over him and escorted him back to the mansion, led him away from the alley and his parents and the blood and the rain.

Bruce opened his mouth to respond, but the lump in his throat had lodged too tight. If he waited any longer, he wasn't sure if he could ever work up enough courage again.

So he tore his gaze away, got out of the car, and, without a backward glance, headed toward the flashing lights.

The murmur and shuffling of the crowd of onlookers grew louder as Bruce neared the block with the barricade. Officers were trying unsuccessfully to clear the area—people would disperse, then slowly drift back. One police officer was shouting in vain for everyone to return to their homes.

Over a loudspeaker from the concert hall, they could hear a man's deep voice spelling out new demands for the police. His voice rang across the night. "We want the city's treasury transferred over to our accounts within the hour," he called out. "If you do so, we will release some of our hostages to you. If you fail, then we will start sending out some bodies. It's your choice, Gotham City."

Not if I can help it, Bruce thought. He paused in a narrow side street, hidden from view. Double-checking the intersection, he then headed in a small side door that led into an empty skyscraper lobby. His footsteps echoed as Bruce hurried straight to an elevator and hit the button for the lowest level.

Alfred was right. The Seco Financial Building's basement level connected directly to the city's underground tunnels—including one running underneath the kiosk across from the concert hall. It would get him past the police barricade. Now Bruce entered the subterranean space and walked along the empty corridor, ignoring the construction materials on either side.

As he reached the end of the hallway, he found the elevator that would take him back up to the surface. He took a deep breath, then got on. As he did, he sent Alfred a message. If he was lucky, the drone would already have made its way toward him.

"Here we go," Bruce whispered.

Reaching street level, the elevator stopped and the doors slid open.

A whirlwind of sound hit him. The roar of helicopters overhead. The *pop-pop-pop* of gunfire as a SWAT team tried to break the drones' formation. The blare of an officer's voice from a megaphone, demanding the Nightwalkers stand down. Bruce looked on in horror from the kiosk as the drones pushed the line of heavily armed police back even farther. Across the street from him, a cluster of drones guarded one of the doors leading into the concert hall. Behind him, a full block away, was the barricade of police cars trying to keep people back from the fighting.

Bruce glanced down at his phone, his hand trembling. His drone had reached the edge of the police barricade. GCPD would see it any second now. Once he made a run for it, he couldn't afford to stop moving.

This was his last chance to stay out of the fight.

His muscles tensed. *Now, Alfred,* he mouthed silently.

A burst of commotion came from the barricade—a chorus of screams. Bruce looked on as an Ada drone leaped over the barricade, completely unharmed by the police's attempts to shoot it, and then made its way toward him. The two drones nearby turned their heads, rearing up—but when Bruce's drone drew closer, they relaxed, recognizing one of their own.

Bruce didn't hesitate. He hurtled across the street toward the concert hall. Behind him, he could hear the police raise the alarm.

"Hold your fire! *Hold your fire!* Civilian in the vicinity!"

In a few split seconds, Bruce had sprinted past the drone barrier and onto the path leading into one of the concert hall's side entrances. The elastic, metallic armor of his suit seemed to give each of his movements strength, enhancing his agility and making each leap feel like little effort. He felt as if he were inside a gym simulation, running a circuit with the ease that came from years of practice. His breaths were steady. Behind him, he saw the two hostile drones advancing on his own. Already, someone from inside was overriding the controls that prevented them from firing on each other. He'd hoped he would have more time—but as he looked on, one of the hostile drones reared up, pointed an arm at Bruce's drone, and opened fire.

The second drone caught sight of Bruce hovering near the locked side entrance. It craned its neck, then lunged over in his direction. Its eyes flashed scarlet, a clear warning, and it raised its arm at him. *"Stand down, civilian,"* it said. *"You are not cleared for this area."*

Was Madeleine behind the eyes of this drone, looking at him? Would she even recognize him, with his disguise on? And if she *did* know it was him . . . would she still attack? Bruce crouched, tense, as the drone stared him down, waiting for him to step away. He stayed where he was. The drone reared higher.

"You are under arrest for resisting police orders," the drone said. *"Hands in the air."*

Bruce narrowed his eyes. "Go ahead, then," he replied as if he were talking directly to Madeleine.

The drone hesitated for a second—perhaps it was *her* hesitating.

Then it raised its weapon. A slight blue glow came from the end of its arm. *It's going to attack.*

The arm shot toward him. Bruce threw himself to the side a split second before the arm struck him—instead, it smashed into the door, shattering it in an explosion of glass. Bruce shielded his neck and face with his arms. As the drone shifted in his direction and reared back to attack again, he sprang to his feet and lunged through the gaping hole in the door. The drone followed in pursuit.

Bruce entered a narrow corridor. Two Nightwalker guards dressed all in black hoisted rifles and pointed them at him. Their jaws dropped in surprise as the drone crashed in after him. Bruce reacted on instinct—he dove into a roll in front of them and swung a leg out at the first guard, knocking him clear off his feet. As he fell, the drone reached forward and caught him, its grip closing tight around the man's chest and lifting him up in the air. The man let out a shout—he pointed his rifle at the drone and opened fire. The shots ricocheted off the metal surface. Bruce ducked. The bullets hit the second guard in his legs. He fell to the floor, screaming.

Bruce seized the injured guard by his arm and dragged him down the corridor and around the corner to safety as the drone behind them realized it had seized one of the Nightwalkers. A glitch that would need fixing.

The injured guard gave Bruce a bewildered look, but Bruce didn't have time to explain that he wasn't here to hurt people. He left the man where he was and sprinted on.

Bruce had been in this concert hall twice before in his life—he recognized this level as the corridor that led into the smaller of two lobbies. Where were the Nightwalkers holding the hostages? Behind him, he could hear the shouts of the first guard, who had been released by the drone. "Someone's inside!" he was saying. "I— I don't know—maybe a cop—he had a black helmet on—"

Bruce toggled one of the panels on the side of his helmet—and suddenly the walls around him turned grid-like and transparent, heat signals of six Nightwalkers lit up behind the walls, each one turned in his direction and heading his way. He glanced up at the ceiling. That looked transparent now, too—and three floors above him, he saw a dense cluster of heat signals, all gathered in what must be the upper mezzanine area of the concert chamber.

The hostages.

His corridor suddenly opened up into a lobby, the gala's silk ribbons and long banners now jarringly out of place. Bruce took a sharp turn away from the center of the room as several heat signals from an adjacent hall rushed closer to him. As they reached the lobby, he darted into an empty corridor and continued sprinting. Shouts went up behind him. They had slowed in confusion, trying to figure out where he'd gone. Bruce turned his attention toward the nearest stairwell. There were clearly heat signals coming from inside it, but only three—if he played his cards right, he could get past them. He reached the end of the hall and slammed himself into the stairwell door. An emergency siren blared.

Bruce looked up the stairwell. He didn't need his heat tech to see that two Nightwalkers were running down toward him, their boots echoing on the metal steps. As he went, he took out the small, round bomb from his backpack. He ran to meet them, jumping up the steps two at a time. As he reached the top of the first flight, he threw the bomb against the wall as hard as he could.

An ear-ringing *boom* rang out in the stairwell. Smoke exploded from the bomb and surged up in the blink of an eye, engulfing everything in near pitch-black. Bruce had the sudden unnerving feeling that he was back inside his mansion when the Nightwalkers' leader had vanished in a cloud of smoke. Bewildered shouts came from the Nightwalkers on the upper flights. Through his shades, Bruce could still see the grid outline of the stairs and the heat signals of his attackers. One of them fired shots, each one looking like a faint red-gold burst. He darted up through the smoke like a ghost.

Halfway up the second flight, he came face to face with the first Nightwalker.

The man opened his mouth in a shout, raising his weapon. But it was too late. Bruce struck him viciously in the side of his jaw. The blow hit true; the man's limbs sagged instantly. Bruce caught him before he hit the ground, then set him down, limp and slumped, against the stair railings. He continued up.

Two more Nightwalkers came into view. Bruce darted to the floor as the first one fired at him, sending bullets whizzing past his shoulder. *Don't think, just move.* He caught the first by his legs and sent him careening backward. The second flung her elbow at him, aiming for his neck—but Bruce spun out of the way as another round of bullets chipped against the wall. He vanished into the gloom of smoke before the two could turn back on him.

A voice suddenly rang out over the hall's speaker system. It was a voice Bruce recognized, and for an instant, he paused on the stairs.

"Stop." It was Madeleine. *She was here after all.* "Turn back now, or you risk the hostages' lives."

Her words sent fury coursing through Bruce's blood. Perhaps she had been the Nightwalkers' boss all along. *When you target my friends,* he thought, *it is always a fight involving me.* He hesitated for a split second—what if they really started killing the hostages? *I'm running out of time.* He narrowed his eyes and continued his sprint up the stairwell.

Another Nightwalker sprang into view, but Bruce had seen her coming from afar and was ready. He lashed out before she could open fire—his knee caught her hard in the ribs, and she went down with a hoarse cry. His boots clanged against the steps.

Finally, he reached the top of the stairs. He kicked the stairwell door open and emerged onto the curving lobby of the concert hall's balcony level. His boots hit the carpet. With his shades, he saw through the walls to where the concert chamber itself was at the end of the curving hall. The hostages were there. Bruce broke into a run again. As he went, he tapped his ear.

Alfred's voice came on. "The police are in," he said. "Through the opening you made."

Bruce started to reply, but he never got the chance. At that moment, the door leading to the concert chamber's balcony swung open, bringing Bruce to a skidding halt.

Madeleine.

She stood with a gun in her hand. It was strange to see her without a glass barrier to divide them, as if she had walked right out of some alternate reality and into his. She looked entirely different from how he remembered her in Arkham Asylum. Gone was her white prison jumpsuit. She now dressed from head to toe in dark blue, military-grade clothes—steel-toed boots, gun holsters at her wide belt, a long-sleeved shirt behind her bulletproof vest. Her hands were hidden under black leather gloves. Her long hair was tied tightly up into a high bun.

How many versions of her was he going to meet? Her eyes no longer contained that familiar, mysterious, playful look. There was nothing amused about her—this was not the girl who stretched like a languid dancer, who pressed a slender finger to her lips to tease him, who curled up into a tight ball on her bed or wrapped her arms around her knees. This was the real Madeleine, cold and hard and made of steel. Someone capable of committing three murders.

"Who are you?" she said, pointing her gun directly at him.

How could he have ever felt for this girl? She was a complete stranger now—maybe she had always been a stranger, and he had never known anything about her. Would he die at her hands tonight? Would she sleep soundly after doing it?

None of that mattered. She had Dianne and Lucius, and he wasn't leaving tonight without them. He took a steady step forward.

The corners of her lips turned up, and she straightened, tilting her head at him in her familiar, mocking way. "Ah," she said. "You."

She'd figured out his identity from his gait. As sharp as ever. She shifted her gun away from him and straight toward the concert chamber door. At the same time, the door swung open, revealing a Nightwalker dragging a struggling person with him. Bruce's heart stopped.

It was Dianne. She fought against the arm wrapped around her neck, her face a livid portrait of both terror and rage, but the Nightwalker hung tightly on.

The Nightwalker was Richard Price.

Bruce was so startled to see his former friend's face that he nearly called out before remembering that no one was supposed to know he was here. *Richard?* A member of the Nightwalkers?

Behind Richard's menacing expression, though, was raw fear. And in that second, as Bruce met his eyes, he realized that Richard was just as terrified of being here as Dianne. As Bruce himself.

Madeleine aimed her gun at Dianne's head. "Don't move any closer," she commanded Bruce.

He froze, glaring at Richard. "Let her go," he snapped, his voice coming out distorted.

Richard seemed to make a move, as if he almost wanted to do what Bruce said—but Madeleine gestured once at him with her gun. He immediately went back to doing what he was told. His eyes seemed red at the corners, like he'd been crying.

Madeleine nodded at Bruce's backpack. "Toss your toys over. Now."

Bruce met Dianne's frightened dark eyes. She didn't seem to know who he was, but she tried shaking her head, bravely telling him not to do it. He pushed the straps off his shoulders and flung the backpack to Madeleine. She caught it neatly, then slung it over her shoulder.

"Thanks," she said. Then her eyes darted to somewhere behind Bruce, and she gave an almost imperceptible nod.

Bruce started to whirl around, but before he could, something heavy hit him hard behind his neck. Stars exploded before his eyes. He staggered forward. The world closed around him, black and suffocating. As he hit the floor, the only thing he could hear was Dianne's scream.

CHAPTER 24

The first thing Bruce heard when he came to was Madeleine's smooth, familiar voice. Her words drifted somewhere above him. He tried to turn in her direction, but pain lanced through his head, as if a thousand knives were stabbing into his skull. He uttered a hoarse groan and stopped.

"You should be stripping his helmet off," someone unfamiliar said.

"*I'll* worry about him, not you," Madeleine replied.

"But the boss wants his info, and if—"

"If you'd like to take it up with him, be my guest. Now, stop wasting my time."

A reluctant silence. "Yes, of course."

Bruce tried to concentrate through his haze of pain. Madeleine wasn't the boss, but she definitely had some sort of rank in the Nightwalkers organization. What had she done with Dianne? Where had they taken her? Why hadn't Madeleine killed him yet? What info did they want from him? He stayed still as he became more conscious of his surroundings, keeping his eyes closed and his breathing even in an attempt to convince anyone around him that he wasn't listening.

"What the hell was that rogue drone?" Another voice. "I thought you checked to make sure all the patches were updated at the same time."

"It didn't come from us," Madeleine said. "It wasn't on our grid—I don't have the serial number on file."

"Must have come from somewhere else, wherever WayneTech keeps their stash."

"You have Lucius Fox down in the first row. Go ask him yourself."

At the mention of Lucius's name, Bruce missed a beat in his breathing.

Were they inside the concert chamber right now? Their voices didn't echo the way they should, had they been overlooking the concert stage, and it was quiet. No shuffling feet of hostages, no occasional weeping or frightened murmur. After a moment of concentration, Bruce could make out the faint buzzing of an air conditioner somewhere. An admin office? A supply room?

"He's coming around," Madeleine said, her voice drawing near. He opened his eyes. Lightbulbs lined the sides of two large mirrors against one wall, their warm, piercing light making him squint. Below them sat two vanities, each piled high not with creams and brushes and cosmetics, but with rifles and laptops. *The backstage dressing rooms*, Bruce thought groggily.

He turned his head and saw Madeleine sitting on a chair beside him, her hair loose now, her elbows leaning casually on her knees, her fingers interlaced. She was studying his helmet but didn't reach out to touch it. Behind her stood three Nightwalkers, two men and a woman, all staring grimly at Bruce with their guns drawn.

How odd, it occurred to him, that their roles had now reversed—that he was her prisoner, and she his keeper.

"Is he a cop? Is he going to survive?" the third Nightwalker, the youngest of the trio, now spoke up. Bruce's vision sharpened enough to realize that it was Richard speaking. His face looked completely drained, and he clutched awkwardly at the gun at his belt as if he'd never used it before. "I—" Richard now went on after swallowing hard. "I didn't ask to stay on—I don't want to be here—"

"You seemed okay with giving us a code into your dad's account," Madeleine replied without looking back.

Richard blanched. Then his face contorted in guilt and anguish. "I thought you just wanted his money! I thought you—and now you—"

"Ellison, Watts, get the new kid out of here," Madeleine interrupted, nodding once toward the door. "It's like listening to a goddamn broken record. Go."

The Nightwalkers needed no second bidding. They immediately straightened and filed out of the room without another word, leaving him alone in the room with her.

Bruce's mind whirled. Was Richard being held here against his will? He and his father had had their differences, but it didn't sound like Richard had any idea the Nightwalkers would break into his home and kill his father. Maybe he had been blackmailed into doing other things, too.

When the door finally clicked shut, Madeleine sighed and gave him a disappointed look. "Take off your helmet, Bruce," she said.

Bruce reached up and slowly pulled the helmet off his head. Cool air hit his exposed face. "Where's Dianne?" he demanded. "If you hurt her—"

Madeleine smiled, although the expression appeared bittersweet. "I thought that was you," she said. "Calm down. Your friend's unharmed, if a little upset."

"Let her go." He glanced toward the door. "And Richard Price, too."

Madeleine rolled her eyes. "I didn't force him to be here, you idiot. Boss recruited him of his own free will. Richard thought he was only getting a little revenge, thought he'd just cost his dad some money. Fool."

What? In a flash, Bruce pictured Richard's disgusted expression at their graduation, the revelation that his father had cut him out of his trust fund. Then he thought of the police lights gathering at the Price family's home. The mayor's murder. Had Richard been responsible for opening up Bruce's home for the Nightwalkers to infiltrate it? Would he really sell out his own father for revenge?

You're going to regret that. Those had been Richard's last words to him before tonight. The memory chilled Bruce to the bone, and his fists tightened. *Had he sold out Bruce to the Nightwalkers?*

"How long has he been working with the Nightwalkers?" Bruce asked her.

"A couple of months."

A couple of months. At the benefit on the night of Bruce's birthday, had Richard asked him for WayneTech access in an attempt to steal weapons for the Nightwalkers? Was working with the Nightwalkers the reason why Richard seemed better at fighting than Bruce remembered—why he knew moves that their coach hadn't taught?

"And how would you know that?" Bruce pressed. "You've been at Arkham that whole time."

Madeleine smiled a little. "You weren't the only one who helped me escape from Arkham."

Connections were flashing through Bruce's mind now, sending his heart racing. The city's government—and the mayor—had power over and access to everything in Arkham. And Richard had access to the mayor. Bruce thought of Madeleine's folded creations, of his theory of her secret messages. She'd mentioned an insider giving tips to the Nightwalkers before. Had *Richard* been the one helping the Nightwalkers receive Madeleine's signals via the security cams? Had he made sure the right workers gained access to her cell so that she could escape?

Richard wasn't just a friend who wanted to exploit their relationship. He was a desperate son, eager for approval, enraged at being denied it, and so determined to get back at his father that he'd gotten himself involved too deeply with the Nightwalkers.

Bruce was shaking—from rage against his former friend or from grief for him, he wasn't sure. *You walked right into their trap, Richard*, he thought bitterly. But Madeleine had tricked Bruce, too, hadn't she?

"What did you promise him, for doing all that?" Bruce asked through gritted teeth.

"It's more what we promised him we *wouldn't* do," Madeleine replied with a shrug.

The rest of his family. His mother, his sister. Had the Nightwalkers threatened them, too?

"You're a pack of animals," Bruce snarled.

"And I told you to get out of Gotham City."

"You sent your hit men to kill me and Alfred in my own home." The rage leaked thick from Bruce's words, and he made no effort to stop it. "How *generous* of you."

Madeleine made an annoyed sound in her throat. "You honestly think I made that decision from Arkham? Don't be stupid. Besides, they weren't there to kill you. We needed you for more than that."

"So you were in on it after all. Don't lie. You've done enough of that."

"It's not a lie," Madeleine said with a shrug. "I only told you what I knew at the time. I didn't have to help you—not that you seem to listen."

"And what was it that you wanted? Access to my accounts? You wanted me to fund your terror campaigns, just like your past victims?"

"You already did." She gave him a taunting nod. "Thanks for your generosity."

"Yeah, I noticed," Bruce snapped. "How did you get into my accounts?"

"The same hack I used to get into the minds of your corporate drones." She winked. "Pretty advanced tech your people are developing there, Bruce. Not advanced enough, but it did take me quite a few tries."

"And that's why I'm not dead yet? You need me for access to everything else I own?"

Irritation flashed across her face. It was all Bruce needed to see to confirm that Madeleine *had* tried—and failed—to hack into his new, secured accounts. She would need him to personally open them up for her.

Madeleine nodded at the door behind her. "I don't want you dead for a variety of reasons. Boss thinks I can break into all of your funds. But it seems like you have some locks on your remaining ones that only you can crack open." She leaned against her knees. "I told you to keep away. But now that you're here, they're going to want you to open up the rest. And they're not going to be nearly as nice about it as me."

The boss. Bruce remembered the man he'd seen in his house, confronting him moments before the police burst in through the doors. Had that been the voice on the loudspeakers, too, demanding ransom? At the look on Madeleine's face, he narrowed his eyes. "You framed me," he choked out. "You left a note that sent me to an interrogation room with the police—you put me behind bars. Real *nice*. Why should I believe anything you say?"

Madeleine gave him a wounded look. "You don't think I meant what I said in my note?"

Bruce strained against his bonds. "Don't insult me. And to think I actually believed you might've been more than a coldhearted killer. I guess I was wrong. What else don't I know about you, Madeleine? Is that even your name? Do you lie just for fun? Does it make you happy, messing with my mind? Do you enjoy making up stories just to mock me?"

Madeline winced, momentarily cutting through Bruce's anger. "You think you've figured me out, don't you?" she said.

"Wouldn't have to if you were an honest person."

The two of them glared at each other in silence. The strange pull between them that Bruce had felt all throughout their visits in Arkham returned in full force, permeating the heavy air.

Finally, he shook his head. "Who are you?"

Madeleine stared at him for a long moment. She pursed her lips, as if trying to find the right words to say, and for the first time, Bruce thought that maybe she was actually preparing to tell him the truth, *a* truth, any truth. She looked toward the lit mirrors, where their reflections stared back at her.

"My real name *is* Madeleine Wallace," she began. "And I'm one of the leaders of the Nightwalkers."

These words sounded true, solid. So had her words in the past, of course . . . but Bruce stayed silent, willing her on.

"Everything I told you about my mother is true," she continued. "She was a brilliant teacher. She taught me and my brother everything she knew. Both of us started coding at an early age—but I was her real prodigy, the one who kept at it when my brother started getting really sick." Her gaze returned to Bruce. "She lost her job trying to take care of him. That much you know. She did what she had to do."

"And so she killed the doctor."

"Wouldn't you?" Madeleine replied coolly. "Tell me, noble Bruce, what would you have done if your parents had been shot not by some random burglar, but murdered by an upstanding doctor? If you were orphaned in the ghetto instead of in your gated neighborhood? If you weren't so rich and white and famous? Would you be the same person you are today? Or would you see justice differently? Do you think we all walk through the world with the same privileges as you?"

The memory Bruce carried of his parents' death shifted momentarily—he imagined his mother and father poisoned by someone in a medical uniform, imagined their killer going free instead of being put away in jail. *Do you think we all walk through the world with the same privileges as you?*

"And what about everything else you've told me?" he asked, forcing the questions away. "Why did you leave that note in your cell? Why did you lead me to the Nightwalkers' underground room and sabotage your own team?"

"I knew we had mostly cleared that room out. I needed to give you something, in order to have you trust me. That was the point behind all of our conversations, Bruce—you were part of my ticket out. You're sweet. And helpful."

A liar, and an exploiter. He wanted to lunge at her, to hurt her for all of her falsehoods.

"As for my note—I left that so that the police would arrest you, of course." Madeleine rolled her eyes in exasperation. Bruce stared carefully at her; something about her exaggerated gesture seemed to signal that she was hiding what she truly felt. "If they held you behind bars, then no one could get to you."

Then no one could get to you. "You . . . were trying to protect me?" he asked incredulously.

Madeleine sighed. Another crack in the wall, another emotion hidden beneath her shell. "What do you think?" she muttered. "You were on the hit list long before I ever knew you personally. I was telling the truth about that, you know. I told you to escape the city immediately. Instead, you went home and stepped into an obvious trap."

"I went inside to save Alfred," Bruce replied. "I wasn't about to leave him behind."

Madeleine shrugged. "At your own peril."

Bruce leaned forward. It was all he could do—and even this small gesture sent his head spinning with pain. "I don't understand why you wanted to save me," he said.

Madeleine gave him a sad smile. She drew closer to him, until she was barely a few inches from his face. He could feel her warm breath against his skin, and the brush of her dark hair against his arm. "I haven't always told you the truth, Bruce Wayne," she murmured. "But I told the truth in that letter." And before he could say anything else, she closed the distance between them and pressed her lips to his.

It was as if something between them had now suddenly snapped, leaving Bruce reeling. *Don't.* But he felt himself kiss her back, felt her leaning into him. What was she trying to do? What did this mean? His thoughts whirled, and his muscles tensed in warning—but he closed his eyes and kissed her harder, unwilling and unable to break this bond. She made a soft, yearning sound in her throat. Maybe he was dreaming again, and he would be shaken awake in a cold sweat . . . but her lips were warm and soft, and the brush of her lashes against his cheeks felt like feathers. Heat rushed through him. His heartbeat roared in his ears. *Don't do this.* But he couldn't help himself. He wanted more of this. Of *her.*

Finally, she broke away. Her breaths were shallow, and she blinked at him, her expression momentarily vulnerable.

"I don't understand," Bruce found himself whispering. He leaned instinctively forward, aching to kiss her again. "What are you doing?"

For once, Madeleine looked as bewildered as he felt. She leaned away from him, frowned, and tried to compose herself. The calm demeanor she usually wore flickered. "I chose to go to Arkham," she finally replied. "But I didn't anticipate meeting you there."

"Why would you *choose* to go to Arkham?"

At that, her expression hardened again. Some of the momentary heat between them cooled. "You aren't going to stop me, nor any of the other Nightwalkers. There is plenty that still matters more to me than you."

"And what about those murders?" Bruce pressed. He leaned closer to her when she refused to look at him. "Did you really commit them?"

For the first time, she hesitated at this question.

"You were protecting someone, weren't you?" Bruce asked again. "You took someone else's fall, admitted to the crimes—you went to Arkham in someone else's place. That's why you said you chose to go to Arkham, right?"

"And what makes you say that?" Madeleine's voice had turned very quiet, reinforcing his suspicions.

"Because you're far too smart to be caught by the police with blood all over you," he replied.

The sound of approaching footsteps outside silenced them both. Madeleine straightened; a warning light glinted in her eyes, and she quickly distanced herself from Bruce as the door opened. Two of the Nightwalkers who had previously been inside now returned, and with them came a third person.

Bruce's attention fixed immediately on the newcomer. He recognized this man. It was the same tall, looming silhouette he'd seen in his house, pointing a gun straight at him—it was the same man who had been wearing a mask and goggles, whose outfit had gleamed a strange metal in the dim light. Bruce recognized the way he walked—easy and dangerous, like a tiger. But this time, the man's mask was off, and his face was exposed.

Bruce's breath caught in his throat. The resemblance was uncanny. Same slender dark eyes, same pale white skin, same black hair—although his was short and wild, a thick mess that he now ran a hand through. And unlike Madeleine's more reserved, calculating expression, this man's face was full of fire. Bruce didn't even need to know him to know that his temper ran on a short fuse. But what really caught Bruce's attention was the gleam of metal against his exposed skin. Bands of what looked like steel lined the sides of both of his forearms, running up to his elbows. His elbow joints were completely metal. That predatory gait he had was possibly due to the enhanced joints in his knees, giving him far greater control than an average human.

Madeleine gave him a wry look, but in it, Bruce saw affection that could only mean one thing. "Took your time today, *Boss*," she said, adding a taunting lilt to the final word.

This man—the Nightwalkers' infamous leader—was Cameron Wallace. Her brother.

Bruce could only stare for a moment as Cameron gave his sister a single, humorless smirk. "Too much fun to be had out there," he replied, nodding toward the door and the concert hall balcony beyond, and then at the captive guards who were now kneeling on the ground before them, heads bowed. "And in here."

"What's going on?" Madeleine asked.

"No thanks to these guys, we hear a few police have managed to make their way through an underground tunnel to be within the concert hall's perimeters. They have a few rogue drones with them." Cameron shoved one of the guards hard enough to send him toppling sideways. "If I'd wanted the police to trickle in, I would've given you all the order to let them do so. Now you've made my life harder."

"Don't do it, Cam," Madeleine said, her voice tight. "We've done enough." But even as she said it, Cameron pulled out a gun from his belt holster and pointed it at the first guard. The guard started shaking his head frantically.

"I did that," Bruce spoke up. Everyone turned to look at him. "I turned the police onto that underground path you missed. I sent the rogue drones. They're mine, after all. Not yours."

"Is that so?" he said, looking between him and Madeleine. "Then that must mean you're Bruce Wayne. What a pleasure. Remember me? We met at your home."

"Cam," Madeleine snapped, the warning growing in her voice.

"Good work getting him here, sis," Cameron replied. He turned his attention back to the sobbing guard. Then he pulled the trigger.

Bruce flinched but didn't look away, his ears ringing. The man fell to the floor with a scream as the bullet ripped through his side. Blood sprayed onto the wall. Cameron shot the two other guards in rapid succession—one in his arm, the other in his hand.

"*Cam*, damn it!" Madeleine jumped to her feet and shoved her brother hard, making him stumble back a step. "We don't have time for this, and you're wasting perfectly good people. *Your* people. Do I need to remind you that we're in a standoff right now?"

"Cheer up, sis. I'm not putting bullets through their heads because of you." Cameron scowled at her and swung the gun onto his shoulder. "They're not 'perfectly good people' if they can't stop a police assault. Now we have cops on the hall's property." He nodded for the others to drag the wounded, sobbing guards out of the room. "One bullet for each mistake," he called out after them. "So make sure you make fewer of them."

"And now you have three injured guards," Madeleine snapped back. "What happens if we need to be on the move? Leave them to be caught by the police and interrogated? Drag them along? You're slowing us down, you idiot."

"I didn't say I'd *never* put bullets in their heads," Cameron replied. "So drop it."

Bruce looked numbly at the carpet. There were streaks of blood leading to the door, and on the other side, he could still hear the wounded Nightwalkers' cries. They rang in his head. So *this* was the boss—a man who everyone had suspected to be dead, to have died as a boy. Suddenly, the cryptic way Madeleine talked about everything made sense.

As Madeleine fumed, Cameron grinned at her and gave her a nudge. "Have you been enjoying your little date night in here?" He swiveled to Bruce and gave him a once-over. "You have some remarkable reflexes, Wayne. It's too bad you're not one of us. You've quite enraptured my baby sister."

Madeleine shot him an annoyed look. Bruce looked at her brother, then back at her. "You told me he was dead," he said. "I read the obituary online."

"It's not hard to fake a death, Bruce," Madeleine replied. "After Cameron almost died, Mom left the country with his body and got a foreign doctor to perform an experimental procedure that saved his life—hence, the artificial joints you see. He's been . . . different, ever since then." She looked at her brother again with a bitter roll of her eyes. Bruce watched them carefully. Had Cameron's procedure not only strengthened his body—but also warped his conscience? "Being off the grid is helpful for a lot of things, Cameron. Isn't it? You tend not to be a primary suspect when you murder people." There was sharpness in her voice.

"*You* were the real killer," Bruce said to Cameron. "You slit the throats of those people, and you made Madeleine take the fall for you."

"I don't make her do anything," Cameron replied.

"I *chose* to take it," Madeleine said. "I was responsible for hacking the home systems at each victim's house. That was my job. Cameron executed." There, in her voice, was a strange sarcasm again— and this time, Bruce understood that it meant Madeleine had neither planned nor approved of the way Cameron murdered their victims. "I saw what our mother went through in the prison system. I wasn't about to see another family member endure it—especially not Cameron, who our mother gave up her life to protect."

Cameron smiled at his sister. "It's good to have you back," he said. "Now we can actually move forward."

"Move forward?" Bruce asked.

"Do you know why I killed each of those moneybags, Wayne?" Cameron said. There was a savage light in his gaze. "It's because they were corrupt to the core." Madeleine made an unhappy face, but he shook his head. "Had you not been Bruce Wayne, you would've gotten a much harsher prison sentence for interfering with the police. I'd bet my life on it. So forgive me when I say that I *relish* stealing the millions in their bank accounts, cutting their throats, and then using that same money to destroy the corruption they all stand for." He shrugged, giving Bruce a wink. "It's invigorating, wouldn't you agree?"

"They weren't supposed to die," Madeleine interjected. She frowned again at her brother. "Let the loss of their wealth be their pain."

"And have them avoid the justice they deserve?" Cameron scoffed before looking at Bruce. "Each of those so-called *philanthropists* earned money from Gotham City's privatized jails. Tell me, then, whether or not they deserved to die."

"They didn't deserve to die like that," Bruce said angrily. "No one does. Maybe not even you."

"I'm already dead. Got my certificate to prove it," Cameron said.

"And I was next?" Anger cut through Bruce's voice.

"That was my plan. Although someone seems to have alerted you to it." At that, Cameron shot Madeleine a scathing look. Bruce looked at her, too. Perhaps she had been watching out for him after all.

Bruce turned to Madeleine. "You *honestly* think that this cycle of theft, murder, and destruction is worth it?"

Madeleine lifted her chin. "I believe this is a wake-up call to Gotham City, yes," she replied. "I have no patience for the ruling class that protects the greedy."

"And what about me?" Bruce said quietly. "Do you believe I deserve the same fate as all the other people you allowed to die?"

"You aren't supposed to be here," Madeleine said in a tight voice.

Cameron looked at her and sighed. "You really took a liking to this one, didn't you?" When she didn't reply, he shook his head and started heading toward the door. "Doesn't matter anyway. Wayne, it's time we finished our business with you. Show Madeleine how to access the rest of your accounts, and we'll do our transaction quickly and quietly."

Good. Keep them going. "Why should I?" Bruce snarled. "Because you'll put a knife to my throat if I don't? Like all the others?"

Cameron lifted an eyebrow at him like he was talking to a child. "Because, Bruce Wayne, if you don't—there are a lot of hostages out there on the balcony who will have to answer for your stubbornness."

Bruce glanced at Madeleine. She only gave him a grave stare. "Don't make me do this," she murmured, shaking her head slightly.

Cameron didn't hear her. Instead, he just opened the door and stepped out. "Don't take too long, sis," he called over his shoulder. He left, leaving them alone for a moment.

"Madeleine," Bruce said in the silence. "This isn't really you. I can see it on your face."

She didn't answer, determinedly looking toward the door, but her body leaned instinctively in his direction, and he felt the warmth of her nearness. "It doesn't matter," she replied quietly, even as uncertainty tainted each word. "Our goals remain the same."

"And what will happen to me, after your brother's done with me?" Bruce hissed. "Do you think he will let me walk out of here alive? Do you think he'll just hand me over to the police?" He glanced toward the door. "Do you think he'll just let his hostages go?"

Madeleine didn't reply right away—and in her moment of hesitation, Bruce saw the truth. "You do care," he whispered. He leaned closer, desperate to see that something in their connection, whatever it was that they had, was real.

"I never wanted you here, Bruce," Madeleine whispered, her eyes hard.

"Why?"

She glanced to her side and looked like she was about to say something—but then thought better of it.

"*Why*, Madeleine?" Bruce said softly. "Because I'll tell you the truth right now—I really thought I liked you. And in spite of everything, I still feel something for you. Don't take this path."

Madeleine looked bleakly at him. "This story can't end happily for us," she finally replied, tearing her eyes away and standing up. "So let's just finish this."

CHAPTER 25

Madeleine led him out of the dressing room toward the concert floor. Bruce analyzed their surroundings. There were at least a dozen Nightwalkers up along the balconies, each one dressed in full military-grade gear, their backs turned to the floor below.

How many had taken the hall? How were the police doing, working on breaking in? Bruce scanned the space, searching for a way out. His eyes settled on the door leading back into the stairwell. He hadn't taken the outer stairwell all the way up—if he had, it would have led to the concert hall's flat roof.

He turned his eyes away as they continued on, but his thoughts lingered on it, ideas spinning rapidly.

Madeleine led them up a flight of curving stairs, where they stepped through a balcony door. The light here was much dimmer, a warm hue that Bruce associated with the moments when the orchestra was still tuning. Crowds of people were seated in the rows, their backs turned to Bruce and Madeleine, almost as if they were show attendees—except each one of them sat tensely, unspeaking, their faces turning occasionally to look at the armed Nightwalkers standing at each section.

Bruce's gaze scanned the hostages, searching for Dianne and Lucius. Some were crying. Others looked deathly pale, on the verge of fainting. Still others had bound hands, perhaps from struggling. He recognized the deputy mayor, then several of the city council members who had attended his last charity banquet.

And *Richard*. Bruce saw him guarding one aisle. It must be surreal for him, standing here overlooking all the black drapes in mourning for his father, Bruce thought, while knowing he was responsible for what had happened. With every movement that anyone near him made, he startled like a rabbit.

Madeleine kept her face turned stiffly away from the hostages, as if it helped her continue by not looking at them. Bruce kept searching the faces, a knot in his throat.

There. Lucius was seated in the front row, stone-faced, staring out toward where the balcony overlooked the main stage.

And Dianne.

She was seated at the edge of the very last row, right next to where a Nightwalker stood guard. It took every inch of Bruce's discipline to not rush over to her right now. Beyond her was the aisle leading out to the exit door. She looked scared, but alert. Most of all, *unharmed*. If they had to move quickly, he knew she would be able to do it.

His attention returned to Madeleine. She seemed more shaken than usual, lost in thought.

Madeleine finally led them to where a network of laptops had been set up on the floor near the top of the carpeted aisle. She motioned for Bruce to sit in front of them, and then joined him. The Nightwalkers who had escorted them moved forward, setting up guard in front of them.

The laptops displayed long chains of numbers and letters against a black screen. Bruce picked out a couple of strings of code—mentions of the Ada drones. This was the makeshift command center Madeleine had set up to take over the robots. Bruce looked at the other computers. On the farthest screen from him was a window showing one of his accounts. The second screen showed another. Both were accounts that had recently been installed with Lucius's new security.

This is my chance.

"Let's make this quick, Bruce," Madeleine said stiffly as she began typing. "Give me access to your remaining accounts, and we can be done."

"And then what?" Bruce countered. "Your brother puts a bullet in my head? Makes me an example?"

Madeleine remained silent, her delicate face a mixture of pain and determination. "Just do it, Bruce," she whispered.

If your accounts are opened with the wrong code, Lucius had told him, *it'll send our security network an alert and remotely disable the offending computer in an instant.*

These laptops were also what Madeleine was using to control the Ada drones, and based on the way Cameron had talked about the drones, they were the only things keeping the Nightwalkers in charge of this situation. If he could disable the laptops, it might disable Madeleine's control over the drones.

"Let the hostages go," Bruce said to her, holding her gaze with his own. "The people in here aren't all corrupt officials. They're decent people. Some of them are my friends. If you let them go, I'll open my accounts."

Madeleine stared back at him. Then, finally, she nodded. "You have my word. Hand over your accounts, and I will send *some* of the hostages out of here."

Some was better than none; Bruce would have to think of something fast to free the rest. In the meantime, he said, "Make sure Lucius Fox and Dianne Garcia are among them." He hesitated. "And Richard Price, the mayor's son."

"Done."

Taking a deep breath, Bruce steadied himself, and looked back at the screens displaying his accounts. This was the money that his parents had left him, that they had worked their whole lives for and put carefully away for their son.

Bruce was about to make sure the Nightwalkers regretted ever targeting it.

He leaned over and typed the code out for Madeleine on each one.

It looked as though he'd logged in.

Madeleine didn't seem pleased or satisfied. Instead, she seemed disappointed. "I'm sorry," she whispered.

"Me too."

Even as they stared at each other, he knew the security system was kicking into gear, and that soon the commandeered drones would hopefully reset back to their original purpose. He had little time to get the hostages out of here.

"Time to keep your end of the bargain," he said to her in a bitter tone.

Madeleine looked away from him and rose. "Cameron," she called to her brother. "We're releasing some of the hostages."

Cameron gave her an incredulous look. "Why the hell would I want to do that?"

"*I* want to. We've made a deal with Bruce Wayne over here. He's given us access to the rest of his funds. We're in." She looked down at the laptops for an instant. "So we're releasing some of the hostages. It'll make the police linger back a bit longer, if there are civilians coming out."

Cameron shot Bruce an ugly look. For an instant, Bruce thought he might not acquiesce to his sister's demands—but then he let out a loud sigh and waved his gun at several of the Nightwalkers, including Richard. Madeleine called out for Dianne, Lucius, and a dozen other hostages to step forward. Lucius went with a grim face, and Dianne moved warily, her eyes flickering in Bruce's direction. As they did, two guards shoved them forward, forcing them to stumble, and ushered them out through the balcony doors. Richard tried to imitate the other Nightwalkers' actions, but his expression was uncertain and vulnerable.

Bruce watched them go. *Faster,* he thought, looking back at Madeleine's screens.

Cameron wandered back toward them. He still had his gun slung across his shoulder, and he paused to look Bruce up and down. At a glance from Madeleine, Bruce stood up, too.

"Apparently this one's now calling the shots for you," Cameron said.

"Well, we're done with him now," Madeleine said, dusting off her hands and stretching her back.

"I suppose we are," Cameron replied, his eyes still on Bruce. Bruce stared quietly back at him, even as his muscles tensed. Some sixth sense screamed at him.

Madeleine suddenly stiffened, too. She glanced at her brother with widened eyes. Cameron swung his gun off his shoulder, then pointed it straight at Bruce. "We're done," he said.

Bruce threw himself down at the same time Madeleine swung her arm up at her brother, knocking his aim off as he fired. Bruce felt the heat from the blast as the bullet narrowly missed his head. It exploded against the wall behind him.

"What the hell, Cam!" Madeleine yelled. She hit her brother again, this time squarely on his chin—Cameron staggered backward, dazed for a split second.

Bruce snatched his helmet, which Madeleine had brought with them. He yanked it on, then leaped to his feet and ran. Screams came from the hostages as he tackled the nearest Nightwalker.

Before the others could react, he hit the guard hard in the head, knocking him out cold, and used his body to kick off at the next closest guard. His boot connected with the man's neck. He yanked the guns from each of the fallen guards' hands, and in the same move, ejected the cartridges from them before throwing them over the balcony. There were only three other guards left in the room—they all swung their guns toward Bruce.

"Kill a hostage!" Cameron shouted at them.

"Stand *down*!" Madeleine yelled at the same time.

Confused, the Nightwalkers hesitated—giving Bruce just enough time to kick a gun out of one guard's hands and throw his weight hard at another. A gunshot rang out near him, ricocheting off one of the seats. Bruce glanced over to see Cameron shooting at him. Bruce gritted his teeth, then made a dash past the seats.

Madeleine launched a ferocious kick at her brother's head, catching him in the neck—and as he stumbled, she kicked the gun out of his grasp, sending it spinning across the carpet.

Cameron bared his teeth at her—but a commotion from the halls on the floor below them made them all pause. It was the sound of what seemed like a thousand boots, and shouts suddenly filled the air.

"Police!" came the shouts. "Police! Get down on the ground, now! Hands behind your backs!"

The police. They'd broken past the drone barricade and gotten in. Bruce turned his head toward Cameron and Madeleine, both of whom appeared stunned for a moment. Then Madeleine glanced down at the laptops. *She knows.* The drones had all been disabled. Her laptops had been destroyed, wiped out by Lucius's security virus.

Cameron shouted a retreat order to the rest of his men. The three other Nightwalkers finally lost their nerve. One of them grabbed the nearest hostage, sending others screaming and running for cover. Bruce ducked as another fired a wild shot, the bullet clipping the balcony railing. Then he raced after them. They burst through the balcony doors and back into the hall, where a few police had already made their way to the top of the stairs. Cameron glanced from one end of the hall to the other. GCPD was swarming up from both ends, sealing off any chance of escape. Madeleine looked back at Bruce with a look of shock and betrayal.

"You unlocked the drones," she said.

"Now we're even," Bruce replied.

To his surprise, a tiny smile touched the edge of her lips.

She took off running with Cameron toward the nearest stairwell door. Bruce sprinted after them—then halted for a split second. Near the door stood Richard, frozen in panic at the chaos unraveling around him. He held his gun out in front of him, his arms trembling. He stared at Bruce's helmet with wide eyes and cringed, bracing himself for an attack.

Bruce just stood for an instant, watching his old friend shake. "Get out of here," he said in a low rumble.

Richard needed no second bidding. With everything unraveling around him, he dropped the gun on the floor and ran in the same direction as the hostages.

Bruce had no time to watch Richard go. He bolted through the stairwell door before the police could reach them. Half a flight of stairs ahead of him was Cameron, who seemed to move with a speed and agility that belied everyone else. Cameron had scarcely reached the next step before he was five steps up and sprinting along the second set of stairs. Bruce pushed himself to go faster. All of his concentration, all the skills he had practiced endlessly at the gym and in simulations, now zeroed in on this moment, on the possibility that Cameron might still escape after all of this was over. *No.* Bruce flew up the steps after them.

Cameron paused one flight of stairs above Bruce, giving him enough warning to dodge as Cameron fired down at him. They sprinted up another flight. Cameron stumbled on one of the steps, slowing him down for a couple of precious seconds. Madeleine darted back to help him up. Bruce took advantage of the moment to hop effortlessly up onto the metal railing of the stairs, then leaped up and grabbed the next set of railings above him. He used his momentum to kick off against the railings and swing over them.

Cameron whirled, but Bruce anticipated his reaction. Bruce lunged forward and seized Cameron's arm, feeling the cold metal of his joints. He slammed the gun and Cameron's hand against the wall. The gun dropped and Bruce kicked it away. Several flights below them came the sounds of police as they headed up. They weren't going to catch up in time, Bruce thought. Cameron pulled out one of WayneTech's smoke bombs.

All Bruce could do was shout out a warning to the police below. "Incoming!"

Cameron threw the bomb down the stairwell, and an explosion of smoke engulfed the police.

Cameron struck out again at Bruce. This time, Bruce failed to dodge the hit. The blow was so strong that it sent him careening to one side, his back hitting the railings hard. Cameron fought to grab his neck with both hands. Bruce leaned back as far as he could go without falling over—he lashed out with fists, connecting again, and then barreled into Cameron, sending both of them crashing against the wall.

A click and a cold barrel nudged Bruce in the head. "Let him go," Madeleine said.

She won't shoot me, Bruce thought. But her act was so sudden that it made him freeze. And a moment was all Cameron needed. He shoved Bruce off him, then sprinted up the final flight of stairs and out through the door leading to the roof.

Madeleine stared at Bruce for an instant. The smoke from the bomb had reached them now, shrouding them in haze. "I should've known," she finally said. He knew she was referring to the code that had disabled the drones.

"Turn yourself in," Bruce replied. The helmet deepened his words. "Please."

She held her position for a second longer, then turned away. "They'll have to catch me first," she called back at him. Bruce tried to seize her ankle, but she darted out of the way too quickly and vanished into the smoke. He cursed and ran after her.

The cold night air hit Bruce as he burst out onto the roof. Smoke poured out behind him. For an instant, the space was empty, almost desolate—were it not for the flashing lights coming from the street below, and the shouts of police. Somewhere in the distance came the sound of an approaching helicopter. Bruce turned in a quick circle. Where had they gone?

"You're dead."

Cameron's voice came from behind him. An instant later, Bruce felt an arm lock tightly around his neck right beneath his helmet, both skin and metal pressing hard against his throat. He gasped, fighting for air. One arm rocketed back as he tried to strike Cameron's face with his elbow, but Cameron tightened his grip, choking off more air.

A click. Through the haze, Bruce saw a gun pointed straight at him. At the other end of it was Madeleine, her face grim and determined.

"What are you waiting for?" Cameron growled behind Bruce. "Shoot him. We don't have time to stick around."

Madeleine's dark eyes met Bruce's. He saw her fingers tighten around the gun. "Madeleine," Bruce managed to choke out.

She shifted the gun slightly—so that it pointed at Cameron. "He's not our enemy, Cam," she said calmly. The sound of a helicopter grew louder. "Let him go."

"*What?*" Cameron's voice turned incredulous. "He just ruined our whole operation! He just—"

"He ruined *your* operation," Madeleine interrupted. "My mission was always to seek justice. Bruce Wayne is not corrupt. He is not the person who killed our mother, who cheated you of your treatments when you were dying. And killing him is not justice. Let him go, Cam."

"*Traitor,*" Cameron sneered, even as Bruce felt the strength in his arm waver. "What happened to you, sis?"

At that, Madeleine narrowed her eyes in anger. "We don't have time," she said. And as if to emphasize her point, the glare of a helicopter's spotlight quavered between the buildings beyond the concert hall, sweeping its way toward them.

Cameron loosened his grip and shoved Bruce forward into Madeleine, who lost her balance. In a blind rage, Cameron lunged at her and yanked the gun from her grasp. He swung it toward Bruce and fired.

He missed.

Bruce felt Madeleine shudder once, violently, against him. *She was hit.*

He choked out a hoarse cry. The scene before him went scarlet as every ounce of fury and adrenaline rushed from his head to his limbs. He threw himself at Cameron.

Cameron hit Bruce hard in his side—he collapsed down onto one knee, gasping, and a split second later, another fist came out of the darkness toward him. Even with his helmet's protection, Cameron's metal joints struck him so hard that his head rocketed backward. Everything blurred. Rough hands grabbed him by the collar and dragged him across the roof as he kicked. His instincts flared up. *He's going to throw me off the roof.*

In one move, Bruce reached up and seized both of Cameron's wrists. He twisted around, then yanked Cameron forward as hard as he could. Cameron staggered and lost his balance. Behind them stood the concrete walls around the stairwell door. *Strike now. Don't hold back.* Bruce let out a wrenching yell as he swung at Cameron's head.

The blow landed perfectly. Cameron slammed into the concrete wall. His limbs sagged, and he collapsed. As Bruce stood there, gasping, the light of an approaching helicopter illuminated his silhouette. *The police are coming. I have to get out of here.*

He whirled back to see Madeleine stumbling toward her brother. Her hands were pressed to her stomach, and pain had turned her as white as winter. A rush of wind hit them as the helicopter neared. For the first time, he saw a hint of real fear in her eyes. *No.* He ran toward her.

Behind them, a loudspeaker blared from the helicopter. "Hands up! We will shoot! I repeat—we *will* shoot!" Squinting, Bruce saw the glint of metal—a rifle—from a military helicopter's open doors. The sound of blades chopping through the air was deafening. The soldier holding the rifle took aim. Bruce's eyes widened.

Sparks lit up the ground near them. Bruce grabbed Madeleine's hand and started to run with her for the safety of the concrete wall. Madeleine resisted for an instant, her boots still turning toward her brother in an attempt to defend him, but her movements were weak, unsteady. Bruce was about to shout something at her, when he saw her eyes widen in shock.

Cameron was throwing up his arms in surrender. And he was pointing a finger in *Madeleine's* direction.

He was telling the police to target *her* first. His own sister. To save himself.

Madeleine only had time to look up at the helicopter. The rifle shifted toward her.

No, not her.

Everything seemed to happen in a slow series of snapshots. Bruce let out a hoarse scream and reached for her, pulling them both behind the concrete wall to safety.

"Drop your weapons!" voices shouted at Cameron from the helicopter. Then the sound of shots fired.

Bruce lowered Madeleine carefully to the ground. Over his shoulder, he saw Cameron's body crumpled against the ledge.

Blood pooled underneath him. The police had not been distracted for long.

Bruce turned back to Madeleine. Blood blossomed across her shirt, and she struggled for air in his arms. *No.* He pulled off his helmet so that he could see her face without the barrier of glass that always seemed to separate them. "They're going to take you to the hospital, Madeleine. You hear me? You're going to be okay."

Tears left trails down the sides of her face. She trembled uncontrollably, but her eyes—deep, dark, endless—stayed fixed on Bruce.

"So damn noble," she managed to say, the ghost of a smile appearing on her lips. They were stained red.

Bruce's arms tightened as he pulled her closer. "Save your breath," he replied. Madeleine trembled, and it took him a moment to realize that his vision was blurring from unshed tears. "But keep breathing. You got that? Keep breathing."

"It's . . . too bad," she said, her voice quieting so that Bruce had to lean closer in order to hear her, "that we met like this."

She was saying her goodbyes. Bruce started to reply, but she shook her head. "You're fighting for the wrong side," she said.

As Bruce crouched over her, he found himself wishing that he could convince her, that there was some magic word he could say to her that would show her the sideways view of her world, that perhaps what she had been taught all her life wasn't true, that there *was* true justice out there. He wished there was a magic word he could say to keep her alive. But instead, he found himself staring back into her eyes as the light slowly faded from them.

"I'm so sorry," he finally said.

She tried to focus on him. "Me too."

He put a hand gently against her face, then leaned down and touched her lips with his. Somehow, he thought that perhaps he would feel her kiss him back, that this gesture could keep the breath in her body long enough to save her. But when he pulled back to look again at her face, her eyes were closed.

The sounds of the helicopter still roared above them, and the spotlight was sweeping in their direction. Bruce could hear police kicking at the locked stairwell door, ready to burst onto the rooftop.

He kept his head down and buried his face against Madeleine's, letting himself linger for a final second. Then he forced himself to step away from her body. He pulled his helmet back on and, shrouded in shadows by the concrete wall, ran toward the edge of the rooftop. He hooked a cable to the ledge, flung himself over, and dropped out of view before the light could reach him. The line blurred by in his hands. As he reached the ground, he could hear the police finally break through the stairwell door above. He pictured them flooding the roof. Their attention was fixed on the two bodies. Bruce could hear them shouting Madeleine's name. He forced himself to unclip the cable and blend in with the night.

There was absolutely no reason to weep, Bruce thought as he ran. Madeleine had been a criminal, a thief, a fugitive, and a liar. He told himself this over and over again.

And yet, the tears still came.

CHAPTER 26

Streaks of light. The sound of a camera crew and the rush of uniforms. The roar of the helicopter still hovering over the hall. Bruce heard everything happen around him in a daze, but there was no time to let any of it sink in. He hid his black suit and changed into his own clothing. He found his way through the tunnels, where he came face to face with the police. They took him to the crowd of cars that made up the barricade, where Alfred and Harvey were waiting for him.

Alfred had made up a story about how the Nightwalkers had broken Bruce out of the precinct in order to force his accounts' passwords from him. Bruce explained how he'd used his accounts to disable the drones remotely. Harvey backed up their statements.

If anyone suspected Bruce as the figure in black on the rooftop, no one acted on it.

Dianne was sitting upright, wrapped in a blanket, on a gurney beside one of the barricade's ambulances. When Bruce and Harvey reached her, she stretched her trembling arms out to both of them, hugging them tight. Bruce closed his eyes, taking in the embrace.

At least they were all here. At least his friends were all alive. That was all that mattered.

When he opened his eyes, he thought, for a moment, that he saw a girl with dark eyes walking through the crowd. He thought he could hear her voice. Maybe if he blinked, he would find himself inside the halls of Arkham again, staring through a glass window at a girl who tilted her head at him and wove her hair into a shining black braid.

But when he looked again, she was gone, replaced with crowds of police and reporters, like she'd never been there at all.

The next morning, Bruce woke up back in his mansion and limped his way down to the courtyard. His body felt bruised and sore in a hundred places, but for the first time in a while, he'd slept through the night. No dreams. No haunted halls. It was a surreal feeling, watching the sunlight cut through the windows of his home and cast bright patterns on the floor. As if the previous night had never happened.

Out on the courtyard patio, Alfred had already set out a tray of coffee, eggs, and toast. Bruce gingerly took a seat in a chair, then looked around at the soothing greenery. The morning was so strangely quiet. Only the sound of birds and a distant fountain could be heard. Had it only been last night that the hostage stand-off had taken place at the concert hall, that the roar of helicopter blades and gunfire had filled his ears?

"Morning, Master Wayne."

Bruce turned in his seat to see his guardian come outside with an armful of envelopes. "Glad to see it, Alfred," he replied as Alfred took a seat beside him.

"Lucius stopped by. He wanted to pass along his gratitude to you," Alfred said. "If the police ever come sniffing around Wayne-Tech, he'll make sure to cover for you."

"Does anyone suspect . . . ?"

Alfred shook his head. "Police still have a warrant out for the arrest of an *unidentified assailant in black*. They won't find you, not if Lucius has anything to do with it."

Bruce tried to smile at Alfred. "Did you apologize to Lucius for me, for breaking into his labs?"

"Lucius is quite fine with your thievery, all things considered," Alfred said with a single chuckle, "and would like to see you later today to give his thanks in person, if you're up for it. He says the team at WayneTech will be busy working out the drone security loophole that Madeleine was able to exploit. Quite a loophole, I'd say." Alfred took the stack of envelopes under his arm and tossed them onto the table. "Some cards were dropped off at the front gate for you."

Bruce ran a hand through the stack, recognizing the names and some of the addresses. They were from classmates and friends, teachers, and Wayne Industries employees. His hand paused on one. It was addressed from Richard. He glanced up at Alfred, who simply nodded, and then carefully tore the seal. Inside was a get-well card. When Bruce opened the card, he saw a brief, handwritten message.

Thank you.

Even after all this time, Bruce could still recognize Richard's handwriting. He reread the words. Richard could not have known that Bruce was the suited figure inside the concert hall. *Could he?* Had he recognized Bruce's fighting style, or his voice? Bruce shook his head, light-headed at the thought, and for a moment, he pictured Richard taken into custody at the police precinct. Would Richard reveal Bruce's identity to the police?

It would certainly match Richard's category. Vengeful, bitter, taunting, eager to see Bruce punished a second time. But Bruce sat and studied the message. *Thank you.*

Somewhere in those simple words, he thought, was a silent promise to keep Bruce's secret.

The chaos of the previous night all came back to him now. "I feel like I'm not really here, Alfred," Bruce admitted.

"I know," Alfred said gently. "Give yourself time to heal from all that's happened." He sighed, then studied his young ward. "I feel as if I may have trouble keeping you out of harm's way, Master Wayne, even though you've proven yourself capable of handling it."

Bruce thought back to the feeling of Madeleine lying limp in his arms. His head still felt fuzzy, and he couldn't quite bring himself to ask Alfred what the police would do with her body. Where she would be buried. "I don't think I've proven much," Bruce said.

Alfred gave him a pointed look. "Just try not to give me too many heart attacks. I'm not getting any younger."

The doorbell echoed. Alfred looked at Bruce a moment longer, then rose and headed in to answer the door. Bruce turned his attention back to staring out at the courtyard, until the sound of familiar voices reached his ears. He glanced over his shoulder.

It was Dianne and Harvey, both bearing gifts. Harvey had an extra backpack slung over his black jacket, his blond hair slicked back and a grin on his face. Dianne looked more reserved—healthy and relatively unharmed, even relaxed in a baggy white sweater and striped tights. There was a pensive, haunted light in her brown eyes, but when she saw Bruce, she lit up and straightened.

Bruce abandoned his dark mood at the sight of them.

"I can't believe you're already back on your feet!" Harvey exclaimed, grabbing Bruce's outstretched hand and pulling him in for a hug. He patted Bruce a little too hard, making him wince and laugh. "I heard one of the SWAT team members ended up fighting it out on the roof with the Wallace siblings—heard that *you* had something to do with helping the police find a way into the building. It's all such a mess; no one's really sure what happened? But hell, I'd be spending the rest of the month in bed, streaming movies and polishing off pizzas."

Bruce pulled away and turned to embrace Dianne. "Well, considering *you* actually survived being a hostage," he said, "I don't have much of an excuse."

Dianne wrapped her arms around his neck and hugged him tight. "Thank you, Bruce," she said. "I don't know if I'd be here right now if you hadn't helped the police."

Bruce closed his eyes and hugged her back. She didn't seem to know that he was the one behind the black helmet, that he had been there on the balcony with her, had seen her frightened face. It all seemed so surreal. "Glad you came over," he replied.

"The police don't quite know what to do about you, you know," Dianne said as they settled into chairs beside him. Alfred brought out more eggs and toast, and two more mugs of coffee. "The news reported this morning that the Nightwalkers broke you out of jail to force you to give up your account passwords."

Bruce exchanged a look of relief with Harvey. Harvey still didn't seem entirely comfortable with breaking the law, but Bruce didn't think he would go running to the precinct to turn himself in, either.

"And your clever trick saved the day," Dianne went on. "But then there was the whole thing with, well . . ." She hesitated. "With Madeleine's letter. GCPD is still trying to figure out whether or not to send you to court again."

"They'd be fools to charge you for anything, Bruce," Harvey said. "And you know what that means, coming from me."

Somehow, none of it—the police's indecision, the possibility of a trial—felt like it mattered.

As always, Dianne noticed the shift in Bruce's mood. She nodded at his eggs and toast, neither of which he'd touched, and her face sobered. "Are you going to be okay? I know . . . it must be hard, after everything that happened yesterday." She held out one of her hands, and Bruce saw that it still shook uncontrollably. "I'm hoping this will go away soon. Someday."

"Someday," Bruce replied with a nod, his thoughts lingering on Madeleine. He could still see her body framed by floodlights, still feel the way she'd trembled against him as he held her. It replayed over and over in his mind. He shook his head. He was not the only one traumatized from the previous night. Many people were also picking up the pieces this morning.

Harvey leaned back in his chair and sighed. "I think you might have to resign yourself to being forever on Gotham City's front pages," he said, even though his words were tinged with a note of sadness. "All they want is the latest scoop on your story. They're trying to grab interviews with everyone who even remotely knows you. The tabloids are already making up their own stories about what really happened."

"Shameless." Dianne shook her head. "You're going to have to wear a mask or something to avoid this circus around you."

Bruce wondered what she'd say if she knew about his suit. His attention shifted back to Harvey. He nodded at the backpack his friend was carrying with him. "Hey," he said. "What's that for?"

Harvey looked at him, then took a deep breath. "So," he began hesitantly. "Remember how I turned my dad in?"

Dianne smiled in anticipation of what Harvey was about to say, but Bruce was silent, remembering Harvey's words as he helped Bruce break out of the precinct. He nodded, waiting for Harvey to continue. "Well, it looks like he's going to get some prison time. So I was wondering—that is—" Harvey's voice caught for a moment as he struggled to get the words out. "I was wondering if it'd be okay with you—if I stayed at your place. Just for a while—just for a few weeks until college starts in the fall. I have most of my stuff with me." He nodded at his small, worn backpack. "Of course, if that's too much trouble—"

Bruce's eyes widened a little. Harvey was finally, *finally*, leaving his father behind. For good.

Harvey looked like he was about to start stammering out an

apology, but Bruce leaned forward and stopped him with a steady stare. "Stay," he replied. "Stay as long as you want."

Harvey hesitated a moment longer. "Figured I should be a little brave, too," he said.

Bruce put a hand on his friend's shoulder. "You're braver than I've ever been."

Dianne pulled Harvey into a hug, and Bruce did the same, savoring their company. This, right here, was everything. They didn't have to come over today, he thought; both of them had suffered in their own way last night, and they were probably as exhausted as himself. But here they were anyway, at his side, trying to cheer him up, and he found himself feeling deeply grateful for these friends with whom he could simply *be*.

The world would always have the liars and traitors and thieves, but there were still those who were good at heart.

They stayed until Alfred came back outside, telling Bruce he had another visitor. Bruce excused himself, rose from the table, and left Dianne and Harvey listing out what concerts they could catch before college started. He headed back inside the mansion, where a tall figure waited for him in the foyer.

It was Detective Draccon, standing with a stranger Bruce hadn't met before. She turned at the sound of Bruce approaching, then held her hand out to shake his. In one of her hands, clutched awkwardly, were a bundle of flowers and a card. "Hello, Bruce," she said. She nodded to the man at her side. "This is Detective James Gordon."

The detective offered Bruce a kind look as they shook hands. He was young, but something about him—his thick brows, his deep-set eyes against his weathered, fair skin—made him look wiser than his years. "An honor, Mr. Wayne."

"You too, sir," Bruce replied.

"Gordon's coming in from Chicago," Draccon added. "He'll be filling my space at GCPD."

Bruce looked sharply at her. "Filling your space?"

"I've been offered a promotion in Metropolis and will be leaving GCPD at the end of the month to head their security force."

At that, Bruce couldn't help but smile a little. "Congratulations, Detective," he said.

"It's thanks to you, really." Draccon waved the flowers uncomfortably, until Alfred put her out of her misery by taking them and going off to find a vase. "The guys at the precinct wanted to send that," she said as she adjusted her glasses. "Once you're feeling better, we'd like to invite you down to formally accept a certificate of honor for your actions."

Bruce looked down at the open card. Inside were scrawled a bunch of signatures. "After all I've put you guys through?" he said, offering Draccon a wry grin. "This is too much."

Draccon put a hand on her hip, but she was smiling, too. "Just take the damn flowers, Wayne, before I change my mind."

"What's the certificate for?"

"For taking decisive action and saving both officers' and civilians' lives," Gordon answered. "That took serious courage, Mr. Wayne, disabling the drones."

Draccon shrugged as if unsure how to praise him. "For your heroics," she added. "We couldn't have accomplished any of this without your help."

"Well done," Gordon said.

Bruce hesitated. "And Richard Price?" he ventured. "What's going to happen to him?"

"There will be charges against him," Draccon answered. "But he's been very cooperative in helping us track down any Nightwalkers who escaped. We'll make sure to adjust his sentence to match what happened to him. I know he's your friend, Bruce, and he's been quite remorseful."

Bruce imagined Richard's life going forward, without a father, with guilt hanging over his shoulders after falling in with a crowd that had changed his life. Maybe after serving his time, Richard could find some solace and peace with his remaining family. "Thank you, Detective," Bruce said.

Draccon gave him a kind smile. "Look, Bruce—I know I originally came down hard on you. When you first landed yourself in community service, I wanted to remind you that you can't just go around doing whatever you like." She paused. "But you have your reasons for seeking out justice. I've actually enjoyed working with you these past couple of months, through all the ups and downs. You're a good kid, Bruce, with a good heart. And with what you've seen and suffered, that's not nothing."

"Thank you, Detective," Bruce decided to say. *Was* he good? He had hurt those he loved before; he had disobeyed orders a hundred times over. But perhaps there was something at the end of all that, something that would make more sense to him as he stepped into his parents' legacy.

One edge of his lips tilted up. "So . . . do I have more probation to look forward to? Not that I don't enjoy probation."

At that, both detectives let out a chuckle, and for a moment, Draccon sounded more like herself. "Not this time, no," she confirmed. "Given the situation you were involved in, and what you contributed, you've been granted a full pardon and your record will be cleared of anything from this case." She fixed Bruce with a stern frown. "Don't push your luck, though. Let's make this the last time you cross hairs with GCPD."

"The last time," Bruce said firmly. "I doubt I'll ever be involved with anything this intense again."

Draccon pursed her lips. "I suppose not." This time, Bruce noticed an uneasy expression pass on the detective's features, as if there was still something else on her mind.

Gordon leaned forward. "We found evidence linking Cameron Wallace to the three murders originally put on Madeleine—we didn't know he was alive, so our DNA evidence against her is looking less conclusive. She was there, but she likely didn't commit the murders."

Bruce nodded numbly, trying not to picture Madeleine's still body. When he looked at Detective Draccon, he noticed the grimace on her face again. The curious part of his mind flared up. "What aren't you telling me, Detective?"

From behind Bruce came Alfred's voice as he returned from the kitchen. "You might as well tell him, Detective," Alfred said. "He'll find out on his own, one way or another."

Draccon rubbed her temple once, then straightened her blazer. "Madeleine . . . her body vanished from the hospital an hour after we took her in."

Bruce stilled. "What?"

"We tracked her to the airport, where we learned that she had already managed to take a flight out of the country."

Madeleine hadn't died. Not even close.

She was *alive*.

She had fooled the medical teams into taking her to the hospital, and in the chaos she had slipped away. Bruce thought back to her pale face, her tears, her farewells. Another, final con.

He couldn't help lowering his head and letting out a single laugh. *Of course she found a way to free herself.*

"Well," Bruce said, after a long pause. "She must have found a way to wire all that money to herself, wherever she is now."

Gordon cleared his throat, and Bruce looked at him. "What?" he asked.

"Madeleine didn't take the money from the Nightwalkers' accounts," he replied.

Bruce paused at that. "She didn't?"

"No," said Gordon. "She funneled everything into a charity. The Gotham City Legal Protection Fund just received a donation in her mother's name, in the millions."

At that, Bruce looked back and forth between the detectives.

The Gotham City Legal Protection Fund—that was the charity his mother had always contributed to with her benefits, the group that defended those who couldn't afford to defend themselves in court. And Madeleine had just given away the Nightwalkers' money to it. As the detectives fell into conversation, Bruce found himself looking out the windows and wondering what had gone through her mind as she did it, what had prompted the move.

Perhaps she no longer believed that they were fighting for opposite sides. Perhaps he had changed her just as she had changed him. Perhaps it was a final gesture of goodwill, whether they'd been friends, or enemies, or more.

Or, perhaps, after all the lies between them, this was her way of telling him the truth of who she really was.

ONE MONTH LATER

CHAPTER 27

A full moon illuminated the streets of Gotham City tonight, painting its corners black and white and silver.

Bruce tore down the freeway in a new car, lost in thought. Earlier in the day, he had joined Harvey at the airport to see Dianne off as she flew to England; later in the week, he would do the same with Harvey as his friend headed off to college. And soon, Bruce would step into university life himself, right here in Gotham City, and into the shoes of his parents as Lucius and Alfred continued to groom him for Wayne Industries.

It seemed like life had organized itself again, that all the blocks of his future had aligned in the appropriate order and that he knew exactly what he needed to do. Everything was back to normal.

And yet, as Bruce drove, he still felt like he didn't quite know where he was going. The GPS in his car kept dinging, reminding him that he needed to make a turn eventually if he was going to head back home. But he kept driving forward, passing one intersection after another. His thoughts lingered on the pockets of his life that still, after everything, seemed unfulfilled. Waiting.

A half hour later, he realized that he had ended up right in front of the Gotham City Concert Hall.

Bruce parked his car in the empty lot, then pulled on his long coat and walked toward the building. The streets here that had once teemed with police and flashing lights were now empty, and the concert hall itself sat shrouded in shadows, instead of illuminated by floodlights. A cold breeze blew about him, and he hiked up the collar of his dark coat so that only the upper half of his face could be seen. There was no event at the hall tonight, but the outer stairwell doors were unlocked, and so he went in, taking the stairs all the way up to the hall's roof.

Once there, he headed to the ledge, where he could see the glittering lights of the entire city.

It seemed strange that only a few months ago, he had set foot inside Arkham Asylum and found himself face to face with a girl who seemed to exist in a realm between black and white, who seemed a force of evil, then of good, and then everything in between. He could still remember their first meeting—her, seated against the wall with her eyes glancing briefly in his direction, her expression unreadable, her thoughts hidden behind the dark wall of her gaze. What had gone through her mind during that first moment? What had she seen in him? Just another billionaire mark, her ticket to escaping from Arkham? Or had she seen someone worth talking to?

Bruce reached into his pocket and pulled out the letter that Madeleine had left him before her escape from Arkham. He had folded and refolded it—first into a flower, then into the diamond, then back again—so many times now, following the lines that she'd originally made, that the creases were starting to fray, leaving fine tears in the paper. He read the words again.

> *Dear Bruce,*
> *We're not a very smart match, are we? I can't think*
> *of a story where the billionaire and the murderer end*

up happily ever after. So let's call us even: thank you for
helping me get out of this place, and you're welcome for
the months of entertainment. I hope you'll remember me.

xo,

MW

Bruce studied her words for a moment. When he'd first read it, he had found her note mocking, taunting him for being so foolish as to allow her to escape; now the words sounded wistful, even nostalgic, a letter yearning for something that would never be. A final note to him, in case their paths never crossed again. Maybe she had even done that on purpose. It was difficult to tell, with her.

In spite of himself, he could feel a small smile turning his lips up at the memory of their conversations together, the knowledge that she was still out there, somewhere, no doubt carving a new path for herself.

Maybe they weren't a smart match, but fate had matched them anyway. And someday, in some future, perhaps they would be matched again. He wondered what he would say if he ever saw her again. He would tell her that he wished they could have met in a different world, without glass between them.

Finally, he refolded the note and put it carefully back into his pocket. Bruce closed his eyes, breathed, and listened to the evening settle in. Somewhere deep in Gotham City, he could hear the sound of sirens, defenders of justice beginning another night of work. The wind picked up, combing his dark hair back and pulling at the tail of his coat, stretching it out so that it almost looked like a cape.

From a distance, Bruce was almost certainly invisible, a tiny silhouette lost against the shadows of the concert hall and the city behind it. There were no lights in the sky for him, no faces turned up in his direction, no one calling his name. No one might ever know that he stood there, a silent sentinel watching over his city.

But looking out, all he saw was an ocean of light, the shimmering heart of Gotham City spread out before him. He didn't know everything his future held for him, not yet, but he knew that whatever it was, it would remain here.

It looked like a place worth protecting.

It looked like home.

ACKNOWLEDGMENTS

I don't entirely understand how I lucked into writing a story about Batman, but I do remember how quickly I said "Yes!" to this project. My earliest memory of the Dark Knight is from *Batman: The Animated Series;* I would watch that show with my head propped up in my hands, imagining what it would be like to soar around a city and defeat bad guys. Batman was my introduction to a nuanced character—to the idea that no matter how little appreciation you get or how much the dark side tempts you, you still need to get up and fight the good fight. To me, that rings true now more than ever.

Batman has the Justice League, and in writing this story, I had one, too:

To Kristin Nelson, my wonderful agent and friend, who thinks of everything and then some. To my brilliant editor, Chelsea Eberly—thank you for being in the trenches with me as we steered Bruce Wayne's story into its final form, by (technology) hell or high water. We made it!

I'm so grateful to the entire team at Random House for welcoming me with open arms and warm enthusiasm: Michelle Nagler,

Jenna Lettice, Barbara Bakowski, Alison Impey, Dominique Cimina, Aisha Cloud, Kerri Benvenuto, Lauren Adams, John Adamo, Adrienne Waintraub, Tara Grieco, Kate Keating, Hanna Lee, Regina Flath, and Jocelyn Lange. Thank you, thank you, thank you all for your kindness, your invaluable editorial help, your design and marketing/publicity savvy, and your extreme awesomeness. To the wonderful team at Warner Brothers—Ben Harper, Melanie Swartz, and Thomas Zellers—and everyone at DC, thank you for entrusting me with the story of young Bruce Wayne and for giving me the chance to say "I'm Batman." This will always be a highlight in my life.

To my fierce, brilliant Amazon of a friend, the inimitable Leigh Bardugo (aka Wondugo): this batty author couldn't have made it without you. Thank you for everything.

My wonderful Dianne—this book was for you from the beginning, you smart lady, but you knew that. Thank you for indulging my Batman questions and having in-depth Bruce Wayne discussions with me over afternoon tea, as one does. Your brain is full of the best things!

To the fabulous Dhonielle Clayton, for all your insight, wit, wisdom, and friendship. To my dear Amie Kaufman, JJ, and Sabaa Tahir—thank you so much for cheering me on whenever I needed it most. I aspire to be each of you.

To Primo, my super hero of a husband—thank you for the many nights of Batman talk, for watching all the Batman things with me, and for being your awesome, fun, kind self. It's like we love each other or something.

Finally, to readers and defenders of justice everywhere: thank you for being the real Dark Knights of our world. Super heroes inspire us because they represent the best that humanity can offer. They are our reminders that we, too, can bring about change and do good. You don't need a billion dollars and a Batcave to be like Batman. You just need your brave, badass heart. Keep on fighting.

ABOUT THE AUTHOR

MARIE LU is the author of the highly anticipated *Warcross*, the #1 *New York Times* bestselling series The Young Elites, and the blockbuster bestselling Legend series. She graduated from the University of Southern California and jumped into the video game industry as an artist. Now a full-time writer, she spends her spare time reading, drawing, playing games, and getting stuck in traffic. She lives in Los Angeles with her husband, one Chihuahua mix, and one Pembroke Welsh corgi.

marielubooks.tumblr.com

 @Marie_Lu

SELINA KYLE IS CATWOMAN.
TIME TO SEE HOW MANY LIVES
THIS CAT REALLY HAS.

DON'T MISS THIS NEW DC ICONS STORY FROM
#1 *NEW YORK TIMES* BESTSELLING AUTHOR
SARAH J. MAAS!

CHAPTER 1

The roaring crowd in the makeshift arena didn't set her blood on fire.

It did not shake her, or rile her, or set her hopping from foot to foot. No, Selina Kyle only rolled her shoulders—once, twice.

And waited.

The wild cheering that barreled down the grimy hallway to the prep room was little more than a distant rumble of thunder. A storm, just like the one that had rolled over the East End on her walk from the apartment complex. She'd been soaked before she reached the covert subway entrance that led into the underground gaming warren owned by Carmine Falcone, the latest of Gotham City's endless parade of mob bosses.

But like any other storm, this fight, too, would be weathered.

Rain still drying in her long, dark hair, Selina checked that it was indeed tucked into its tight bun atop her head. She'd made the mistake once of wearing a ponytail—in her second street fight. The other girl had managed to grab it, and those few seconds when Selina's neck had been exposed had lasted longer than any in her life.

But she'd won—barely. And she'd learned. Had learned at every fight since, whether on the streets above or in the arena carved into the sewers beneath Gotham City.

It didn't matter who her opponent was tonight. The challengers were all usually variations of the same: desperate men who owed more than they could repay to Falcone. Fools willing to risk their lives for a chance to lift their debts by taking on one of his Leopards in the ring. The prize: never having to look over their shoulders for a waiting shadow. The cost of failing: having their asses handed to them—and the debts remained. Usually with the promise of a one-way ticket to the bottom of the Sprang River. The odds of winning: slim to none.

Regardless of whatever sad sack she'd be battling tonight, Selina prayed Falcone would give her the nod faster than last time. That fight . . . He'd made her keep that particularly brutal match going. The crowd had been too excited, too ready to spend money on the cheap alcohol and everything else for sale in the subterranean warren. She'd taken home more bruises than usual, and the man she'd beaten to unconsciousness . . .

Not her problem, she told herself again and again. Even when she saw her adversaries' bloodied faces in her dreams, both asleep and waking. What Falcone did with them after the fight was not her problem. She left her opponents breathing. At least she had that.

And at least she wasn't dumb enough to push back outright, like some of the other Leopards. The ones who were too proud or too stupid or too young to get how the game was played. No, her small rebellions against Carmine Falcone were subtler. He wanted men dead—she left them unconscious, but did it so well that not one person in the crowd objected.

A fine line to walk, especially with her sister's life hanging in the balance. Push back too much, and Falcone might ask questions, start wondering who meant the most to her. Where to strike hardest. She'd never allow it to get to that point. Never risk Maggie's safety like that—even if these fights were all for her. Every one of them.

It had been three years since Selina had joined the Leopards, and nearly two and a half since she'd proved herself against the other girl gangs well enough that Mika, her Alpha, had introduced her to Falcone. Selina hadn't dared miss that meeting.

Order in the girl gangs was simple: The Alpha of each gang ruled and protected, laid down punishment and reward. The Alphas' commands were law. And the enforcers of those commands were their Seconds and Thirds. From there, the pecking order turned murkier. Fighting offered a way to rise in the ranks—or you could fall, depending on how badly a match went. Even an Alpha might be challenged if you were stupid or brave enough to do so.

But the thought of ascending the ranks had been far from Selina's mind when Mika had brought Falcone over to watch her take on the Second of the Wolf Pack and leave the girl leaking blood onto the concrete of the alley. Before that fight, only four leopard spots had been inked onto Selina's left arm, each a trophy of a fight won.

Selina adjusted the hem of her white tank. At seventeen, she now had twenty-seven spots inked across both arms.

Undefeated.

That's what the match emcee was declaring down the hall. Selina could just make out the croon of words: *The undefeated champion, the fiercest of Leopards . . .*

A thump on the metal door was her signal to go. Selina checked her shirt, her black spandex pants, the green sneakers that matched her eyes—though no one had ever commented on it. She flexed her fingers within their wrappings. All good.

Or as good as could be.

The rusty door groaned as she opened it. Mika was tending to the new girl in the hall beyond, the flickering fluorescent lights draining the Alpha's golden-brown skin of its usual glow.

Mika threw Selina an assessing look over her narrow shoulder, her tight braid shifting with the movement. The new girl sniffling in front of her gingerly wiped away the blood streaming from her swollen nose. One of the kitten's eyes was already puffy and red, the other swimming with unshed tears.

No wonder the crowd was riled. If a Leopard had taken that bad a beating, it must have been one hell of a fight. Brutal enough that Mika put a hand on the girl's pale arm to keep her from swaying.

Down the shadowy hall that led into the arena, one of Falcone's bouncers beckoned. Selina shut the door behind her. She'd left no valuables behind. She had nothing worth stealing, anyway.

"Be careful," Mika said as she passed, her voice low and soft. "He's got a worse batch than usual tonight." The kitten hissed, yanking her head away as Mika dabbed her split lip with a disinfectant wipe. Mika snarled a warning at her, and the kitten wisely fell still, trembling a bit as the Alpha cleaned out the cut. Mika added without glancing back, "He saved the best for you. Sorry."

"He always does," Selina said coolly, even as her stomach roiled. "I can handle it."

She didn't have any other choice. Losing would leave Maggie with no one to look after her. And refusing to fight? Not an option, either.

In the three years that Selina had known Mika, the Alpha had never suggested ending their arrangement with Carmine Falcone. Not when having Falcone back the Leopards made the other East End gangs think twice about pushing in on their territory. Even if it meant doing these fights and offering up Leopards for the crowd's enjoyment.

Falcone turned it into a weekly spectacle—a veritable Roman circus to make the underbelly of Gotham City love *and* fear him. It certainly helped that many of the other notorious lowlifes had been imprisoned thanks to a certain do-gooder running around the city in a cape.

Mika eased the kitten to the prep room, giving Selina a jerk of the chin—an order to go.

But Selina paused to scan the hall, the exits. Even down here, in the heart of Falcone's territory, it was a death wish to be defenseless in the open. Especially if you were an Alpha with as many enemies as Mika had.

Three figures slipped in from a door at the opposite end of the hall, and Selina's shoulders loosened a bit. Ani, Mika's Second, with two other Leopards flanking her.

Good. They'd guard the exit while their Alpha tended to their own.

The crowd's cheering rumbled through the concrete floor, rattling the loose ceramic tiles on the walls, echoing along Selina's bones and breath as she neared the dented metal door to the arena. The bouncer gestured for her to hurry the hell up, but she kept her strides even. Stalking.

The Leopards, these fights . . . they were her job. And it paid well. With her mother gone and her sister sick, no legit job could pay as much or as quickly.

The bouncer opened the door, the unfiltered roar of the crowd bursting down the hall like a pack of rabid wolves.

Selina Kyle blew out a long breath as she lifted her chin and stepped into the sound and the light and the wrath.

Let the bloodying begin.

DAUGHTER OF IMMORTALS.
DAUGHTER OF DEATH.
THEIR FRIENDSHIP
WILL CHANGE THE WORLD.

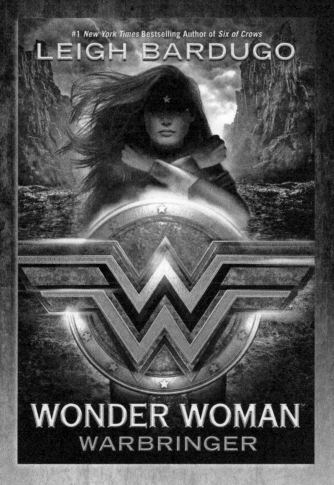

TURN THE PAGE TO SEE HOW
DIANA'S BATTLE BEGINS
IN THE NEXT DC ICONS STORY!

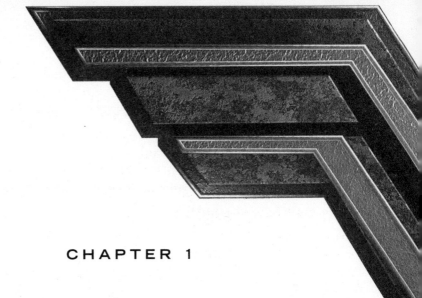

CHAPTER 1

You do not enter a race to lose.

Diana bounced lightly on her toes at the starting line, her calves taut as bowstrings, her mother's words reverberating in her ears. A noisy crowd had gathered for the wrestling matches and javelin throws that would mark the start of the Nemeseian Games, but the real event was the footrace, and now the stands were buzzing with word that the queen's daughter had entered the competition.

When Hippolyta had seen Diana amid the runners clustered on the arena sands, she'd displayed no surprise. As was tradition, she'd descended from her viewing platform to wish the athletes luck in their endeavors, sharing a joke here, offering a kind word of encouragement there. She had nodded briefly to Diana, showing her no special favor, but she'd whispered, so low that only her daughter could hear, "You do not enter a race to lose."

Amazons lined the path that led out of the arena, already stamping their feet and chanting for the games to begin.

On Diana's right, Rani flashed her a radiant smile. "Good luck today." She was always kind, always gracious, and, of course, always victorious.

To Diana's left, Thyra snorted and shook her head. "She's going to need it."

Diana ignored her. She'd been looking forward to this race for weeks—a trek across the island to retrieve one of the red flags hung beneath the great dome in Bana-Mighdall. In a flat-out sprint, she didn't have a chance. She still hadn't come into the fullness of her Amazon strength. *You will in time*, her mother had promised. But her mother promised a lot of things.

This race was different. It required strategy, and Diana was ready. She'd been training in secret, running sprints with Maeve, and plotting a route that had rougher terrain but was definitely a straighter shot to the western tip of the island. She'd even— well, she hadn't exactly *spied*. . . . She'd gathered intelligence on the other Amazons in the race. She was still the smallest, and of course the youngest, but she'd shot up in the last year, and she was nearly as tall as Thyra now.

I don't need luck, she told herself. *I have a plan.* She glanced down the row of Amazons gathered at the starting line like troops readying for war and amended, *But a little luck wouldn't hurt, either.* She wanted that laurel crown. It was better than any royal circlet or tiara—an honor that couldn't be given, that had to be earned.

She found Maeve's red hair and freckled face in the crowd and grinned, trying to project confidence. Maeve returned the smile and gestured with both hands as if she were tamping down the air. She mouthed the words, "Steady on."

Diana rolled her eyes but nodded and tried to slow her breathing. She had a bad habit of coming out too fast and wasting her speed too early.

Now she cleared her mind and forced herself to concentrate on the course as Tekmessa walked the line, surveying the runners, jewels glinting in her thick corona of curls, silver bands flashing on her brown arms. She was Hippolyta's closest advisor, second in rank only to the queen, and she carried herself as if her belted indigo shift were battle armor.

"Take it easy, Pyxis," Tek murmured to Diana as she passed. "Wouldn't want to see you crack." Diana heard Thyra snort again, but she refused to flinch at the nickname. *You won't be smirking when I'm on the victors' podium*, she promised.

Tek raised her hands for silence and bowed to Hippolyta, who sat between two other members of the Amazon Council in the royal loge—a high platform shaded by a silken overhang dyed in the vibrant red and blue of the queen's colors. Diana knew that was where her mother wanted her right now, seated beside her, waiting for the start of the games instead of competing. None of that would matter when she won.

Hippolyta dipped her chin the barest amount, elegant in her white tunic and riding trousers, a simple circlet resting against her forehead. She looked relaxed, at her ease, as if she might decide to leap down and join the competition at any time, but still every inch the queen.

Tek addressed the athletes gathered on the arena sands. "In whose honor do you compete?"

"For the glory of the Amazons," they replied in unison. "For the glory of our queen." Diana felt her heart beat harder. She'd never said the words before, not as a competitor.

"To whom do we give praise each day?" Tek trumpeted.

"Hera," they chorused. "Athena, Demeter, Hestia, Aphrodite, Artemis." The goddesses who had created Themyscira and gifted it to Hippolyta as a place of refuge.

Tek paused, and along the line, Diana heard the whispers of other names: Oya, Durga, Freyja, Mary, Yael. Names once cried out in death, the last prayers of female warriors fallen in battle, the words that had brought them to this island and given them new life as Amazons. Beside Diana, Rani murmured the names of the demon-fighting Matri, the seven mothers, and pressed the rectangular amulet she always wore to her lips.

Tek raised a blood-red flag identical to those that would be waiting for the runners in Bana-Mighdall.

"May the island guide you to just victory!" she shouted.

She dropped the red silk. The crowd roared. The runners surged toward the eastern arch. Like that, the race had begun.

Diana and Maeve had anticipated a bottleneck, but Diana still felt a pang of frustration as runners clogged the stone throat of the tunnel, a tangle of white tunics and muscled limbs, footsteps echoing off the stone, all of them trying to get clear of the arena at once. Then they were on the road, sprinting across the island, each runner choosing her own course.

You do not enter a race to lose.

Diana set her pace to the rhythm of those words, bare feet slapping the packed earth of the road that would lead her through the tangle of the Cybelian Woods to the island's northern coast.

Ordinarily, a miles-long trek through this forest would be a slow one, hampered by fallen trees and tangles of vines so thick they had to be hacked through with a blade you didn't mind dulling. But Diana had plotted her way well. An hour after she entered the woods, she burst from the trees onto the deserted coast road. The wind lifted her hair, and salt spray lashed her face. She breathed deep, checked the position of the sun. She was going to win—not just place but win.

She'd mapped out the course the week before with Maeve, and they'd run it twice in secret, in the gray-light hours of early morning, when their sisters were first rising from their beds, when the kitchen fires were still being kindled, and the only curious eyes they'd had to worry about belonged to anyone up early to hunt game or cast nets for the day's catch. But hunters kept to the woods and meadows farther south, and no one fished off this part of the coast; there was no good place to launch a boat, just the steep steel-colored cliffs plunging straight down to the sea, and a tiny, unwelcoming cove that could only be reached by a path so narrow you had to shuffle down sideways, back pressed to the rock.

The northern shore was gray, grim, and inhospitable, and Diana knew every inch of its secret landscape, its crags and caves, its tide pools teeming with limpets and anemones. It was a good place to be alone. *The island seeks to please*, her mother had told her. It was why Themyscira was forested by redwoods in some places and rubber trees in others; why you could spend an afternoon roaming the grasslands on a scoop-neck pony and the evening atop a camel, scaling a moonlit dragonback of sand dunes. They were all pieces of the lives the Amazons had led before they came to the island, little landscapes of the heart.

Diana sometimes wondered if Themyscira had called the northern coast into being just for her so that she could challenge herself climbing on the sheer drop of its cliffs, so that she could have a place to herself when the weight of being Hippolyta's daughter got to be too much.

You do not enter a race to lose.

Her mother had not been issuing a general warning. Diana's losses meant something different, and they both knew it—and not only because she was a princess.

Diana could almost feel Tek's knowing gaze on her, hear the mocking in her voice. *Take it easy, Pyxis.* That was the nickname Tek had given her. Pyxis. A little clay pot made to store jewels or a tincture of carmine for pinking the lips. The name was harmless, meant to tease, always said in love—or so Tek claimed. But it stung every time: a reminder that Diana was not like the other Amazons, and never would be. Her sisters were battle-proven warriors, steel forged from suffering and honed to greatness as they passed from life to immortality. All of them had earned their place on Themyscira. All but Diana, born of the island's soil and Hippolyta's longing for a child, fashioned from clay by her mother's hands—hollow and breakable. *Take it easy, Pyxis. Wouldn't want to see you crack.*

Diana steadied her breathing, kept her pace even. *Not today, Tek. This day the laurel belongs to me.*

She spared the briefest glance at the horizon, letting the sea breeze cool the sweat on her brow. Through the mists, she glimpsed the white shape of a ship. It had come close enough to the boundary that Diana could make out its sails. The craft was small—a schooner maybe? She had trouble remembering nautical details. Mainmast, mizzenmast, a thousand names for sails, and knots for rigging. It was one thing to be out on a boat, learning from Teuta, who had sailed with Illyrian pirates, but quite another to be stuck in the library at the Epheseum, staring glazed-eyed at diagrams of a brigantine or a caravel.

Sometimes Diana and Maeve made a game of trying to spot ships or planes, and once they'd even seen the fat blot of a cruise ship on the horizon. But most mortals knew to steer clear of their particular corner of the Aegean, where compasses spun and instruments suddenly refused to obey.

Today it looked like a storm was picking up past the mists of the boundary, and Diana was sorry she couldn't stop to watch it. The rains that came to Themyscira were tediously gentle and predictable, nothing like the threatening rumble of thunder, the shimmer of a far-off lightning strike.

"Do you ever miss storms?" Diana had asked one afternoon as she and Maeve lazed on the palace's sun-soaked rooftop terrace, listening to the distant roar and clatter of a tempest. Maeve had died in the Crossbarry Ambush, the last words on her lips a prayer to Saint Brigid of Kildare. She was new to the island by Amazon standards, and came from Cork, where storms were common.

"No," Maeve had said in her lilting voice. "I miss a good cup of tea, dancing, boys—definitely not rain."

"We dance," Diana protested.

Maeve had just laughed. "You dance differently when you know you won't live forever." Then she'd stretched, freckles like dense clouds of pollen on her white skin. "I think I was a cat in another life, because all I want is to lie around sleeping in the world's biggest sunbeam."

Steady on. Diana resisted the urge to speed forward. It was hard to remember to keep something in reserve with the early-morning sun on her shoulders and the wind at her back. She felt strong. But it was easy to feel strong when she was on her own.

A *boom* sounded over the waves, a hard metallic clap like a door slamming shut. Diana's steps faltered. On the blue horizon, a billowing column of smoke rose, flames licking at its base. The schooner was on fire, its prow blown to splinters and one of its masts smashed, the sail dragging over the rails.

Diana found herself slowing but forced her stride back on pace. There was nothing she could do for the schooner. Planes crashed. Ships were wrecked upon the rocks. That was the nature of the mortal world. It was a place where disaster could happen and often did. Human life was a tide of misery, one that never reached the island's shores. Diana focused her eyes on the path. Far, far ahead she could see sunlight gleaming gold off the great dome at Bana-Mighdall. First the red flag, then the laurel crown. That was the plan.

From somewhere on the wind, she heard a cry.

A gull, she told herself. *A girl,* some other voice within her insisted. *Impossible.* A human shout couldn't carry over such a great distance, could it?

It didn't matter. There was nothing she could do.

And yet her eyes strayed back to the horizon. *I just want to get a better view,* she told herself. *I have plenty of time. I'm ahead.*

There was no good reason to leave the ruts of the old cart track, no logic to veering out over the rocky point, but she did it anyway.

The waters near the shore were calm, clear, vibrant turquoise. The ocean beyond was something else—wild, deep-well blue, a sea gone almost black. The island might seek to please her and her sisters, but the world beyond the boundary didn't concern itself with the happiness or safety of its inhabitants.

Even from a distance, she could tell the schooner was sinking. But she saw no lifeboats, no distress flares, only pieces of the broken craft carried along by rolling waves. It was done. Diana rubbed her hands briskly over her arms, dispelling a sudden chill, and started making her way back to the cart track. That was the way of human life. She and Maeve had dived out by the boundary many times, swum the wrecks of airplanes and clipper ships and sleek motorboats. The salt water changed the wood, hardened it so it did not rot. Mortals were not the same. They were food for deep-sea fishes, for sharks—and for time that ate at them slowly, inevitably, whether they were on water or on land.

Diana checked the sun's position again. She could be at Bana-Mighdall in forty minutes, maybe less. She told her legs to move. She'd only lost a few moments. She could make up the time. Instead, she looked over her shoulder.

There were stories in all the old books about women who made the mistake of looking back. On the way out of burning cities. On the way out of hell. But Diana still turned her eyes to that ship sinking in the great waves, tilting like a bird's broken wing.

She measured the length of the cliff top. There were jagged rocks at the base. If she didn't leap with enough momentum, the impact would be ugly. Still, the fall wouldn't kill her. *That's true of a real Amazon*, she thought. *Is it true for you?* Well, she *hoped* the fall wouldn't kill her. Of course, if the fall didn't, her mother would.

Diana looked once more at the wreck and pushed off, running full out, arms pumping, stride long, picking up speed, closing the distance to the cliff's edge. *Stop stop stop*, her mind clamored. *This is madness.* Even if there were survivors, she could do nothing for them. To try to save them was to court exile, and there would be no exception to the rule—not even for a princess. *Stop.* She wasn't sure why she didn't obey. She wanted to believe it was because a hero's heart beat in her chest and demanded she answer that frightened call. But even as she launched herself off the cliff and into the empty sky, she knew part of what drew her on was the challenge of that great gray sea that did not care if she loved it.

Her body cut a smooth arc through the air, arms pointing like a compass needle, directing her course. She plummeted toward the water and broke the surface in a clean plunge, ears full of sudden silence, muscles tensed for the brutal impact of the rocks. None came. She shot upward, drew in a breath, and swam straight for the boundary, arms slicing through the warm water.

There was always a little thrill when she neared the boundary, when the temperature of the water began to change, the cold touching her fingertips first, then settling over her scalp and shoulders. Diana and Maeve liked to swim out from the southern beaches, daring themselves to go farther, farther. Once they'd glimpsed a ship passing in the mist, sailors standing at the stern. One of the men had lifted an arm, pointing in their direction. They'd plunged to safety, gesturing wildly to each other beneath the waves, laughing so hard that by the time they reached shore, they were both choking on salt water. *We could be sirens,* Maeve had shrieked as they'd flopped onto the warm sand, except neither of them could carry a tune. They'd spent the rest of the afternoon singing violently off-key Irish drinking songs and laughing themselves silly until Tek had found them. Then they'd shut up quick. Breaking the boundary was a minor infraction. Being seen by mortals anywhere near the island was cause for serious disciplinary action. And what Diana was doing now?

Stop. But she couldn't. Not when that high human cry still rang in her ears.

Diana felt the cold water beyond the boundary engulf her fully. The sea had her now, and it was not friendly. The current seized her legs, dragging her down, a massive, rolling force, the barest shrug of a god. *You have to fight it,* she realized, demanding that her muscles correct her course. She'd never had to work against the ocean.

She bobbed for a moment on the surface, trying to get her bearings as the waves crested around her. The water was full of debris, shards of wood, broken fiberglass, orange life jackets that the crew must not have had time to don. It was nearly impossible to see through the falling rain and the mists that shrouded the island.

What am I doing out here? she asked herself. *Ships come and go. Human lives are lost.* She dove again, peered through the rushing gray waters, but saw no one.

Diana surfaced, her own stupidity carving a growing ache in

her gut. She'd sacrificed the race. This was supposed to be the moment her sisters saw her truly, the chance to make her mother proud. Instead, she'd thrown away her lead, and for what? There was nothing here but destruction.

Out of the corner of her eye, she saw a flash of white, a big chunk of what might have been the ship's hull. It rose on a wave, vanished, rose again, and as it did, Diana glimpsed a slender brown arm holding tight to the side, fingers spread, knuckles bent. Then it was gone.

Another wave rose, a great gray mountain. Diana dove beneath it, kicking hard, then surfaced, searching, bits of lumber and fiberglass everywhere, impossible to sort one piece of flotsam from another.

There it was again—an arm, two arms, a body, bowed head and hunched shoulders, lemon-colored shirt, a tangle of dark hair. A girl—she lifted her head, gasped for breath, dark eyes wild with fear. A wave crashed over her in a spray of white water. The chunk of hull surfaced. The girl was gone.

Down again. Diana aimed for the place she'd seen the girl go under. She glimpsed a flash of yellow and lunged for it, seizing the fabric and using it to reel her in. A ghost's face loomed out at her from the cloudy water—golden hair, blue gaze wide and lifeless. She'd never seen a corpse up close before. She'd never seen a boy up close before. She recoiled, hand releasing his shirt, but even as she watched him disappear, she marked the differences—hard jaw, broad brow, just like the pictures in books.

She resurfaced, but she'd lost all sense of direction now—the waves, the wreck, the bare shadow of the island in the mists. If she drifted out much farther, she might not be able to find her way back.

Diana could not stop seeing the image of that slender arm, the ferocity in those fingers, clinging hard to life. *Once more*, she told herself. She dove, the chill of the water fastening tight around her bones now, burrowing deeper.

One moment the world was gray current and cloudy sea, and

the next the girl was there in her lemon-colored shirt, facedown, arms and legs outstretched like a star. Her eyes were closed.

Diana grabbed her around the waist and launched them toward the surface. For a terrifying second, she could not find the shape of the island, and then the mists parted. She kicked forward, wrapping the girl awkwardly against her chest with one arm, fingers questing for a pulse with the other. *There*—beneath the jaw, thready, indistinct, but there. Though the girl wasn't breathing, her heart still beat.

Diana hesitated. She could see the outlines of Filos and Ecthros, the rocks that marked the rough beginnings of the boundary. The rules were clear. You could not stop the mortal tide of life and death, and the island must never be touched by it. There were no exceptions. No human could be brought to Themyscira, even if it meant saving a life. Breaking that rule meant only one thing: exile.

Exile. The word was a stone, unwanted ballast, the weight unbearable. It was one thing to breach the boundary, but what she did next might untether her from the island, her sisters, her mother forever. The world seemed too large, the sea too deep. *Let go.* It was that simple. Let this girl slip from her grasp and it would be as if Diana had never leapt from those cliffs. She would be light again, free of this burden.

Diana thought of the girl's hand, the ferocious grip of her knuckles, the steel-blade determination in her eyes before the wave took her under. She felt the ragged rhythm of the girl's pulse, a distant drum, the sound of an army marching—one that had fought well but could not fight on much longer.

She swam for shore.

As she passed through the boundary with the girl clutched to her, the mists dissolved and the rain abated. Warmth flooded her body. The calm water felt oddly lifeless after the thrashing of the sea, but Diana wasn't about to complain.

When her feet touched the sandy bottom, she shoved up, shifting her grip to carry the girl from the shallows. She was eerily light, almost insubstantial. It was like holding a sparrow's body between her cupped hands. No wonder the sea had made such easy sport of this creature and her crewmates; she felt temporary, an artist's cast of a body rendered in plaster.

Diana laid her gently on the sand and checked her pulse again. No heartbeat now. She knew she needed to get the girl's heart going, get the water out of her lungs, but her memory on just how to do that was a bit hazy. Diana had studied the basics of reviving a drowning victim, but she hadn't ever had to put it into practice outside the classroom. It was also possible she hadn't paid close attention at the time. How likely was it that an Amazon was going to drown, especially in the calm waters off Themyscira? And now her daydreaming might cost this girl her life.

Do something, she told herself, trying to think past her panic. *Why did you drag her out of the water if you're only going to sit staring at her like a frightened rabbit?*

Diana placed two fingers on the girl's sternum, then tracked lower to what she hoped was the right spot. She locked her hands together and pressed. The girl's bones bent beneath her palms. Hurriedly, Diana drew back. What was this girl made of, anyway? Balsa wood? She felt about as solid as the little models of world monuments Diana had been forced to build for class. Gently, she pressed down again, then again. She shut the girl's nose with her fingers, closed her mouth over cooling mortal lips, and breathed.

The gust drove into the girl's chest, and Diana saw it rise, but this time the extra force seemed to be a good thing. Suddenly, the girl was coughing, her body convulsing as she spat up salt water. Diana sat back on her knees and released a short laugh. She'd done it. The girl was alive.

The reality of what she'd just dared struck her. All the hounds of Hades: *She'd done it. The girl was alive.*

And trying to sit up.

"Here," Diana said, bracing the girl's back with her arm. She couldn't simply kneel there, watching her flop around on the sand like a fish, and it wasn't as if she could put her back in the ocean. Could she? No. Mortals were clearly too good at drowning.

The girl clutched her chest, taking huge, sputtering gulps of air. "The others," she gasped. Her eyes were so wide Diana could see white ringing her irises all the way around. She was trembling, but Diana wasn't sure if it was because she was cold or going into shock. "We have to help them—"

Diana shook her head. If there had been any other signs of life in the wreck, she hadn't seen them. Besides, time passed more quickly in the mortal world. Even if she swam back out, the storm would have long since had its way with any bodies or debris.

"They're gone," said Diana, then wished she'd chosen her words more carefully. The girl's mouth opened, closed. Her body was shaking so hard Diana thought it might break apart. That couldn't actually happen, could it?

Diana scanned the cliffs above the beach. Someone might have seen her swim out. She felt confident no other runner had chosen this course, but anyone could have seen the explosion and come to investigate.

"I need to get you off the beach. Can you walk?" The girl nodded, but her teeth were chattering, and she made no move to stand. Diana's eyes scoured the cliffs again. "Seriously, I need you to get up."

"I'm trying."

She didn't look like she was trying. Diana searched her memory for everything she'd been told about mortals, the soft stuff—eating habits, body temperature, cultural norms. Unfortunately, her mother and her tutors were more focused on what Diana referred to as the Dire Warnings: War. Torture. Genocide. Pollution. Bad Grammar.

The girl shivering before her on the sand didn't seem to qualify for inclusion in the Dire Warnings category. She looked about the same age as Diana, brown-skinned, her hair a tangle of long, tiny braids covered in sand. She was clearly too weak to hurt anyone but herself. Even so, she could be plenty dangerous to Diana. Exile dangerous. Banished-forever dangerous. Better not to think about that. Instead, she thought back to her classes with Teuta. *Make a plan. Battles are often lost because people don't know which war they're fighting.* All right. The girl couldn't walk any great distance in her condition. Maybe that was a good thing, given that Diana had nowhere to take her.

She rested what she hoped was a comforting hand on the girl's shoulder. "Listen, I know you're feeling weak, but we should try to get off the beach."

"Why?"

Diana hesitated, then opted for an answer that was technically true if not wholly accurate. "High tide."

It seemed to do the trick, because the girl nodded. Diana stood and offered her a hand.

"I'm fine," the girl said, shoving to her knees and then pushing up to her feet.

"You're stubborn," Diana said with some measure of respect. The girl had almost drowned and seemed to be about as solid as driftwood and down, but she wasn't eager to accept help—and she definitely wasn't going to like what Diana suggested next. "I need you to climb on my back."

A crease appeared between the girl's brows. "Why?"

"Because I don't think you can make it up the cliffs."

"Is there a path?"

"No," said Diana. That was definitely a lie. Instead of arguing, Diana turned her back. A minute later, she felt a pair of arms around her neck. The girl hopped on, and Diana reached back to take hold of her thighs and hitch her into position. "Hold on tight."

The girl's arms clamped around her windpipe. "Not that tight!" Diana choked out.

"Sorry!" She loosened her hold.

Diana took off at a jog.

The girl groaned. "Slow down. I think I'm going to vomit."

"Vomit?" Diana scanned her knowledge of mortal bodily functions and immediately smoothed her gait. "Do *not* do that."

"Just don't drop me."

"You weigh about as much as a heavy pair of boots." Diana

picked her way through the big boulders wedged against the base of the cliff. "I need my arms to climb, so you're going to have to hold on with your legs, too."

"Climb?"

"The cliff."

"You're taking me *up the side of the cliff*? Are you out of your mind?"

"Just hold on and try not to strangle me." Diana dug her fingers into the rock and started putting distance between them and the ground before the girl could think too much more about it.

She moved quickly. This was familiar territory. Diana had scaled these cliffs countless times since she'd started visiting the north shore, and when she was twelve, she'd discovered the cave where they were headed. There were other caves, lower on the cliff face, but they filled when the tide came in. Besides, they were too easy to crawl out of if someone got curious.

The girl groaned again.

"Almost there," Diana said encouragingly.

"I'm not opening my eyes."

"Probably for the best. Just don't . . . you know."

"Puke all over you?"

"Yes," said Diana. "That." Amazons didn't get sick, but vomiting appeared in any number of novels and featured in a particularly vivid description from her anatomy book. Blessedly, there were no illustrations.

At last, Diana hauled them up into the divot in the rock that marked the cave's entrance. The girl rolled off and heaved a long breath. The cave was tall, narrow, and surprisingly deep, as if someone had taken a cleaver to the center of the cliff. Its gleaming black rock sides were perpetually damp with sea spray. When she was younger, Diana had liked to pretend that if she kept walking, the cave would lead straight through the cliff and open onto some other land entirely. It didn't. It was just a cave, and remained a cave no matter how hard she wished.

Diana waited for her eyes to adjust, then shuffled farther

inside. The old horse blanket was still there—wrapped in oilcloth and mostly dry, if a bit musty—as well as her tin box of supplies.

She wrapped the blanket around the girl's shoulders.

"We aren't going to the top?" asked the girl.

"Not yet." Diana had to get back to the arena. The race must be close to over by now, and she didn't want people wondering where she'd gotten to. "Are you hungry?"

The girl shook her head. "We need to call the police, search and rescue."

"That isn't possible."

"I don't know what happened," the girl said, starting to shake again. "Jasmine and Ray were arguing with Dr. Ellis and then—"

"There was an explosion. I saw it from shore."

"It's my fault," the girl said as tears spilled over her cheeks. "They're dead and it's my fault."

"Don't," Diana said gently, feeling a surge of panic. "It was the storm." She laid her hand on the girl's shoulder. "What's your name?"

"Alia," the girl said, burying her head in her arms.

"Alia, I need to go, but—"

"No!" Alia said sharply. "Don't leave me here."

"I have to. I . . . need to get help." What Diana needed was to get back to Ephesus and figure out how to get this girl off the island before anyone found out about her.

Alia grabbed hold of her arm, and again Diana remembered the way she'd clung to that piece of hull. "Please," Alia said. "Hurry. Maybe they can send a helicopter. There could be survivors."

"I'll be back as soon as I can," Diana promised. She slid the tin box toward the girl. "There are dried peaches and pili seeds and a little fresh water inside. Don't drink it all at once."

Alia's eyelids stuttered. "All at once? How long will you be gone?"

"Maybe a few hours. I'll be back as fast as I can. Just stay warm and rest." Diana rose. "And don't leave the cave."

Alia looked up at her. Her eyes were deep brown and heavily

lashed, her gaze fearful but steady. For the first time since Diana had pulled her from the water, Alia seemed to be truly seeing her. "Where are we?" she asked. "What is this place?"

Diana wasn't quite sure how to answer, so all she said was "This is my home."

She hooked her hands back into the rock and ducked out of the cave before Alia could ask anything else.